Praise for Anthony Bid᠁

Praise for *Amus᠁*

"Bidulka's *Amuse Bouche* is an effervescent first novel that is much like the tasty French hors d'oeuvres from which it takes its name."
— *Quill & Quire (Toronto)*

"First-rate mystery...by any standards."
— *The StarPhoenix (Saskatoon)*

"Bidulka unravels his tale with skill and gentle humour but his real strength lies in his characters and his evocation of...community in a smaller city."
— *The Voice (Ottawa)*

"*Amuse Bouche* is a novel that entertains and broadens horizons; something...all literature should do."
— *NewWinnipeg (Winnipeg)*

"Bidulka's Quant is a wonderfully 'comfortable' raconteur."
— *Outlooks (Calgary)*

"Suspense, humour, and ambiguity surround the colourful characters that meander throughout the pages of [Amuse Bouche], taunting and teasing you to dare to guess 'who did it?' "
— *Swerve (Winnipeg)*

"[*Amuse Bouche*] is populated with a broad variety of interesting and very human characters, written with warmth and a genuine sense of humour."
— *FFWD (Calgary)*

'Choice of the Week' — "Anthony Bidulka paints the Prairies a lighter shade of noir with *Amuse Bouche*."
— *The Georgia Straight (Vancouver)*

"Bidulka has talent and this *Amuse Bouche* promises lots of tasty things to come."
— *The Globe and Mail (Toronto)*

"Bidulka serves up strong characters and an intriguing plot...one hopes this book itself is only an amuse bouche...for those that are to follow."
— *Lavender Magazine (Minneapolis/St. Paul)*

"Bidulka is so entertaining that he makes you consider a visit to that prairie province once famed for wheat."

– The Blade (Laguna Beach, California)

"With first novel *Amuse Bouche*, Anthony Bidulka shows a certain *je ne sais quoi*."

– in newsweekly (Boston)

Praise for *Flight of Aquavit*:

"...there is sincerity and just a hint of sage world-weariness about the self-questioning lifestyle and relationships the author draws from his charming, vulnerable detective."

– Canadian Book Review Annual

"Bidulka treats the reader to enough red herrings with which to open a fishmarket and more than one writer's fair share of keen observations and appealing *bons mots*."

– Outlooks (Calgary)

"I was surprised at how 'comforting' it was to be reunited with familiar characters—almost like returning to school after summer break."

– Outlooks (Calgary)

"...the pages turn at a frantic speed, each suspenseful chapter a chaser for the preceding."

– Swerve (Winnipeg)

"...Quant is a delight to spend time with..."

- StarPhoenix (Saskatoon)

"Between Quant's quips and hard-boiled comments and the colourful cast that includes enough suspicious characters to fill a rogues' gallery, readers will find that Detective Russell Quant is a fun guy..."

- tobe (Ottawa)

"There's plenty of action here, and Bidulka spreads it out with witty dialogue, smart commentary, and plenty of good, sharp writing."

– Globe & Mail (Toronto)

"...Bidulka takes off and runs with it into a fast, compelling plot..."

- The Free Press (London)

"Bidulka manages to spin a compelling detective story with colourful characters, hilarious situations, and touching relationships."
— *Midwest Book Review*

Praise for *Tapas on the Ramblas*:

"The best thing about Bidulka's mysteries is the cast of by now well-developed, endearing characters. *Tapas on the Ramblas* is a solid follow-up to his Lambda Literary Award-winning *Flight of Aquavit*."
— *Quill & Quire (Toronto)*

"There's intrigue at every destination, and each is as richly detailed in the writing as Saskatoon is in books past."
—*Xpress (Ottawa)*

"...leaves us salivating for a taste of what is next to come in the world of Russell Quant."
—*Outlooks (Calgary)*

"Bidulka-brand cliff-hanging suspense is still a trademark of the Quant series, but now accompanied with more action, an almost dizzying array of plot twists, and an intriguing conclusion that's a tempting promise for more."
—*Swerve (Winnipeg)*

"*Tapas on the Ramblas* is the third in the Russell Quant series, and the books seem to get better and better."
—*BooksnBytes*

"...a Russell Quant tale is highly entertaining, from strange beginning to amusing, twisted end."
— *The Edmonton Journal (Edmonton)*

"*Tapas on the Ramblas*...like its predecessors carries the reader along on an exuberant joy ride of action with sporadic pit stops for mayhem, menace and occasional romance."
— *Wayves (Halifax)*

"In *Tapas on the Ramblas*, Bidulka has really hit his stride. Bidulka...shows himself to be a writer firmly in control of his story and able to give full rein to his considerable wit and wry observations."
— *Wayves (Halifax)*

"One of the book's most enjoyable aspects is its lively descriptions of foreign places…it is clear that Bidulka has traveled there himself and his novel captures the flavor of those travels quite vividly."

– Altar Magazine (Brooklyn, NY)

"*Tapas on the Ramblas*…is not your mama's mystery."

– OutTraveler (Los Angeles, CA)

Praise for *Stain of the Berry*:

"Saskatchewan's master of all things mysterious is back with *Stain of the Berry*…Bidulka's Quant mysteries always crackle with action, suspense, intricate plotting…"

– Planet S (Saskatoon)

"A terrifying stain is marring the beauty of the Prairies."

– Swerve (Winnipeg)

"…the best of the series."

– Globe & Mail (Toronto)

"If you've missed the previous three novels set in Saskatoon and featuring gay sleuth Russell Quant, you'll want them first."

– Globe & Mail (Toronto)

"…death will lead Quant into a strange but wide-ranging problem that proves quite disconcerting, and dangerous. It's a strong mystery that calls on all his ingenuity."

– The StarPhoenix (Saskatoon)

"Bidulka is no slouch when it comes to snappy dialogue and campy one-liners that more than tip the hat to classic noir…"

– NOW Magazine (Toronto)

"…an Arctic escapade worthy of James Bond."

– NOW Magazine (Toronto)

"With this fourth book, Bidulka really comes into his own as a writer— the stakes are higher, the sense of menace much more realized throughout and the deepening of the mythology of the series makes everything come that much more to life."

– Outlooks (Calgary)

"Bidulka ups the chill factor, notch by notch, making the …Boogeyman specter into a palpable presence."

– Lavender Magazine (Minnesota)

"This enjoyable series, which boasts an amiable and chatty…hero, really fires on all cylinders…"

– reviewingtheevidence.com

"Bidulka is a relaxed and fluent storyteller who creates some memorable characters…"

– reviewingtheevidence.com

"The strength of the books lies, as it so often does, in characters…I don't see my admiration for the writer or his character waning any time soon."

– CanadaEast (New Brunswick)

"This novel is the most complex in the series."

– Lambda Book Report (New York)

"…the storyline brings a smile as pages turn with gorgeous images and smells of summer.…"

– Feminist Review

"Bidulka's characterization is excellent. He has a way of nailing a person with a few words to evoke a strong mental image."

– Spinetingler Magazine

"Quant…makes for a riveting hero…the kind of friend you want to have—unless you're a killer."

– Mystery Scene Magazine (New York)

"Bidulka is clear evidence that writing in the mystery genre does not automatically preclude character development or emotional connection with the reader."

– Wayves (Halifax)

"Bidulka's skill makes the story so vivid that we feel as if we are the friend holding the flashlight while Quant explores the tunnel ahead."

– Wayves (Halifax)

"This thriller is guaranteed to keep you on the edge of your beach blanket."

– Frontiers Magazine (Los Angeles)

"...Bidulka brings a fresh voice to Canadian crime fiction, with a sense of humour that is often outrageous and always original; he provides his readers with a cleverly crafted tale full of twists and turns, and challenges readers to broaden their perspectives."

– The Sherbrooke Record (Sherbrooke, QC)

"The ending...is as satisfactory as any I have recently encountered, but I was not expecting it. Yet the author plays scrupulously fair with the reader."

– reviewingtheevidence.com

"Despite all the darkness in the novel, this is the author's most joyful to date. It is also his finest, a work that radiates a deep sense of humanity and wisdom."

– reviewingtheevidence.com

"Bidulka is an experienced writer...and it's apparent from the first three lines."

– Wayves (Halifax)

"My first reaction in reaching the end of this book was to head to my computer to find how to get a hold of the four earlier books in the series..."

– Wayves (Halifax)

"...a satisfying episode in Quant's ongoing professional saga."

– PGN (Philadelphia)

"Russell Quant is a hero who is humble, vulnerable, but intelligent, resourceful, and all too human."

– Midwest Book Review

"All dangers aside, though, when you're through with this riveting book, you might find yourself booking the first flight to Cape Town. See you on the plane!"

– Mystery Scene Magazine (New York)

"Despite many reminders of how messy and even unpleasant human existence can be, there is a peacefulness about this novel that is new to the series."

– Lambda Book Report (Los Angeles)

"The novel is by all odds the author's most masterful to date..."

– Lambda Book Report (Los Angeles)

Aloha,
Candy Hearts

Also by the author

Amuse Bouche
Flight of Aquavit
Tapas on the Ramblas
Stain of the Berry
Sundowner Ubuntu

Aloha,
Candy Hearts

A Russell Quant Mystery

Anthony Bidulka

INSOMNIAC PRESS

Library and Archives Canada Cataloguing in Publication

Bidulka, Anthony, 1962-
    Aloha, candy hearts / Anthony Bidulka.

ISBN 978-1-897178-76-8

    I. Title.

PS8553.I319A64 2009   C813'.6   C2009-901093-3

The publisher gratefully acknowledges the support of the Canada Council, the Ontario Arts Council and the Department of Canadian Heritage through the Book Publishing Industry Development Program.

Printed and bound in Canada

Insomniac Press
192 Spadina Avenue, Suite 403
Toronto, Ontario, Canada, M5T 2C2
www.insomniacpress.com

  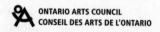

In the middle of the North Pacific Ocean is an island nicknamed "The Gathering Place." Its population sits at under a million, the area code is 808, and the average temperature is 25°–30° C (75°–85° F). This island is Oahu, Hawaii.

The people of Hawaii are known throughout the world for their spirit of *Aloha*. This spirit can only be described as an inner warmth: a feeling of love, respect, and hospitality. This spirit comes from the very soul of this ancient people.

This book is dedicated to my longtime *ku'uipo* and brand new *pilikua*, Herb, who would spend every vacation, weekend off, and special occasion in Hawaii if he could (and with dozens of trips already logged, he has given it a good try), and to his lovely oasis that, because of his presence there, has become mine as well.

Herb's love affair with the islands—Oahu in particular—began in childhood and has deepened with time and maturity. Although the experience has recreated itself many times and in many ways, some favourites (and favourite memories) endure: the Surf Club on Kuhio, Waikiki Shore with its perfect slice of Waikiki Beach and view of Friday night fireworks, the scent of plumeria, POG & vodka on the beach, ahi tuna poke, La Mer and Orchids at the Halekulani, sunset hula by Kanoe Miller, Starbucks and oat bars, Holly's cottage in the hills, Evil Jungle Prince at Keos, music radio and newspaper on the beach, perfect Mai Tais at the Royal Hawaiian, swimming with dolphins, jogging down the Ali Wai, watching videos at Hulas, climbing up Diamond Head, grocery trips to Daiei, walking Kalakaua, spotting the green flash at sunset, towels from ABC, the juiciest fruit from Henry's, Pat and Jack Brattus, long afternoon walks down the beach, finding perspective, the first breath of moist, tropical air as we step off the aircraft, the many family and friends we've laughed with there, and anticipating years and years and years of the same.

Much *Aloha*.

Early on, when I was first settling on a concept for this sixth Quant book, I had Russell investigating a rather dark case surrounding a suicide club and a nasty character who preyed on terminally ill people who'd come to believe that taking their own lives (or having someone do it for them) was a better way out. Although I ultimately decided the storyline wasn't what I was looking for, I've stored it away for potential use in the future. That being said, I owe a debt of gratitude to the people who helped develop the concept and flesh it out with wonderful detail, including Jo-Anne, Brian, my sister Hope, Ted, my niece Kim, and Della. Your willingness to share your special talents and brainpower is much appreciated.

In the summer of 2005, I had the opportunity to speak at the annual Association of Canadian Archivists conference. I knew little about the process of archiving, but found the subject fascinating and thought it might make good fodder for a book one day. That day has arrived. I never forgot the many fine professionals I met that evening, and called upon two of them, Tim Hutchinson and Cheryl Avery, of the University of Saskatchewan Archives, for help when I was developing this story. Tim and Cheryl provided invaluable insight. Thank you for your generous donation of time and information. Any errors I've made in this regard are solely my creation.

I also want to say a special hello to Louis Volz who won his place in Russell Quant lore at the 2008 Human Rights Campaign National Dinner in Washington, DC.

I need to thank: James Fuester who, upon hearing the title of this book, immediately sent theme and décor suggestions for the launch party (...sandy beaches of turbinado brown sugar and meringue froth...) and both Jim and his very "cool" mom for my very own Bidulka Michigan football sweatshirt, T-shirt, and PEZ – awesome!; once again the EY alumni group led off by Shelley B— I can't think of a better crowd to celebrate with; everyone who came to the *Sundowner Ubuntu* book launch to share in the fantastic food and drink prepared by the pros at Prairie Ink, and African rhythmic dancing of Kahmaria Pingue, Kirsty, Kristen and drummer Marnie—each launch just gets better and better thanks to all of you—the spirit of *ubuntu* is truly in abundance in Saskatoon;

Karen for the way cool telegram; JorDan for the special African feast (Kelly, Rhonda, Jan, Paul, Dori, Rob, Jill, Shelley, David for sharing it with us, and Nigel {as Russell Quant}, Catherine {as Jane Cross} and Herb {as narrator} for the awesome dramatic re-enactment from *Flight of Aquavit*); all the entrants of the World of Russell Quant Wine Gift Basket Contests—special thanks to Book & Brier, Little Sister's wine and cheese afternoon attendees, and Chronicles of Crime; my fellow "Men of Mystery" Neil Plakcy and Mark R. Zubro; the Bloody Words gang for laughing at the right spots and the opportunity to MC a spectacular gala; Caro Soles for your wonderful "Touring Texas with Tony" article; only my hairdresser knows for sure—thanks Shelley for keeping my poster up all year long – Salon Pure rocks!; Kevin Hogarth and Clipper for marathon photo session with great results; Wayne Gunn and Raymond-Jean Frontain for your especially kind words; Dori for the cool black golf shirts; Sheila for all you do for *Acreage Life*; Robert and Ted for a great evening in New Orleans; Ward for Ubuntu in a frame; Carrie S—terrific to finally meet in DC—you're my cemetery goddess; My Facebook Fan Club—special thanks to Shawn, and officers Mark, Bonnie and Dyl!; Vicki for inviting me to TypeM4Murder; Bev J for our office parties for two!; newlyweds Graham and Randall for suggesting a title for a Hawaiian-themed Russell Quant—*Poison in the Poke*—before I'd even written it— sadly there was no poison in the poke…this time; David Rimmer of After Stonewall Books for all you do; and to the absolute best circle of family and friends that any guy could have…much love.

Special affection and appreciation is reserved for my talented colleague and friend from Florida, author Neil Plakcy, whose own detective, Kimo Kanapa'aka, appears on these pages. As a great fan of TV series crossovers (remember when The Six Million Dollar Man showed up on *The Bionic Woman*?), I was thrilled with the idea of our two detectives appearing together. Neil and I have attended conferences and toured together many times, so it only made sense that our characters should finally meet. I'm sure their adventures are only just beginning.

To all the people in the industry—booksellers, reviewers, interviewers, distributors, events coordinators—thanks for paying attention to Russell Quant and for keeping reading alive.

Insomniac Press continues to believe in the world according to Russell Quant—thanks Mike and Gillian. And Gillian, thanks for being my date to the Arthur Ellis Awards dinner!

This book was pulled into production six months earlier than originally planned, and editor Catherine Lake jumped on board with no notice, having to make room for it in her busy life. Thank you for the willingness to do so and grace under pressure.

Truly, the best part of what I do is the people who read these books. I've been lucky enough to meet many of you over the past half dozen books at readings, on tour, at conferences, or just on the street or in a grocery store. And if that's not enough, I wake up every morning to find wonderfully inspiring, encouraging, and uplifting emails and messages sent to me from places across the street to the other side of the world. I cannot thank you enough for this. It is that extra bit of special that I never anticipated when I first began to write, and have come to treasure.

For dear, sweet, cousin Lorraine. Forever unforgettable.

And Herb.

Chapter 1

"Russell Quant, will you marry me?"

I gulped.

The old, vine-fortified *banyuls* I'd been blissfully sipping, along with our shared Grand Marnier and *lilikoi* soufflé, suddenly turned sticky in my throat. I wished for a draft to cool my rapidly crimsoning cheeks. Although only seconds passed before I responded to the unexpected question, it seemed as if the world around me had slowed to half speed. Visions of my life passed before my eyes. Or at least the last seventy-two hours of it.

The telephone call had been unexpected. There are no sweeter six words than: come to Hawaii for the weekend. With the possible exception of: Your ticket is paid for, Russell. That's when the cyclone first hit. After that, it was such a whirlwind, I hadn't even been aware that I was being swept off my feet—until those final six words: Russell Quant, will you marry me?

We were staying on Waikiki beach in Oahu, at the plush Halekulani Hotel. Halekulani means "House Befitting Heaven."

And from what I'd seen so far, I was so becoming an angel. Our days began with boogie boarding or kayaking in the mornings. Afterwards we'd grab a bite at House Without a Key, the hotel's outdoor gathering place immortalized by the Charlie Chan novel of the same name. Then it was time for lazing on the beach or around the pool with its stunning orchid mosaic. In the early evening, after cleaning up, we'd return to House Without a Key, wearing our tropical whites and shirts that billowed in the perfect breeze and find a spot under the kiawe shade tree. From that glorious place, we'd sip on surprisingly strong Mai Tais (regular ice, not crushed), watch the sunset, and enjoy the hula of a former Miss Hawaii. This wasn't the hip-rattle-roll stuff you get at the tourist luaus either. This was graceful hula, accompanied by ukulele, steel guitar, slack key, and the lilting falsetto vocals unique to traditional Hawaiian music. Later we'd have dinner at popular eating spots like Keo's or Alan Wong's. But tonight, the eating experience had been ratcheted up a notch or two.

We were dining at La Mer, on the second floor of the hotel. The menu featured "neo-classic French" cuisine. I didn't know what that meant, but I liked it all the same. I liked it a lot. It might have been the champagne they served us before our butts were even in our chairs. Or the unimpeded view of Waikiki beach, the Pacific Ocean, and Diamond Head. Or the fact that they brought a little stool just to set my camera on. Or maybe it was the fillet of *opaka-paka* baked in rosemary salt crust. And still, despite it all, I was completely oblivious to the portentousness of all this luxury and excess. I thought he was just *really* happy to see me.

Then came THE QUESTION.

Even though I never took my green eyes off his cocoa brown ones, I was acutely aware of our waiter, Raymond, standing not far off. He'd obviously been in on the whole thing. I could feel his ear-to-ear grin even though I couldn't see it. And I was pretty sure a few neighbouring diners were also monitoring the drama at our table. How could they resist? Two well-dressed men seated at the best table in the house, a tropical paradise as our backdrop, the sultry haziness of too much, too-expensive wine that begs close acquaintance from perfect strangers, romantic island music, one of us with a ring in his hand and hopeful look on his face, the other with a wide open mouth and shock on his (that would be me).

For a second I looked away. At Raymond. He gave me an encouraging nod. My eyes fell back on Alex Canyon. I gave him my answer.

"Yes."

I had a couple of hours to kill at the Honolulu International Airport after seeing Alex off on his flight to Australia before my own flight home to Canada. Alex is a private and corporate security specialist and had been working a job in Melbourne for the past couple of months. Hawaii had been playing the role of handy halfway point for our not-regular-enough liaisons. It was going to be weeks before we saw each other again. That seemed like a good enough reason to head for the nearest bar to drown my sorrows.

The place had a name, I'm sure, but I decided to call it Hawaiian Kitsch. It was stuffed to the rafters with everything Hawaiian, from surfboards to drinks served in fake coconuts. It was also stuffed with *haole* (non-Hawaiian) customers. It seemed everyone was desperate to get one last hit of island flavour before they returned to their real lives, sadly lacking in plumeria leis, grass skirts, and *kalua* pig burgers. There wasn't even an empty stool at the bar to be had. My eyes jumped from table to table assessing whether anyone was about to leave. It didn't look that way, so I decided to forgo the drink and simply find a comfy spot near my gate and dig into the Josh Lanyon book I'd been saving for the plane.

This far ahead of departure, I had plenty of choice spots to pick from, and selected one with a good view of the tarmac. Even tarmacs in Hawaii somehow manage to look tranquil and tropical. I settled in with a bottle of water (poor replacement for a double gin and tonic) and a bag of the licorice I always keep in my carry-on.

Half an hour later, having difficulty concentrating on my book with my head full of this and that, I heard loud voices. Someone wasn't happy. I looked around to find the source, half-thinking I wanted to shoot them an irritated look for interrupting my nonreading. What I found were three guys, about a hundred metres off: two Hawaiians and a *haole*.

One Hawaiian was much smaller than the other two guys, short and wiry, with a tortoise-like face, and looking extremely jumpy. He was the one doing all the caterwauling. The other two were showing him something—ID maybe? Weapons?—and I guessed they were either some kind of airport security or the Hawaiian version of mafia hit men. From my experience as a once-upon-a-time-cop, and something about the stance of the two big guys, I was betting on the former. Either way, things did not look so good for the tortoise.

And just like that, the jittery-looking guy took advantage of a passing parade of Japanese tourists, and, using them as a shield, made a dash for it, heading my way.

I heard a muffled "Stop! Police!" come from one of the pursuers, temporarily waylaid by the tourists. I instinctually leapt to action. Things were happening so fast, I didn't have much time to make plans, other than to decide I had to do what I could to stop the fleeing man. He was barrelling (not very tortoise-like) toward me at breakneck speed. I was either going to have to get into a footrace with him through the airport terminal, or find a way to stop him.

I never made the high school football team. It wouldn't have been difficult, though, growing up in Howell, Saskatchewan. Most graduating classes numbered under a dozen, and were half female, a statistic that practically guaranteed a spot for anyone who wanted to suit up. But despite being built as sturdy as a tree by grade nine, it just wasn't for me, so I never tried out. But, from my days at the police academy, I do know a thing or two about tackling goons.

My airport runaway was moving too fast to assure a quick takedown from behind. Instead, I needed to break his momentum. That's the thing about speed—the faster you're moving forward, the faster you go down when you meet with an obstacle. I decided to be that obstacle.

Timing myself as carefully as I could, with bowed head and hunched back, I propelled myself into tortoise's path.

He never saw me coming. I felt the man's body fold over mine as I rolled over the floor, and looked up just in time to see two legs flailing in the air. Success!

I'd barely come to a stop before the two cops were on the guy like icing on cake. For big fellows they moved like cheetahs. In one slick move, the *haole* had the smaller guy up and in cuffs, while his partner pushed his nose into the tortoise face and said some words that probably weren't very nice.

I stood up and was brushing myself off when I saw the Hawaiian cop coming over.

"Hey," he said as he approached, his dark eyes covering every inch of me.

He was tall, well-built, and casually dressed for a cop, in nice fitting jeans and a worn, surfer's T-shirt, the kind The Gap sold to kids who'd probably never been on a board. But something told me this guy was one-hundred-percent authentic. And he certainly wasn't a kid. The face was handsome, and on closer inspection didn't look all Hawaiian after all; there was some other influence in his exotic features. Strong jaw. Sharp cheekbones. Nice lips. I only noticed the lips because I thought I detected a slight grin there.

"I'm sorry," I said, palms out. "I know I shouldn't have interfered. It's just that I used to be a cop."

The guy cocked an eyebrow. "Instinct, right?"

I nodded. "Yup. Never goes away, I guess."

Surprising me, he reached out and took my left hand in his. Aw crap. Was I gonna get a set of stainless steel bracelets for all my trouble? Was I about to share a cell with tortoise man?

Instead, the cop turned my hand palm up and inspected a scrape I must have gotten from my tumble.

"You need some medical attention."

"Nah, nah," I said looking at the wound. "It'll be fine. I'll just clean it up in the bathroom."

"Uh, if you're done chit-chatting over there," the other cop called over with a funny look in his eye, "maybe you could pay some attention to the perp we got over here?"

The Hawaiian released my hand and shot his partner a well-practiced look of annoyance just as the other officer's radio bleeped for his attention.

"You'll have to excuse Ray," the Hawaiian said. "He's not real good in public."

I smiled. He smiled back. I felt an odd tingle in some odd spots and inwardly chastised myself. I really needed that drink.

"Thanks for giving us a hand with Huei. He must have forgotten that the Honolulu police frown on people leaving the island when we have an arrest warrant with their name on it."

"Maybe his memory isn't what it used to be."

"That must be it."

"Hey, Kimo," the other cop said as he dragged a sullen-looking Huei closer. "That was the chief. One of us gotta hang out here to unruffle the feathers of some airport guys who wanna know why we're disturbing their passengers. They say they'll be right down. Which probably means half an hour. You wanna do that while I take in our friend here?"

Kimo winced at the idea, but nodded. "But I'm only waiting ten minutes. After that I'm heading for the surf."

Ray grunted agreement and led his charge away.

"Looks like I've got a few minutes to wait," Kimo said. "Can I buy you a coffee to thank you for your heroics?"

I could tell he wasn't exactly serious about the "heroics" part, but who was I to turn down coffee with a handsome surfer dude cop?

After scoring a couple of drinks from a nearby vendor, we returned to where I'd left my stuff and took spots next to one another.

"Let me see," Kimo began in serious earnestness, "you're at the airport, you have a carry-on, I see a ticket in your pocket; my superior detecting skills tell me you're heading home."

I laughed. "Yeah. I can see you must be one of Hawaii's best and brightest."

He smiled easily. "Where's home for you?" he asked.

"Saskatchewan."

He tried to repeat the name of the province. He blundered badly, but with a pleasing boyish smirk that made up for it.

"It's a tough one," I allowed.

"I can relate," he said. "With a name like Kimo Kanapa'aka."

I felt obliged to try it out. It came out something like: Kimokalawakala. I grimaced. "Sorry."

"Just Kimo is okay."

"I'm Russell. Russell Quant."

We each took a sip of our coffees while regarding the other with inquiring eyes. That done, we put our cups on our laps and tried out matching silly grins. We were strangers cast together unexpectedly but somehow drawn to one another. The silence wasn't exactly comfortable, but I didn't care. There was something immediately likeable about this guy.

"I'm glad to see you smile," he finally said. "I was thinking you looked a little miserable when I first saw you. I hate to see anyone leaving Hawaii without a big, fat grin on his face."

"Could have been because I was on the ground after tackling your bad guy."

"Nah, *brah*, it was before that. I noticed you when we were staking out the terminal looking for Huei."

Had Mr. Hawaiian surfer dude, he-man cop been checking me out? "Oh really?"

"We were about to apprehend a criminal," he explained, possibly having read my mind. "As a former policeman, I'm sure you know that in a situation like that, a good cop is always fully aware of his surroundings and exactly who and what is around him."

"Oh," I said, a little disappointed. "Of course."

"So why were you sitting here looking so miserable? Bad book?"

He really had been fully aware of me and what I'd been doing. I was impressed. "I wasn't miserable, really." I told him. "Just a little bummed out. I won't see my...fiancé..." The word felt weird coming from my mouth, as if I'd just made it up. "...for a few weeks. So I guess I'm a little sad about that."

Kimo bobbed his head in an empathetic gesture. "That's too bad. How come? Your *ku'uipo* from here then? That why you won't see her, she lives here?"

"She's a he," I told him, followed by a sip of coffee.

The man's eyebrows rose over his eyes.

I shrugged and grinned. "Yeah, that's right," I said, "I'm Canadian."

After a beat, he grinned back and said, "Me too."

I realized what he was really telling me. He was a *gay* Hawaiian surfer dude, he-man cop. Very cool. We clinked coffee cups and drank a toast.

"Where's the wedding gonna be?" he asked. "Here on the island maybe?"

My eyes widened. Never even thought about it. "I dunno."

"When's the big day?"

"I dunno."

"Are you big, white wedding kind of guys, or into something small and intimate?"

Jeepers! Who was this guy? A reporter for the Oahu six o'clock news? "I dunno."

Kimo frowned. "You have actually *met* the guy who you think is going to marry you, right?"

I gave him a face that said, "Very funny, smartass."

He gave me an apologetic look. "Okay, okay. So what's your fiancé's name?"

And for one horrible moment that lasted an eon, my mind went blank.

Kimo let out a nervous chuckle. He checked his watch as if hoping it was time to go. "You're kidding me, right?"

"Alex!" I finally got out. "His name is Alex. Alex. Alex. Alex."

"Russell," he asked, his face suddenly serious. "Did you just meet this guy, *brah*?"

"No! Of course not. It's just all so new for me. He only asked me to marry him last night. I haven't quite processed it yet." I was beginning to feel a little uneasy with the way the conversation was going. It was time to take it on a less intrusive detour. "So you're a cop?"

He nodded.

I eyed up the T-shirt and silver bracelet embossed with surfboards. "And a surfer?"

He gave me a strange look before answering, "I like to surf, yeah."

"Is that...a good hobby?" It didn't come out quite as I'd meant it to.

Kimo chuckled. "You mean for a guy my age?"

I gave him a mischievous smile. "Well, I'm sure there are many seniors' surfing competitions you'd do really well in." Even in the short time we'd spent together, there was something about this guy that told me our senses of humour jived.

He made a move as if pulling a knife from his heart. "You wound me, *brah*."

We shared a look. The kind that two people attracted to one another, but knowing it can't ever go anywhere, share. We drank some more coffee.

During the nearly six-hour flight from Honolulu to Vancouver, and the layover until I could board my plane for Saskatoon, I did more reading and eating than sleeping. So by the time I was winging my way home, I was ready for a nap. I snuggled into the CRJ's seat with about seventy other passengers and prepared for some shut-eye. But fate had another plan. It began with a series of sighs from the seat next to me.

I admit to being as curious as the proverbial cat. How can I not be, given my chosen career? So, although I was a little vexed by the noisy exhaling, it wasn't surprising that I found myself abandoning the promise of pleasant dreams for a peek at my neighbour.

The man sitting next to me was a little odd in appearance to say the least. If there were a human version of Mr. Magoo, he would be it. Through the slit of one eye, I could make out a hugely bulbous nose, sticky-outy chin, wobbly jowls, sunken mouth, and a completely hairless, perfectly round head. His eyes, nearly hidden behind pouches of skin, sat below eyebrows shaped like inverted "V"s. Although it was summer, and the forecast for our evening arrival was balmy, he wore some kind of trench coat with a uniquely patterned scarf of orange and blue wound about his neck. If I had to guess, I'd say he was nearing seventy.

Just as I was about to lose myself back to sleep, the man sighed again. This time it was accompanied by a gentle but definite "har-rumph." I saw that he was intently studying a piece of paper. His scrunched-up mouth was travelling from one side of his face to the other, as if worrying over a particularly recalcitrant piece of gum.

I saw a crew member making his way down the aisle with water. Deciding that wouldn't be a bad idea, I sat up and waited to be offered some. I exchanged a polite glance with Magoo.

"Good evening," he said. "I hope I didn't wake you."

"No," I lied. "I never sleep long on planes."

He nodded absentmindedly as he returned his attention to the paper on his lap.

Dropping my seat table, I accepted water from the steward.

After one more sigh, the man carefully folded the paper and placed it in the breast pocket of his coat. He looked over at me with a lopsided, lip-less smile. "Going home?"

He even sounded like Mr. Magoo. Or was it Thurston Howell III from *Gilligan's Island*? "Yes," I told him. "It's nice to get away, but always nice to come back home too."

"That's refreshing to hear from a young person," he said. "I suppose with the local economy booming the way it is, more and more youngsters like you are staying in Saskatchewan."

I was enjoying being called a youngster. Especially since I'd just turned thirty-eight. A few years back, my ultra-stylish friend Anthony had cajoled me into using a line of Clinique skin products for men. I guess they were worth the ultra-stylish cost. Although I steadfastly refuse to wear a moisturizing mask to bed. "Yes, I hear that's true."

"What line of work are you in?"

"I'm a private detective."

That answer is always good for a reaction. And Mr. Magoo did not disappoint. He shifted in his seat to get a better look at me. Although the flaps covering his eyes were nearly impenetrable, I spied a flash of blue, brilliant as a newborn's.

"No!" he said, truly astonished.

I'd run into this before. I dug a business card (you never know when you might meet a potential client) from a pocket of my cargo shorts and handed it to him. He studied it carefully before burying it in his jacket pocket.

"So you investigate murders and that sort of mayhem?"

I nodded. It was the truth. I had been involved in at least a few murder cases—granted, sometimes peripherally—since leaving the Saskatoon Police Service several years earlier. There was Tom Osborn found afloat in Pike Lake. James Kraft shot in a New York City hotel room. The drag queen who looked like Phyllis Lindstrom from *The Mary Tyler Moore Show* pushed off the side of an ocean liner. And Tanya Culinare, who jumped from the eighth-floor balcony of her Broadway Avenue apartment. Oh yeah, I investigated murders all the time.

"I wouldn't have thought there'd be much call for that sort of thing in a city the size of Saskatoon," the old man commented.

At about a quarter of a million people, Saskatoon is not a big city. And indeed, in between my higher profile cases, most of my time as a prairie detective is spent chasing down errant husbands, runaway kids, lost pets, and, in one instance, discovering whether a local restaurant had indeed used Mrs. Galabruch's perogy recipe and passed it off as their own. But no one needed to know about that. I nodded again and said, "A hot economy has benefits for my line of work too. More people, more action, more crime." Gosh, I love prosperity.

His mouth made a chewing motion as he considered what I'd said. Then he asked, "You wouldn't be interested in something a little less dramatic, then?"

I was very interested. Not only do I like being able to pay my bills (that damn Clinique stuff is expensive), as compelling as my infrequent murder cases are, they aren't necessarily my favourite kind of work. Murder means death. Death means grief. Usually for many people. Death is gruesome. Death is just not a nice thing to spend all your time around. So, although I might outwardly whine about being asked to find out if Sophie Underwill's beagle from down the street is responsible for the daily deposits of doody in Mr. Kindrachski's bed of prize-winning lilies, inwardly I rather enjoy the work.

Then again, sometimes there's nothing better than a good murder.

"I might be," I told Mr. Magoo.

"What about treasure maps?" he asked. "Are you any good with treasure maps?"

Now it was my turn to look astonished. Treasure maps? I suddenly had memories of being eight. I loved movies and books about adventurous pirates in exotic locations in search of treasure. I daydreamed of chests filled with gold and jewels and countless coins. But the man sitting next to me did not at all resemble a pirate: no eye patch, no bandana around unruly black hair, no peg leg or missing teeth. I was going to be disappointed. I was sure of it.

Magoo rifled around in his pocket and pulled out the piece of paper I'd spied him studying earlier in the flight. He pulled down his seat table and flattened the paper on top of it. Although I hate being snoopy—okay, that's a lie—I couldn't help taking a peek. It was a rather crude drawing, a few squiggles and symbols, interspersed with lots of words. The thing looked more like a poem than a treasure map. Treasure maps were supposed to have a compass rose and a trail of arrows over sketched terrain, which usually included mountains and valleys and swamps. And there should be a castle and a few warnings about quicksand or dragons or something good like that. So yup, I was disappointed.

"I don't know what she was thinking when she did this," Magoo muttered. "But I shouldn't be surprised. Helen always was a quirky one."

"I'm sorry," I said. "What exactly is this?"

"Helen, my…friend…left this for me," he said, his fingers busily fumbling over the surface of the paper. "It's a map of Saskatoon."

I leaned in and peered closer. "It is?"

"Sure it is," he said, pointing at a blob that I suppose could have been a castle. "See, that's the Bessborough Hotel." His finger moved from blob to blob. "And there's the river. And the university campus. Downtown."

I thought he was giving the artist greater credit than deserved, but geographically speaking, if I squinted and turned my head just right, I could see a general resemblance to the city where we were about to land.

"And what's all the writing over top of the map?"

"Those are the clues," he whispered in a way that urged me to do the same. "You see, I have to figure these out in order to find it."

"Find what?" I asked, my curiosity gene on full alert.

The man stared at me. For a moment he seemed uncertain, as if suddenly realizing that maybe he'd said—and shown me—too much. Finally, his cartoonish face broke into a conspiratorial smile. "A treasure," he enthused quietly. "If I decipher the clues correctly, I find the treasure. Simple as that. It's like a game."

"I see." The man didn't need to hire a detective. He needed a playmate.

"I've been going over the clues," he said, thick fingers pointing at the first stanza of the treasure map poem. "I think I've got some of them figured out. But the rest, well, I just can't seem to. I need help. I guess maybe I'm getting a little too old for this sort of thing. The brain isn't working at top form anymore."

"Maybe you're just tired," I suggested helpfully.

He nodded. "Travelling does take the stuffing out of me these days. Perhaps I'll be more clear-headed in the morning."

"Yes, I'm sure you will," I assured him. "Why don't you give it another go when you're feeling better? If you still need help after that, you can give me a call. You have my card."

"Do I? Oh, my, yes I do. You just gave it to me! See what I mean? Dotty as a drunken donkey."

I chuckled. "I haven't heard that one before."

"Feel free to use it, my boy."

And with a ping of the seat belt sign, we began our descent into Saskatoon. It was good to be home.

I felt the arm thread through my own just as we entered the second floor arrivals lounge that overlooks the main concourse—okay, the only concourse—of the John G. Diefenbaker International Airport. I looked down at the little person who'd attached himself to my left side. It was Magoo.

"I hope you don't mind," he said, staring up at me with a sweet smile. "I feel like a doddering old auntie, but my gout is acting up, you see. Would you mind escorting me to where the bags come out?"

There was something odd about the smile on his cartoonish face. It didn't quite go with the look in his eyes. Was he ogling me? I couldn't be sure. But how could I turn him down? "Of course not," I said.

Together we traversed the short distance down the escalators to the luggage carousels. Within a few minutes the track began moving and my unexpected companion clapped his hands with glee when his one small, argyle-patterned bag was among the first to arrive. I pulled it off the carousel and handed it to him with a goodbye at the ready.

"What about you?" he asked, seeming a bit discombobulated by the sudden farewell.

"I'm afraid my bags haven't come off yet. Do you need help getting to a taxi?" I offered. "I can come back for my bags after we get you set."

"Oh," he said, looking a bit vague. "No. I have my own car in the lot."

I wondered how he was going to drive if his gout was bothering him as bad as he'd claimed. My mother suffered intermittently with gout, so I knew about the pain associated with it. "Are you sure you can drive? Maybe you should take a cab home tonight. You could come back for your car tomorrow."

"Of course I can drive. Why not?"

"Your gout?"

"Oh. Oh that. Well, I'm suddenly feeling much better."

"That's good news."

He stood there, unmoving, a perplexed look on his face.

"Would you like me to walk you to your car?"

"I wouldn't want you to go to the trouble. Are your bags here yet?"

I searched the conveyor for my luggage. Even though most of the other passengers had already retrieved their bags and begun migrating toward the exits, mine were nowhere to be seen. This was not a good sign, and neither was the approaching Air Canada representative.

"I'm afraid that is all the luggage from this flight," he announced to the half-dozen of us left. "If you could follow me to the booth right over there, I can take your information."

What followed was a chorus of discontent that I knew from past experience was utterly useless. I looked at Magoo and grimaced. "My bad luck, I guess."

He nodded, looking even more disgruntled than I was. His eyes made a quick sweep of the concourse as if looking for something or someone, then he shrugged and said, "Well, m'boy, I guess I'll be off then. It was a pleasure meeting you. I hope we get a chance to talk again soon." And with that, he toddled off.

I joined the unhappy throng at the lost luggage counter.

Twenty minutes later, with Air Canada promising to home deliver my two suitcases as soon as they returned from their own getaway vacation to who knew where, I was in the airport long-term parking lot trying to recall where I'd left my silver Mazda RX-7. I usually park near a walkway, to make spotting the small vehicle a little easier. On the bright side, at least I didn't have to bother with hauling a couple of heavy pieces of luggage after me.

It was getting dark out and I'd just spotted the car when I noticed a flurry of activity not far off. People were gathered in a dim corner of the lot, but something told me this was definitely more than just an impromptu tailgate party. There was unmistakable tension in the air. Voices were raised, and I thought I could hear crying. Something was wrong. I trotted over to take a look.

Squeezing through the circle of gawkers, I finally saw what the fuss was about. Someone had collapsed next to a car. He didn't seem to be moving. A couple of parking lot security guards were attending to him, but the situation didn't look good. Heart attack maybe? I could hear one of the guards talking to a 9-1-1 operator, asking for both an ambulance and police.

Although by virtue of my chosen career I am a professional snoop, I try to hold it to a minimum in times of private misfortune.

I was about to step away from this bad luck story when something familiar caught my eye.

An orange and blue scarf.

I drew in a sharp breath.

It was Mr. Magoo lying lifeless on the ground.

Then I noticed one more thing. Alarm bells started ringing in my head.

I charged forward, and yelled: "Seal off the parking lot!"

Chapter 2

Detective Darren Kirsch was not amused when after asking me—
five separate times—to identify the dead man in the parking lot, all
I could answer was: "Mr. Magoo."

"I'm sorry," I said. I was. "I never asked his name. We were
strangers who met on a plane. We chatted. I helped him with his
suitcase. That's it."

"How did you know he was murdered?"

I winced. It turned out the orange and blue scarf around Mr.
Magoo's throat was tied *very* tightly. He'd been strangled. In the
Saskatoon airport parking lot of all places. It was shocking. On
average, there are fewer than ten homicides each year in my
prairie hometown. Most of those happen within a very specific
area of the city. Most involve alcohol and knives, not an orange
and blue scarf. A quick visual survey of the people still milling
about the murder site revealed that everyone, cops and medical
professionals included, was just as taken aback as I was.

"I didn't know it was murder."

"Then why did you demand the parking lot be sealed off before anyone even suspected the death was suspicious?" Kirsch barked. It was his favourite manner of speaking, particularly to me. We'd worked together years ago when I was still a cop. We enjoyed being thorns in each other's sides ever since. Well, me more than him.

"I told you already. His luggage. I'd helped him, so I knew he had a carry-on and an argyle suitcase."

Kirsch stared at me. He was probably wondering what "argyle" meant.

"They were missing. And the body was too far from the car for him to have already stashed them in the trunk. I assumed he'd been robbed, not murdered. I thought if we stopped people from leaving the parking lot, we might be able to identify the thief by searching cars and finding out who had the luggage. I could have been wrong, I suppose, but I thought it was worth the effort."

The big cop grunted. "I suppose."

"Was that a compliment? Was that a, 'Hey, good call, Russell'?"

Kirsch snarled. Unfortunately for him, despite the requisite dark brooding eyes, shovel jaw, and cheesy mustache favoured by Saskatoon cops, he was simply too teddy bear cute to pull it off.

"Don't leave town," he said as he stalked off. "I'm gonna need to talk with you again."

"I'll look forward to it." I turned to go, then stopped and called out: "Have you been able to identify Mr. M…the dead man?"

"Angel," he called back. "His name was Walter Angel."

As I walked away, a troubling thought entered my mind. Had I read the look in Walter Angel's eyes incorrectly? Had he been ogling me? Or was he afraid?

It was late—after ten p.m.—by the time I got away from the airport. I knew stuffing two happy-to-see me schnauzers in the RX-7 would be a bit tricky, but I was desperate to be reunited with my pups Barbra and Brutus after being away for a whole week. Using my cellphone, I dialled Errall's number and got a two-word reply to my request. "Yeah, fine."

Errall Strane is my landlord, lawyer, sometime dogsitter, sparring partner, and oftentimes reluctant friend. She owns PWC, the downtown building that is home to my workplace, as well as her own one-woman law practice, Beverly Chaney's psychology office, and Alberta Lougheed's psychic realm of bizarreness. Errall was also Brutus's former owner.

Her greeting upon my arrival was just as verbose. She had both dogs on their leashes, waiting for me on the front porch. It was Saturday night, but it was obvious she wasn't entertaining guests. All the windows were dark. Even the front porch light was off. I could barely see her face when she said, "Here," and handed me the leads.

Barbra and Brutus are not effusive dogs. They lean more toward graceful and reserved, but I could tell they were thrilled to see me. As I was them. Their little tails were whirring fast enough to set them into flight, and they were letting out barely restrained whimpers of delight. Errall, on the other hand, was in a black mood. No tail wagging from her. She didn't bother to invite me in.

I took the leads. "Did Barbra and Brutus behave themselves?" They always did, but I liked getting a report anyway.

"Sure."

"Errall," I said, "Is everything all right?" I suspected it wasn't.

"Yep." She pulled back inside the house and turned away, kicking the door shut with her heel.

It was a beautiful August evening, but I didn't dare leave the top down. Not with two antsy dogs in the seat next to me. So I went through the machinations of covering up. I love my little car, but it is twenty years old. It doesn't have any of the push-one-button technology of newer convertibles. I had to unfold the top canopy, flip some flaps and doohickeys, get back in the car, turn a knob, wait for it to lift and fall into place above our heads, flip the flaps and doohickeys again, and then it was done. Barbra and Brutus watched and waited with admirable patience. It was a little tight quarters for all three of us in there, but all the better for a few minutes spent cuddling, petting, patting, and licking (I was the lickee, not the licker). We'd missed each other.

When that was done, I shifted into drive and headed off, planning to go straight home. It was late. I hadn't had much sleep in the past twenty-four hours. Someone I knew, however briefly, had just been murdered. You'd think home was where I'd want to be. But somehow I found myself steering the car in an entirely different direction.

I ended up on a leafy lane in an old part of town. I parked across the street from a charming house painted in hues of burgundy, harvest yellow, and dusk blue. A hand-carved sign swinging from a newel post identified it as Ash House, the home (and business) of Ethan Ash. Ethan was a man I'd met while on a case a couple of years earlier. I waited for a truck to pass before rolling down my window for a clearer view.

What are you doing here, Quant? I asked myself. Barbra snuffled her wet nose into my ear, asking the same thing. Or maybe she was wondering when she could finally get out of the cramped car. Both very good questions.

I shook my head. This was insane. I shouldn't be skulking around outside some guy's house like a lovesick schoolboy. I'm an engaged man. I love Alex Canyon. I'd accepted his offer of marriage. So why, oh why, can't I let this go? Another vehicle passed by. Damn traffic.

For years, my friends had chided me for being devotedly single and liking it. I'd been in love once, a long time ago. But when that was over, it seemed, so was my ability and desire to fall that far again. I'd had my crushes—usually on men who were totally unsuitable or un-haveable—like my best friend's boyfriend, or a Roman Catholic priest, or a guy who lived in New York City, or my best one yet: a murderer. Was I unlucky at love, or just not trying very hard? I'd been happy enough without it. Complete without it. I had great friends and family, a great job, great home, great dogs. I loved my life. But now I *had* fallen in love. Twice. With two different guys. At the same time. Rather inconvenient to say the least.

No, that wasn't true. It couldn't be. I couldn't be in love with Ethan Ash. We first met when I was hired to find a man who turned out to be his ex-lover. Ethan ran Ash House—kind of a frat house for the senior set in Saskatoon. Oldsters who were in pretty good health but maybe needed a little help with day-to-day chores, preparing meals, or just wanted to avoid loneliness, moved into Ash House where Ethan looked after them. He also looked after his twelve-year-old daughter, Simon (short for Simonette).

Ethan is a sweet, caring, gentle bear of a man. He's smart, jovial, and loves to laugh. He's a big, beefy guy, with poker-straight, shiny brown hair, rosy, dimpled cheeks, smiling eyes and an open, friendly face. The natural set of his features seems to be stuck on "happy," but when you catch him unaware, maybe looking a little wistful, his pleasant face turns downright beautiful. And although it's difficult to pinpoint exactly how he does it, sex appeal just oozes from his pores like syrup from a waffle.

When I first met him, I felt an unfamiliar spark—well, actually there were several sparks, in several different parts of my body. During the course of the case I was on, Ethan had been badly beaten and I visited him in the hospital. It was then, while sitting next to his bed, holding his hand, that I first fell in l...

No!

Not love. I had a crush. That's all it was.

Jeez, how old was I? When was I going to stop with the crushes?

Normally, it wouldn't have been a problem. Cases eventually end. Time passes. People move on and I don't see them again. But that didn't happen. As fate would have it, Ethan had become a bigger part of my life. Or at least the lives of my circle of friends.

Ethan and my boutique-store-owing friend, Anthony Gatt, were already acquaintances. Anthony's long-term partner, Jared Lowe, had recently ended his life as a jet-setting, internationally acclaimed supermodel. This was due both to the end of his thirties and the loss of his unblemished beauty when a maniacal stalker threw acid in his face. Although surgeries had taken care of some of the latter, when combined with the former, a screeching halt to his career was the undeniable consequence. So Jared had been looking for new opportunities, and now, he and Ethan were about to become business partners.

An aging Saskatchewan population and booming economy

had combined to make Ash House more successful than ever. The place was bursting at the seams. In shrewd contemplation of this, Ethan had purchased a small acreage just outside the city limits, right before local real estate prices went through the roof. His plan was to build a bigger and better facility (and a home for himself and Simon). But then construction costs went crazy and he needed a bigger loan than he could handle.

Enter Jared with his buckets of modelling profits. With Anthony's guidance, he'd invested his savings wisely and the asset side of his ledger had added up rather nicely over the years. After some research and soul searching, Jared offered to assist Ethan in the financing and building of the new Ash House, with the proviso that he could help run the expanded operation once it was done. Ethan was more than grateful to get the investment dollars, as well as the help with taking care of the much bigger property and its residents. Jared was thrilled to find something he could pour his passion into. He hadn't been looking forward to the nine-to-five world of regular, non-model folk. When completed, the new Ash House would be right up his alley. It would allow him a flexible schedule and the chance to help other people. The fact that some older people had poor eyesight and most simply didn't care about his altered looks, were side benefits he never publicly admitted.

So, like it or not, Ethan was in our lives. My life. And I, god help me, was drawn to him, like metal shavings to a magnet.

I don't like being metal shavings.

My betrothed (that word just makes me want to spend a weekend in the English countryside playing cricket and sipping cordials with women in hoop skirts), Alex Canyon, however, was not in my life. Not in a day-to-day way, anyway. That, I was guessing, was the problem.

Alex is a security expert, hired by people or companies with issues and lots of money to deal with them. The problem was that those issues rarely occured anywhere near Saskatoon, Saskatchewan, Canada. We'd been doing the long-distance thing for more than two years, and for the most part, it had worked out fine. Deep down, I'm an introvert. I like my alone time. I like not having to consider someone else's taste when ordering pizza or watching a movie or selecting a bottle of wine. It's nice. At least that's what I told myself.

Unlike Ethan, Alex is an in-your-face kind of guy. He's aggressive, powerfully built, Clark-Kent-handsome and super masculine, with a dry wit and global intellect. And did I mention smoulderingly sexy?

I suppose being part-time lovers over a long enough period should be enough to tell two people if they are meant to be together. I love Alex, I do, and I know he loves me.

Conclusion: I was being an idiot.

It was time to start the car and get the hell home.

As I prepared to pull away from Ash House, I waited for a white Ford F-150 with a cab over the bed to pass by.

Hey. Wait a second.

A white Ford F-150 with a cab had passed by a minute or so earlier. And a couple of minutes before that, too. What was going on here?

Was someone else staking out the house of the man I had a crush on? That didn't seem right.

I screeched out of my spot and made a sharp right off Elliott onto Wiggins Avenue. The Ford was not far ahead of me. I saw him make another right onto Temperance Street heading for Clarence Avenue. I did the same.

At Clarence, the white truck turned right. If I was a good boy and heading for home, I would turn left. I sat at the intersection and watched the progress of the suspicious vehicle.

He turned off Clarence back onto Elliott. What the hell? The driver was going in circles.

I, of course, had no way of knowing whether White Truck Guy was watching Ash House or one of the many other houses on the tree-lined suburban street. But something told me this was no father waiting to pick up his daughter from a babysitting job. Wisely or not, I made up my mind.

I switched the direction of my turn signal and headed right onto Clarence then turned down Elliott. As soon as I did, the white truck, dawdling down the street, suddenly lurched forward and sped off. The driver had caught sight of me and obviously did not want to be followed.

I sped up. So did the Ford. Once again he swung right onto Wiggins Avenue, then really floored it.

Oooeeee! A car chase! And I wasn't even on a case. Oh well, the Mazda could use the exercise after sitting in an airport parking lot for a week. The dogs seemed happy enough to go along for the ride. So, off I went.

This time the driver kept going straight, heading south, as if his next stop was Antarctica. We were speeding through what was mostly a residential area with uncontrolled intersections. The driver of the Ford was making tracks like he had the uncontested right-of-way. I watched as pretty little streets with their benign yards and mature treescapes whizzed by at double the posted speed. Given the time of night and part of town, the sidewalks were barren. For that I was glad.

Despite the empty streets, this was still unsafe. I knew I had to let the Ford go. As far as I knew, the guy behind the wheel of the white truck had done nothing wrong, except speed. But the fact that he was running away from me told me he'd probably been up to no good. How did he know I wasn't after him to tell him he had a flat tire, or to ask for directions?

I began to slow down. I was pretty sure there were no lights at the upcoming busy intersection with 8th Street. The chase was over. We'd both have to stop there.

Except he didn't.

I watched as the white devil shot across 8th, barely missing being broadsided by a Camaro going one way and a Kia heading the other. I was not so cavalier with my life. The car chase was over—for me.

I screeched to a halt and watched as the truck got away.

I swore a little, but I should have known better. Car chases never turn out well. Either you end up like I did today, with nothing to show for it, or somebody gets run off a cliff and explodes in a ball of fire à la *Charlie's Angels* or *The Rockford Files*. Neither a very appealing result.

Feeling a bit sulky, I made my way back to Clarence Avenue

and headed south for home. This had not been my finest hour. It was time for me to skulk off with my tail between my legs before I did something else stupid.

I squinted and swore a little when a pair of headlights, set on bright, pulled up behind me, getting closer by the second. I checked the rear-view mirror.

Holy Mother of Moby Dick.

It was the same white truck.

I immediately checked for a licence number and swore again when I remembered that Saskatchewan no longer required front licence plates. So instead of a number I could trace to an owner, the plate on the front bumper of my mouse-turned-cat bore a cartoon. It looked like some kind of boat next to something that I took to be a beehive. Made no sense to me, but I had better things to figure out, like what this guy was up to.

A tap on my rear bumper gave me my first clue.

Did this guy really intend to ram me? In the middle of a city street?

True, it had been a little presumptuous of me to follow him just because I saw him circle a street once or twice. I'd overreacted. I knew this and I was sorry. But metal kissing my bumper seemed a little on the excessive side of things.

I stepped up my speed, just to see what he would do.

He followed. Only inches from my rear, the big white mass was indisputably threatening. This guy was serious.

What to do? Home was out of the question. No nearby police station.

We were approaching a four-way stop. I debated zooming through. Maybe a cop would come after us. Where was a hidden spot check when you really needed one?

I looked left. Empty. I looked right. Oh crapola. Some guy was out for a late night bike ride. I wouldn't hit him, but I couldn't guarantee that GI Jackass behind me would be so careful. I didn't want to put anyone else's life in jeopardy. I slammed on the brake and came to an abrupt stop.

The white truck zoomed up behind me and I felt another tap. The asshole revved his engine and slowly began pushing me into the intersection. Thankfully, this was Saskatoon, late at night, on a suburban street. But still!

This guy was really beginning to piss me off.

The cyclist made it safely through the intersection. It was my turn to go. I hit the pedal and raced through. The truck came with me. Hey! This was a four-way stop! Bugger wasn't even going to wait his turn. Now that really burned me.

I'd had enough. This idiot was cruising for a confrontation. I'd just have to give it to him. I'd started this stupid game. I knew that had been stupid. So the first thing I'd do—through clenched teeth—would be to apologize. If that did nothing, all bets were off. What he was doing was dangerous. I had pooches in the car. I didn't want Barbra, Brutus, the Mazda, or me getting hurt over something so ludicrous. At least with a face-to-face, the odds went down to only me potentially getting hurt. (Depending how big the other guy was.) I was hoping, however, that we could deal with this in a more civilized way.

As we progressed southwards, I scoured the street for potential battlegrounds. And then, almost running out of Clarence Avenue, I found the perfect spot: the parking lot of St. Martin's United Church.

I cranked the wheel and made a left into the empty lot. I parked with my nose pointing toward the slat fence that separated the church grounds from its nearest neighbour. The white truck followed me in.

I told Barbra and Brutus to wait for me in the car, and to call 9-1-1 if I wasn't back in ten minutes.

Shifting about to open the driver's side door, I looked out. What I saw took my breath away. The front end of the white truck was rushing right for me. I shrieked—I'm not proud of that—and drew back in shock and surprise. I cringed as I listened to the sickly crunch of the truck's bumper making contact with the Mazda's door, effectively blocking my exit unless I wanted to crawl over the dogs to the other side.

Fortunately, he stopped just short of a full-on bash. The bright lights of the other vehicle filled the inside of the Mazda with enough wattage to make me believe this was some kind of alien abduction. I could barely hear my own heavy breathing over the powerful rumble of the big truck's cruel engine.

Fear quickly turned to anger. "What the hell?" I bellowed, shielding my eyes.

Barbra and Brutus seconded my outrage with one annoyed bark each.

Then came another, unexpected, noise.

My cellphone.

Talk about bad timing for a call.

Then again, maybe it was excellent timing. I obviously needed help.

I reached into my pocket, pulled out the phone, and answered, "It's Russell."

"When I pull back, I want you to drop it out of your window to the ground. Then I'll let you leave," a hushed, whispering voice—male? female? I couldn't quite tell—instructed me. "Or else I'll ram you. *And your little dogs too!*" (Okay, I made up that last part about the dogs.)

"What?" I screamed into the phone. "What are you talking about? Who are you?"

"I know you have it. Now drop it out the window. Or else."

What was going on? Obviously this had nothing to do with the trucker being mad that I'd unnecessarily tailed him. This guy thought I had something he wanted. Trouble was, I didn't.

"You have to believe me, I don't have what you're looking for. You've got the wrong guy here."

Once before, a couple of years ago, I'd caught the attention of a bad guy outside of Ash House. What was with that place? The sooner they moved to the new location the better, as far as I was concerned. That time, I'd initially thought the bad guy had something to do with Ethan. I was wrong. But what about this time?

All I'd been doing was stalking Ethan, minding my own business. Now this guy comes after me? Unless he was a superaggressive Neighbourhood Watch member, he was after the wrong man.

"My name is Russell," I shouted into the phone. "And I'm telling you, you have the wrong guy."

"I know who you are, Mr. Quant," came the weird sounding

voice.

Oh, jeez. How did he know my last name? Jiminy jumping beans, it *was* me he was after. But why?

"I don't have what you're looking for," I told him again.

The engine made a menacing sound, indicating rising rpm's. I felt a shudder as the truck inched into us. Shit, shit, shit! He didn't believe me.

"Wait!" I yelled.

I looked over at the dogs. They were admirably controlled, given the circumstances, but I could tell they were growing increasingly antsy. They could sense something was not right. If they decided I was being threatened, there'd be hell to pay. They'd start jumping about, barking and growling. Not only would that be distracting, there simply isn't room for pandemonium in an RX-7 convertible. I knew I couldn't deal with them and this tense situation at the same time. With as calm a voice as I could muster, I whispered sweet nothings to them. It seemed to work. For now.

"Are you going to do as I say? Or do I ram you?" the voice wanted to know.

Man? Woman? I was still unsure, but the choice of vehicle was making me lean toward man. An ugly one with a thick neck, bitten down fingernails, hairy back, and a low forehead.

"Yeah, yeah, okay," I said, my voice steady for the dogs' sakes. "But I need to get it first. I'm going to hang up now. Call me back in a minute."

I heard the caller begin to protest, but I hung up anyway. I quickly searched the cellphone's directory and hit a speed-dial number.

With each ring I pleaded for an answer. I knew it was late, and Dane and Jim would be asleep, but they were my only hope for immediate help.

"Yeah," came a groggy voice.

"Dane? It's Russell."

"Wha...?"

"Never mind. I'm parked in the parking lot between your house and the church. There's a white truck about to ram into me. I need you to get eggs and tomatoes and whatever else you have in your fridge and start throwing them over your fence at the truck. Do *not* come into the parking lot. I repeat, *do not* come into the parking lot. This guy is dangerous."

I hung up and hoped for the best. As soon as I did, the phone began to jangle. I waited a beat, then answered. "Yeah?"

"Don't hang up on me!" the voice warned.

I already did, you idiot. But I didn't say it out loud. Instead, I said, "Sorry, but I can't talk to you and get...it... at the same time. It's in my bag in the back seat."

"Just get it."

"Okay. Hold on."

Please, please, please, Dane and Jim, I chanted in my head. Remember the time I gave you a jar of my mother's homemade pickles? Surely that has to count for something.

And then I saw a light switch on through the slats of the fence that separated the parking lot from Dane and Jim's yard. Good sign. At least they hadn't fallen back to sleep.

I heard a thump.

Then another. Then an egg splattered all over the centre of my windshield.

Typical gay guys. No aim.

Next came a head of romaine. Then I heard a sprinkling on the hood. Yup. Croutons. It was Caesar salad night.

"What the...?" I heard the voice on the other end of the phone. I guessed some of the produce was making its way onto his windshield as well.

I rolled down my window just a tad. I could hear voices: "Get out of here! Get out! We're calling the cops! Get out!"

I could have kissed those boys. At the least, I'd replace the groceries.

"This isn't over!" I heard the phone voice hiss before the connection was cut.

I watched as the truck pulled back, then squealed out of the lot, barely missing hitting me one last time. Asshole.

As soon as we were in the garage and the Mazda's rotary engine whirred to a stop, Barbra and Brutus began to fuss. They wanted out. Now.

While they raced off to do their business, I assessed the damage to my car. There was a pretty major dent and scrape on the driver's side door, and a few smaller ones on the rear bumper. Then, adding insult to injury, she was covered in smashed and shmooshed produce. Poor baby. I petted the car's hood, yanked a piece of lettuce from under her windshield wipers, and promised to get her into the car spa as soon as I could.

Before lowering the garage door, I did a quick check of the back alley. Although I'd been extra careful to ensure no one was following me home, I wanted to be sure. Last thing I needed was White -Truck Crazy finding out where I lived.

I still had no idea who he (she?) was, or what the "it" was that he was so certain I possessed. How desperate did you have to be to get your hands on something to chase someone down and threaten bodily and vehicular harm? The only thing I knew for sure was that whoever it was in that truck did not want to be identified. He'd not once stepped out of the cab of his vehicle, he'd blinded me with his headlights so I couldn't see in, and he'd done a pretty fine job of disguising his regular speaking voice on the phone.

Was this all some kind of bizarre mix-up? The fact that he knew my name and cellphone number convinced me otherwise.

What a night. Welcome home, Russell Quant. Never a dull moment.

With my luggage lost in space, I wasn't in any particular hurry to get inside to unpack. So I decided to saunter around the backyard until Barbra and Brutus were ready to come in.

My home is my castle, a place where I re-energize and seek refuge from the world. If I could build a moat around it, I would, but I think the city has zoning restrictions on drawbridges. The house is on a large lot at the dead end of a quiet, little-travelled street. A grove of towering aspen and thick spruce neatly hides it from the view of the casual passerby. Inside, the house is a unique mix of open, airy rooms and tiny, cozy spaces, each appealing to me, depending on my mood. The backyard is a wonderful never-

never land of lovingly planted flora, clay pots, metalwork benches, and stone pathways that lead into leafy enclaves hidden
throughout the expanse. At the rear of the lot, accessible by way of
a back alley, is the two-car garage with a handy second storey I use
for storage.

As I entered the backyard, I took a deep breath. As much as I
love to travel, Dorothy was right, there really is no place like home.
It was nearing midnight, but the air was still toasty after a hot day
and perfect for a late night stroll. An arrangement of solar lights
along the pathways, in the flowerbeds, and even hanging from the
boughs of trees, created enough light for me to enjoy the familiar
landscape. I deadheaded a few geraniums, pulled out an errant
weed or two, checked on the progress of my gladiola patch, and
finally settled on a Muskoka chair on the deck. I sucked in a lung-
ful of sweet air and beheld my kingdom. Once my two royal sub-
jects were done relieving themselves and snuffling under bushes
to confirm that no other animal had marked their property while
they were gone, we proceeded inside.

Barbra and Brutus immediately visited their dishes, looking up
at me with disappointment when they found them empty. I tossed
my carry-on onto the kitchen island and filled their bowls with
cool water. Not quite what they were hoping for, but good enough
for a few slurps.

Since it was Saturday night after all, and I was suddenly not
tired, I opened a bottle of 2006 Granada Creek Vermentino for
myself. It was so crisp and clean, it tasted like fruit just turning
from green to gold. Exactly what I was hoping for, and good
enough for several slurps.

Knowing that I'd pocketed a couple of dry doggie treats,
Barbra and Brutus trotted after me down the hallway to my bedroom. I deposited the carry-on and washed my hands and face.
Then we headed to my den, hidden in a cozy corner further down
the hallway, at one end of the house.

I wanted to check my phone messages, hoping for a call from
the Air Canada lost luggage gods. I put the message manager on
speaker and joined the dogs on the inviting, toffee-coloured couch.
All six of our ears perked up when the mechanical voice informed

me that I had fourteen messages. But I'd checked them only three days ago from the island!

Getting home to find real life crashing in all around me is the one part of travelling I hate. I wasn't ready for it. I debated jumping up and switching off the machine, but it was too late. I heard Sereena's voice: rich, clear, and unmistakably imperious in a the-queen-who-lives-next-door kind of way.

"Russell, you'll be home in a day or two. I've been watching over your house as you asked me to. All is well. There was an unfortunate incident with a pollster, but more on that some other time. Missing you dreadfully. I hope you've had a chance to visit Louis Pohl's Gallery. Or have you been spending all your time cavorting on beaches and in bed with Mr. Canyon? Don't forget skincare. And did you try Hoku's at the Kahala? You shouldn't miss the wild mushroom and truffle consommé. Anyhow, enough of that. With Anthony and Jared's wedding coming up the Saturday after you get home, I'll need your assistance with a few small things. I'll expect your call. *Aloha*, darling."

That was Sereena. My next door neighbour. A woman with a pedigree of well-earned mystique. She's a complex, fantastical creature with a mythical past no single person knows the whole of. Somewhere north of middle age, she's an imperfect, damaged, raving beauty with an unrivalled, give-me-all-you've-got outlook on life. It comes from being a survivor who barely survived, a woman of the world in a world that showed her equal parts treachery and extravagance. She's a modern day Cleopatra, except without the lands to rule and fewer asps.

Although I knew my good friends, Anthony and Jared, were indeed taking the plunge in less than seven days, it was still a shock to hear the word "wedding" being spoken. I'd barely had time to swallow that reality when the next message filled the room. Speak of the devil, it was Jared, reminding me that I'd promised to help build the deck for the new Ash House. How drunk was I when I made that commitment? Then came Errall. She'd finally decided to spread Kelly's ashes and wanted me to join her. Was that why she was so morose earlier on? Why hadn't she said anything to me then? There were a few hang ups, a carpet cleaning service offering free, no obligation quotes, and then my mother.

Even though I'd told her exactly where I was going and exactly when I was coming back, she sounded as if I'd disappeared off the face of the earth, had been gone for a decade, and she was wondering when I was planning on seeing her. Another few hang ups. Another call from Errall about wanting me at some PWC meeting. A dentist appointment reminder. A don't-forget-you're-my-best-man-on-Saturday reminder from Anthony. The last call was from Alex.

"Hi sexy," he began, his deep voice rumbling over the miles of cable (or whatever it is that telephone companies use these days). "I miss you, guy. I guess I don't really know why I'm calling. Just feeling a bit punchy after all the flying. Loved our weekend together." There was a pause, then: "I'm glad you said yes."

Even though it was the shank of summer, all I wanted to do was hide myself under a blanket until sometime next week. I glanced at Barbra. With a vaguely accusing look, she gazed at me, at the phone, then back at me. Damn dog. I tried my luck with Brutus. He was snoring by the fireplace. Much better.

I gulped the last of my wine and decided to distract myself by unpacking my carry-on. We padded back to the bedroom. Barbra and Brutus quickly claimed spots on the bed, from where they could keep an eye on me while still being comfortable. I pulled out my Dopp kit and put my airline-regulation-sized toiletries back in their regular places. My book went on the bedside table. I reached into the outside pocket of the bag for the slip of paper the lost luggage guy had given me. It had the claim number and the address for a Web site where I could apparently check the retrieval status of my bag. Along with the claim tag came a second piece of paper. I unfolded it and frowned.

Suddenly I knew exactly what it was the maniac in the white truck had been after.

Chapter 3

Summer Sunday mornings should be for church, brunch with friends, sleeping in, or long walks along the river. Not jangling phones that make it seem as if your skull is home to a New Orleans Dixieland marching band.

My head made just enough of a rotation to catch a glimpse of the call display. Uh-uh. I knew that number. Constable Dudley Do-Right. If Kirsch thought his early bird catches the worm routine was going to work with me, he was sadly mistaken.

I rolled over and ended up with a nice, furry piece of dog ear in my mouth. I couldn't catch a break. I tossed to the other side of the bed. It had been a rough night. I was feeling overwhelmed and I'd been home less than twelve hours. Everyone wanted a piece of me. Alex. Sereena. Errall. Anthony. Alex. Jared. My mother. Darren Kirsch. Alex. It was Sunday for Saint Francis of Assisi's sake. Couldn't they all leave me alone for just one day?

The phone started ringing again.

I had to get away. I considered jumping the next flight back to paradise. By tonight I could be having a rum-soaked Mai Tai in the glorious pinkness of The Royal Hawaiian hotel and eating Peking Duck at Wo Fat. Instead, I let the dogs out, fed them, showered, grabbed a few things, and was out the door before the Clinique was dry on my face.

I wasn't heading for the airport, but I did have something just as adventurous in mind. I was going on a treasure hunt. For some reason, Mr. Magoo, a.k.a. Walter Angel, had decided to slip the treasure map he'd been fretting over into my carry-on. I would have thought I'd have noticed him doing so, but the only time I could think of when he'd have had the chance without my knowing was after we'd deplaned and he'd glommed on to me to help him to the arrivals level. That was the when. The more interesting mystery was: Why?

It didn't take too much skull scratching to figure out that it was the treasure map my friend in the white truck had been after last night.

Right?

Unlike me, White Truck Guy had somehow known that Angel slipped me the map. He followed me, thinking I'd lead him home. Which I would have if I hadn't been so intent on mooning over Ethan Ash. Then I chased him. He chased me back. It hadn't ended up well for either of us. White Truck Guy didn't get what he wanted. The Mazda was dented and scratched. Both vehicles were covered in gooey foodstuffs. To conclude that White Truck went through all that to get the map was a valid theory.

What I was having more trouble with was Walter Angel's motive for giving me the map in the first place. Was he so desperate for me to figure out the clues that he'd hoped I'd change my mind if I had the treasure map in hand? Possibly. But a more sinister option had been flitting through my mind ever since I first laid hands on the thing. He'd slipped the map into my carry-on only minutes before he was murdered. Did one have something to do with the other? What was White Truck Guy's role in all this?

Maybe I was being too suspicious and thinking the worst. Detectives have a predilection for that sort of thing. The map could be nothing more than a benign hobby. Angel could have been murdered for a million other reasons. White truck could have been after something else he thought I had that I didn't.

So that, I told myself, was why I was on the hunt today: to figure out if this treasure map was of any importance at all. It had nothing to do with wanting to avoid the pressures awaiting me in the real world—everything from Anthony and Jared's wedding to carpentry—or wanting to fill my mind with anything but the fact that I would soon have to start planning my own wedding. Ugh. Crikey, I felt like throwing up.

First things first. I headed straight to the car wash to rinse off last night's Caesar salad debauchery. Then it was on to Colourful Mary's for a nice big cup of coffee. My friends Mary Quail and Marushka Yabadochka own the restaurant/bookstore. Its reputation for fabulous food, much of it influenced by the Aboriginal and Ukrainian (respectively) heritage of the couple, far outdistances that of its being the only gay-owned restaurant in Saskatoon.

When I stepped inside, I spotted both Mary and Marushka already hard at work: Marushka in the kitchen, Mary on the floor. Although I was happy to see them, I'd wished they'd at least take a Sunday morning off. As far as I could tell, they worked too many hours, and played too few. With the recent explosive development of the city's south downtown, Colourful Mary's—right in the middle of it all—had become more popular than ever.

Mary suggested and I accepted a sunny table on the outdoor patio. This was really nothing more than the empty parking lot adjacent to the restaurant, but you'd never know it. The space was decorated for the summer months to look like a clearing in a tropical jungle. The floor was littered with flats of plants that looked like undergrowth and piles of rocks on which you could believe a lizard might be sunning himself or a leopard might be hiding behind for protection from the hot midday sun. Tarzan-worthy vines, papier mâché monkeys, colourful plastic parrots, and lethal-looking rubber snakes hung from the gnarled limbs of overhead foliage. Outdoor speakers completed the illusion by playing tracks from *The Sounds of the Amazon*. It was a magical atmosphere, and I could swear the humidity was higher here than anywhere else in the city.

While Mary went to get me a Kenyan coffee and low fat tamarind muffin, I got comfortable in my seat and glanced around. I noticed a few people I knew, including my friend Louis Volz. He was entertaining a large table of family and friends, one of which fit nicely into the theme of the place with her zebra print sarong and rather unique, hyena-like laugh. Louis and I exchanged friendly nods, and then I got down to business. I pulled out the map I'd found in my carry-on.

As I'd noticed when I first saw it on the plane, Walter Angel's treasure map didn't much look like one. The background drawing of Saskatoon was crude at best, meant more, I guessed, as the first hint to the reader of what city they were to look in to find the treasure. The real clues were in the text. Here's where things got interesting. Although there was nary an "Aye, Matey!" or "Beware the Black Spot!" warning in the whole thing, the passages were certainly obtuse and challenging enough. While I waited for my caffeine, I read it over:

Begin where it ended,
For the first of Saskatoon,
Next to baby Minnie,
Margaret tells you what to do.

There it is,
What it is,
Where it is,
But where is what it is where it wasn't?

Morning, noon, night,
Behind a door too high,
Years and weather ingrain,
Now to fame's portrait in a frame.

Beneath the lonely trio
Where consumption did reside,
Nicknamesake toiled to foil
Then died.

Finally it hides,
Below sparkling skies,
Within a golden urn,
Treasure you will find.

It wasn't Yeats or even Keats, that was for sure. But who was I to pass judgment? I could barely manage a dirty limerick.

What did it all mean? Each stanza seemed to refer to a specific place. Reaching one, I hoped, would lead to the next. For a few minutes I studied the last verse. If only I could figure that one out, I'd be set. I wouldn't have to bother with the rest. Sparkling skies? A golden urn? Where the heck could that be? I had no idea. This treasure map wasn't about to let me cheat my way to the prize without doing the work to get there. All I could do was start at the beginning and see what I came up with.

Begin where it ended,
For the first of Saskatoon,

Aww, jeez, I was stumped already. Great detective I was. But I gave myself a break. It was Sunday morning, after all, and I was suffering from jet lag and a lousy night's sleep.

"What's this?" Mary asked as she set both herself and my breakfast down. "Have you taken to writing love sonnets for Alex?"

I smiled at Mary, as always taken in by her glowing, dark eyes. "Nah. It's supposed to be a map to find…something…I'm not sure what."

"So why are you looking for it if you don't know what it is?"

Good question. "Curiosity, I guess. But if my first try is any indication, I'm never going to find it anyway. Listen to this." I read her the first four lines. "What does that mean to you?"

Mary turned the page so she could see it straight on. "I love stuff like this," she enthused, taking a sip from my coffee cup. "These are like clues, right? You have to figure them out to know where to go next. Like a scavenger hunt."

I stared at Mary, surprised by her zest for the project. The things you don't know about your friends. "Yeah." I pulled my coffee closer to me.

"So they're obviously telling you where to start," she said as she mulled over the words and chewed on a piece of my curiously sweet-and-sour muffin.

"Doesn't seem so obvious to me."

"Begin where it ended, for the first of Saskatoon," she repeated. "Hmmm, the first of Saskatoon."

"They're clearly talking about the first settlers," I said, "the pioneers."

Mary gave me a kind but indulgent smile. "That depends on who you think our pioneers were. My people, the Cree, the Northern Plains people, were the first to settle here. They've gathered here for six thousand years, to hunt bison, gather food, find shelter from winter winds, open a restaurant/bookstore."

I smiled at her gentle way of giving me a much-needed history butt-kicking without making it seem like a lecture. I tried for some brownie points: "I've heard that some of the sites discovered at Wanuskewin are older than the pyramids." Wanuskewin is a heritage park just five kilometres outside of Saskatoon.

She nodded. "Uh-huh, that's right. But by the look of this map and the clues, something tells me they're talking about something a little more recent, and a little more white."

"So that would be the Temperance colonists?" I said, scouring my mind for whatever I remembered of city history. "Early nineteen hundreds."

"The first immigrants to Saskatoon arrived in more like the late eighteen hundreds," Mary noted.

"Brought here by John Lake, right?" I said, impressed that my memory banks were beginning to open up. High school social studies class hadn't been such a waste after all.

"On the advice, once again, of one of my people," Mary proudly announced, "Chief Whitecap of the Dakota Sioux. Check out the statue by the river."

Mary was right. A twice life-sized bronze statue of Lake and Whitecap had recently been erected at the base of the Traffic Bridge to commemorate their meeting. Conceived as an agricultural utopia on the unspoiled prairies, far from the wickedness of Toronto and Montreal, Saskatoon was founded in 1883 by the Temperance Colonization Society. It was an organization dedicated to the ideals of capitalism and prohibition. Strange combination, I always thought. John Lake was their representative, come to check things out. Things have changed a bit since he was last here. Especially the no drinking part.

Mary mumbled under her breath as she considered the rhyme. "Where did it end?"

"The river?" I suggested. The muffin was delicious. "They came from wherever they came from, and started building sod shacks by the river. The river was the end of their journey."

"Maybe," she drawled, not sounding convinced.

"What else is there? They came. They worked. They died. End of story."

"That's it!"

A nearby elderly female couple looked over, with worried looks on their time-and-sun-worn faces (big golfers, I was betting).

"Sorry, gals," Mary apologized to the women. "I'm getting a little too exuberant for a Sunday morning, aren't I?"

The women smiled good naturedly and went back to their own conversation.

"What's it?" I asked.

"What you just said," Mary continued, quite enjoying her coup. "They died. That's where it ends for all of us. You need to begin where it ended for the first residents of Saskatoon."

She was on to something. As I sipped my coffee, I scoured my head for something I knew was in there somewhere. Finally I had it. "There's a cemetery near the exhibition grounds."

Mary nodded encouragingly.

"Actually, I think it's even called the Pioneer Cemetery or something like that." I knew that because it was on the way to Diefenbaker Park where they set off fireworks every Canada Day.

Mary looked exultant. "You're right. It's right on the river. That's where the first Saskatoon settlers were buried. That's got to be it, Russell," she agreed. "And look," she said excitedly, pointing at the poem. *"Next to baby Minnie, Margaret tells you what to do."*

I looked at her, a pained look on my face. "I don't get it."

"That cemetery is filled with babies' graves."

I winced.

"I know, it's sad, but that's just the way life was back then. The conditions were harsh—the weather, the food, the insects. Sometimes they didn't have proper clothing and medicine for the children. A lot of these pioneer women were young mothers with little experience, and good doctors were scarce. A lot of babies simply didn't survive."

I shook my head and looked around at the plenty surrounding us. Only a hundred years ago, the thought that someday Saskatonians would be seated in a mock jungle eating muffins and drinking designer coffee from Africa, would have been unthinkable, almost laughable. Those people struggled every day just to stay alive, to start new lives. And this is what it turned into only a few generations later. We truly did owe our pioneers an unfathomable debt of thanks.

"All you have to do, Russell," Mary told me, "is go to Pioneer Cemetery and find a grave for baby Minnie." She stopped for a moment, then said, "More of your people should visit her."

I gave her a questioning look.

"Even though she was so young, she was among the first," Mary said, "to give her life for Saskatoon."

"You are both beautiful and wise," I praised my friend. "And hungry," I added. "You ate most of my muffin."

Nutana Cemetery, also known as Pioneer Cemetery, is located where Ruth Street ends at St. Henry Avenue. It's a narrow rectangular plot along the east bank of the South Saskatchewan River, right before it leaves the city limits. A plaque confirmed that it was indeed Saskatoon's first cemetery. Although a number of graves had subsequently been moved to other sites due to riverbank slumping, the plaque went on to say that members of many of Saskatoon's most notable pioneer families remained, including Robert Clark, who was the first resident to die (while fighting a prairie fire), Grace Fletcher (Saskatoon's first businesswoman), and Edward Meeres (who died in a blizzard). No mention of baby Minnie.

At first, there looked to be about forty or fifty headstones, but as I walked further into the grounds, I saw that there were many more gravesites than visible markers, some with nothing more than a stone stump or rusted steel plate obscured by overgrown grass. There was no way to know where baby Minnie was laid to rest. I mapped out a simple grid that would take me up and down the length of the burial ground, I hoped without missing any of the graves, and began my search.

I was on my fourth lap when I found her. Minnie Caswell. She died in 1896 at only four months old. I mulled this over and wondered if the area in town called Caswell Hill was named for her family. Was that where I was being sent to next? Right beside Minnie, as the poem suggested, was Margaret.

At the base of an impressive monument that had obviously been constructed long after Margaret's death, was a square of marble. The engraving read: In Loving Memory – Margaret Marr – 1853-1889. I shook my head. People certainly didn't enjoy long lives in the early days of Saskatoon. I pulled the poem out of my pocket and read the part pertaining to Margaret: *Next to baby Minnie, Margaret tells you what to do.*

Humph. I read it again. Stared at the stone. Read it once more. I didn't know anything about Margaret Marr, but I did know there was a place in Saskatoon called the Marr Residence. I only knew that because my friend Brenda, a local singer-songwriter, had once been artist-in-residence at Marr Residence. I didn't really know what an artist-in-residence was or what they did when they were in residence, but I was pretty sure I knew what Margaret was telling me to do.

A few minutes later I pulled up next to a white, clapboard, two-storey house on a heavily treed street, just a block up from the river. A white picket fence surrounded the large yard, half of which was given over to a pleasantly landscaped garden. I knew this because a sign on the lawn announced Marr Garden. Another sign on a gate beneath a graceful, arched arbour said "Welcome." How friendly. I decided to take advantage of the lovely space on what was turning into a warm Sunday morning. I entered the garden and made my way down a stone path. At one end of the yard were two benches. One was occupied by an elderly woman who'd obviously had the same idea I did. But instead of solving a treasure map clue, she was knitting. Very sensible. I sat down on the other bench and smiled at her. She scowled back.

I read the next bit of Walter Angel's poem.

There it is
What it is
Where it is,
But where is what it is where it wasn't?

Of all the stanzas, I decided, I hated this one the most. What the heck was this about? I decided that "it" had to be the Marr Residence. Otherwise, why would Margaret send me here? That's where my brilliant thinking process stalled. A sour feeling of hopelessness crept up my spine. I thought about how vital it was that I get every one of these clues exactly right. If I made just one mistake, I would be on a wild goose chase that would never end. What if I was wrong about coming to the Marr House in the first place? What if Margaret was telling me to go to the downtown 7-Eleven rather than here? If that were true, no amount of deciphering "there it is what it is where it is" was going to help me. I could see why Walter Angel thought he might need help figuring the whole thing out.

I studied the gardens. Day lilies. Dogwoods. Several types of bushes. Lots of grass. Ill-tempered old woman. It reminded me of home when I was a kid. Except the ill-tempered old woman part (most of the time). I'd spent so many loooooooong, hot summer afternoons playing outdoors. You couldn't go anywhere in that farmyard without catching a whiff of Mom's flowers. Wherever she found a spare patch of fertile dirt, she planted something. Peonies. Sweet peas. Snapdragons. Wild rose bushes. As summer moved on, the fruit trees matured and I'd snack on crabapples and raspberries. There was no mystery why my own backyard looked the way it did. I'd brought some of my childhood memories with me.

As I sat there, appreciating the mini-park, a peculiar thought came to me. Suppose the old gal was grouchy for a reason. Suppose she'd been sitting on that same bench ever since whoever wrote this poem wrote it, waiting for a treasure hunter like me to come along and ask her to solve the riddle of this stanza.

I smiled again at the woman. She hadn't taken her eyes off of me ever since I sat down. Amazing, really, how she could knit and be a crotchety vigilante at the same time.

"Excuse me," I called across to her. "You wouldn't happen to be waiting for...someone...would you?"

She continued to stare and knit, but uttered not a single word. I got to thinking maybe she needed some sort of code word or something. "Margaret sent me," I told her, my voice low and conspiratorial.

The creases in her forehead deepened.

"There it is," I began, giving her a "y'know what I'm talking about" wink. "What it is." Dramatic pause. "Where it is."

The busy hands stopped moving in mid-knit. The woman's eyes narrowed into slits and her nose began to quiver. Ah hah! I was right!

"But where," I began meaningfully, "is what it is where it wasn't?"

She got up and left.

Shit.

I stood and looked around, hoping no one had witnessed the silly and ultimately fruitless exchange. Thankfully, it seemed I was alone.

After a bit of a stretch, I walked around the property some more, waiting for inspiration. Eventually I found myself at the front of the house. There was a bronze plaque next to the front door. What would detectives and treasure hunters do without plaques? I read the first part out loud: "Built in 1884 by the Marr family, the Marr Residence is the oldest building in Saskatoon on its original location and one of the first to be built in the settlement. During the Rebellion of 1885, the residence served as a field hospital for the Canadian militia." Interesting, interesting, interes...wait...my brain was clicking now.

There it is...the Marr Residence.

What it is...the oldest building in Saskatoon.

Where it is...on its original location.

But where is what it is...the oldest building in Saskatoon...*where it wasn't?*

The poem wanted me to answer the question. The answer was where I needed to go next. That had to be it! Or so I hoped.

I had an idea. According to what I'd just read, the Marr Residence was one of the first to be built...but it wasn't *the* first. It was the oldest building in Saskatoon on its *original* location. Was there a house older than this one still standing in Saskatoon, but not on its original location? That would be *what it is where it wasn't.* Wouldn't it? My head was hurting.

Fortunately this was a Sunday in August, which, according to a poster in the front door's window, meant the Marr House was open today. I pulled open the screen door, turned the knob of the wooden door behind it, and indeed, it was unlocked. I stepped into the porch and just as I reached for the door into the house, it opened, revealing a middle-aged woman with a beaming face.

"Hello," she greeted me warmly. "I saw you out here. I thought I'd come say hello. Have you been to the Marr Residence before? Can I answer any questions for you?"

I debated using the code word thing again, but quickly abandoned the idea as passé. Maybe it worked for World War II double agent operatives and the Pink Panther, but it just wasn't doing anything for me. Maybe one of these days...

"Actually, yes," I told her. "I see by the sign out front that this house is the oldest in Saskatoon on its original location. I was wondering if you knew whether there is an older house in town that isn't?" Let's see how good she is with riddles.

"You mean Trounce House?"

I wanted to hug this woman. "Uh, yeah, I think so. Is that what it is where it wasn't?" Couldn't hurt to ask.

She gave me a blank look, then, "I don't know about that, but Trounce House is actually the oldest house in Saskatoon. It was built in 1883, a full year before the Marr house. Wait until you see it. It's just the cutest, teeniest, weeniest little brown thing. And if you can believe it, the family ran a store out of a lean-to addition, and even rented one of the rooms. And it only had three! Isn't that something?

"It's not far from here. Up on Tenth Street just off of Broadway. You'll have to go down the back alley to see it, though. They moved it to the back of the property to make room for another bigger house at the front. And that," she smiled sweetly as she reported, "is why it's not the oldest house on its original location."

I thanked the woman profusely, got the address, and headed for Trounce House.

I didn't get too far. Just as I hit Broadway Avenue, my cellphone rang. It was my home security company. Someone was trying to break into my house.

Chapter 4

Barking is not a means of communication favoured by Barbra and Brutus. They much prefer pointed looks or wet noses in delicate places. Barking is meant to call attention to something irregular. So when I screeched to a halt in front of my house and heard them, I knew my dogs were not pleased.

I hopped out of the car and was almost run over by a speeding vehicle.

White truck. Ford F-150.

Holy moly! The same damn vehicle I'd almost been flattened by the night before! What the hell? How had he found me? Then again, I knew he had my name and number. It didn't take a professor to look up my address in the phone book.

I could hear my house alarm blaring in competition with increasingly agitated howling and growling. I wanted to go after the white truck, but the screaming alarm won out over the mysterious vehicle. This time.

I bolted up the pathway to my front door. The alarm was making a ghostly whooping loud enough to wake Dracula from a day-time nap. Upon any activation of the alarm, my home security company was instructed to first contact me. If that failed, they were to call Sereena. If they couldn't reach Sereena, it was time to dispatch the boys in blue. Fortunately, I'd been available to take their call and, because I was only a few minutes away from home, asked them to hold off on alerting the police until I had had time to check things out.

I unlocked the front door and Barbra and Brutus bulldozed into me like Dalmatians fleeing Cruella De Vil. After a few reassuring words and head pats, I raced into my house, disabled the alarm, and did a quick inventory of each room. My last stop was the kitchen. And there it was. One of the windows in the nook area had a large crack in it.

Zipping out the back door, I found a shattered clay pot on the deck below the window. The crack, and ensuing alarm, hadn't been caused by an unfortunate bird collision. This was no accident. Someone had tried to get into my house. Fortunately the glass had held, but the impact caused the alarms to go off and scare away the would-be intruder.

I could see how he or she would choose the back side of the house for the break in. My backyard is extremely private, with no easy sightlines from outside the property. Even so, it was a pretty ballsy move in broad daylight. That being said, I was pretty sure that whoever did this was not an experienced burglar. Tossing a clay pot against a window? Come on.

Back in the house, I further placated the dogs with a couple of their favourite treats. They appeared satisfied, and after wolfing down the bits of faux bacon, insisted on being let out into the back-yard to carry out their own investigations of the distressing incident. Grabbing the cordless phone from the kitchen, I followed them out and settled on a chair around the patio table. I called the alarm company to confirm everything was all right, then left a message with a window company (it was Sunday) about replacing the glass. When I set the handset back on its cradle, I noticed the indicator light was furiously blinking. Again. I didn't need to check the calls. I could pretty much make a good guess who they were from. Instead, I called Darren Kirsch. Sunday or not, I knew he'd be in the office working on his juicy new murder case.

At first he actually scoffed when I told him I wanted to report a break-in. He took me more seriously when I added that I had some information on Walter Angel he might be interested in. With some persuasion, he finally agreed to meet me for lunch. I used (cringingly) one of my mother's favourite lines: You have to eat anyway.

It's an odd sight indeed. At the corner of 21st Street and Spadina Crescent, downtown Saskatoon, right across from the Bessborough Hotel, is a bright red, double-decker bus. It never moves. It just sits there, looking like something from *EastEnders*. Come the first warm day of spring, one side flips open and, voila, it becomes a wildly popular hotdog stand until the first flake of snow flies in the fall.

Kirsch and I each ordered a Riverbank dog loaded with good stuff like hot chili peppers, sauerkraut, and spicy salsa. While we waited for our order, I tried my hand at small talk, and Kirsch tried his hand at grunting and scratching his butt. He was wearing a pair of what I think of as Texas Ranger sunglasses, with reflective surfaces he could see out of, but no one could see in. I knew that as a cop, it was sometimes preferable that bad guys and/or suspects not catch a glimpse of whatever might be going on in your eyes—anger, doubt, maybe fear. But come on, this was lunch with me.

Once the food and cold drinks arrived, we took our bounty across the street into Kiwanis Park. We found an empty bench facing the South Saskatchewan River and started chewing and sipping.

Seeing as I was the one to call this meeting, I knew I'd have to start the dialogue. Otherwise I wouldn't put it past the burly cop to finish his meal and walk off without uttering a single word.

"Have you made any progress on Angel's murder?" I asked with what I thought was respectful politeness.

"None of your business. Next."

With few people do I have as short a fuse as with Darren Kirsch. And now he'd pissed me off. "You know," I said with mock sincerity, "I really love it how our relationship has progressed over the years and blossomed into something I've really come to cherish. I hope you feel the same."

Darren gave me his snarly-Elvis-lip-curl.

I mimicked it back.

Hotdog halfway between lap and mouth, he stared at me for a count of two. His jaw was tight, his lips tighter. And then, he couldn't help himself, his face broke. He grinned. And that was it. That smile was exactly why I even bothered to keep up a relationship with the big lug. Every so often, the broomstick wedged in his ass at birth dislodged just enough to reveal a real person with a decent sense of humour. Well, that and the fact that as a private dick it helped to have a contact in the local police department. And none of the other cops returned my calls.

If I let him be, Constable Darren Kirsch would likely slip into comfortable homophobia like many men of his background, position, and mentality. But I wasn't about to let that happen. I'd been muscling my way into his life ever since we first met at the police academy several years back, and I wasn't giving up anytime soon. I think he finally got that, and, for the most part, had given up trying to resist with any real force. He didn't know it yet, but I'd won. The prize? Well, that part wasn't so clear, nor was the reason I'd played the game to begin with. But like many worthwhile things in life, it was the journey that made things interesting and not the destination.

The hotdog found its mark. "We're making inquiries but don't have nothing much yet. This being a Sunday ain't helping any," he muttered, revealing the shocking insider details as he stuffed the last of his lunch into his mouth.

I sighed impatiently. Why was I here? I was getting nothing from Kirsch. I looked away and chewed on my own dog.

Why wasn't I spending a lovely Sunday with someone other than this pug? Was I really that desperate to avoid my friends and family? Why? Was it simple post-vacation depression? I glanced down at my ring finger. Or was it because if I saw them I'd have to explain the white gold band I was wearing there?

Kirsch, of course, would never even notice it. Or if he did, he couldn't care less. Another reason I like hanging with the guy. No silly questions about rings.

The cop swiped some mustard off his chin and said, "Quant, this is all great and everything, having lunch in the park and all, but let's cut to the chase. You said you had some information on Angel. Let's have it."

For a second, I hesitated, feeling proprietary over the information I had. But I quickly realized the error in my ways. There had been a murder, and I might know something that would help solve it. It was my duty—private detective or not—to divulge that information. So, I told him about the map, how I'd come to be in possession of it, and my halting success thus far in deciphering it.

Kirsch listened with the intensity of a practiced interrogator. His eyes were narrowed and his brain chugged away so speedily I could almost hear it through his thick skull. When I finished, he waited for a second or two to ensure there was nothing more, then he asked with a face that was nearing what I might call fuming: "And you never thought to tell the police about any of this before now?"

"As I already explained, I didn't know I had the map until I got home last night."

"You knew about the map's *existence* on the plane," he correctly pointed out, his voice growing increasingly annoyed. "You knew about it when the man who it belonged to was found strangled to death in the parking lot at the Saskatoon airport. You knew about it when you were being questioned by members of the Saskatoon Police Service. You've known it had been slipped into your carry-on for the past twelve hours. Quant, I should arrest your ass right now for withholding significant evidence in a murder investigation."

Despite the fact that he was right about everything, I was indignant. "All that may be true, but I didn't know—and I still don't for that matter—if this map has anything to do with Walter Angel's death."

He eyes narrowed even further, like knife slits in his face; the frown stayed where it was. "Then why are you coming to me now? What's changed your mind?"

I told him about the threatening white truck. Well, most of it. I left out the bit about first seeing it while I was parked outside Ethan Ash's home, all doe-eyed.

The look on the policeman's face changed. Despite our tendency to get under each other's skin—on purpose—neither of us wanted the other to be in true danger. It suddenly occurred to me, as it had to Darren Kirsch, that I was.

His measured voice was low as he warned me: "You have something the murderer wants, Quant."

I gulped. I hate when that happens.

"When you searched the body," I began haltingly, "did you happen to find a business card, say, with my name on it?" If the answer was no, I'd have a pretty good idea how White Truck Guy had gotten my cellphone number. And, it would pretty conclusively tie him to the murder.

Kirsch shook his head. I figured as much.

The cop held out a hand. "It's time you handed over the map."

The disturbed look on his face told me what I already knew. Giving him the map wasn't going to make one little bit of difference to the killer. Not unless he or she was watching us right this second. Not if they suspected I'd never hand over the map to the police without making a copy for myself. (Which of course, I had.)

It wasn't that I didn't trust the SPS to do a thorough job. But I just wasn't the kind of guy to put my fate entirely in the hands of the police. Sure, the SPS was a good police force. I'd been a part of it once upon a time. But in the early hours of a murder investigation, their focus was going to be widespread. Mine, however, would be laser sharp: getting my butt out of the mess I'd landed in.

As the woman from the Marr Residence had told me, Trounce House was indeed teenie, weenie, and brown. I didn't know if it was all that cute, though. It looked like any other old garage or storage shed in need of a major overhaul—except for one thing.

A fence, maybe four or five feet high, had been built around the structure—quite recently by the look of it—as if it were in need of protection. Or maybe to keep it from the prying eyes of nosey tourists with a *Sights of Saskatoon* guide book? I wondered how many people walked down this nondescript back alley every day just to see the oldest structure in Saskatoon? Would they take pictures? Circle around it? If they did, their route would take them out of the public alley directly into the private backyard of whoever lived in the main house. Would they want to touch it? Try to get in? The owners had probably gotten fed up with having a municipally designated historic site next to their barbecue. I felt for them.

Unfortunately, I couldn't comply with their wishes. I needed to get a good look at Trounce House.

I pulled my copy of the treasure map out of my pocket and read the third verse:

Morning, noon, night,
Behind a door too high,
Years and weather ingrain,
Now to fame's portrait in a frame.

Behind a door too high. Hmmmm. At least that gave me something specific to work with. Even from my position on the wrong side of the fence, I could still see several doors on the house. The one at the east end looked to have been the original front entrance. On the alley side was another pair, over what in a newer construction might have been considered a bay window. But the door that caught my attention was up high—*too high* you might say—at the apex of the gabled roof. It might have been a window at one point, but now it was a door, made of the same dog-brown clapboard. That had to be it: the *door too high.* I'd found it.

Elation quickly wilted into frustration. There's an obvious problem with doors that are "too high": they're too high. I needed to get a look behind it. How the heck was I going to do that?

I stood and stared at the door too high for quite some time, considering and abandoning various plans of action. But I wasn't in the mood for failure.

In all the time I'd been in the back alley, I'd yet to see another person, a car, or even a roaming pet. And especially, I'd not seen a white F-150. (I'd taken extra precautions getting to Trounce House, and my stealth had apparently paid off.) So, as interesting as Trounce House was, apparently it didn't draw a big crowd on a regular basis. This was good news for me, especially since the plan I'd finally settled on involved some not-exactly-legal activity I'd rather carry out without witnesses.

This was yet another example, I rationalized to myself, of why I was better suited to pursue the treasure map clues than the police. By the time they had jumped all the hoops to be nicey-nicey with the house owners and get official permission to check behind the door too high, it could take days. My way was much more expedient, if not exactly neighbourly.

The way I saw it, the only way to get to the too-high door was via the roof. If I could get on the roof and scale it to its topmost point, all I'd have to do was reach down, open the door and see what was behind it. Sounded simple. Looked simple.

It wasn't simple.

The first obstacle was getting on the roof in the first place. The damned privacy fence was a problem. It was doing its job, keeping me well away from the historic house. How could I get on the house's roof if I couldn't even get to the house?

As I studied my circumstances, I began to wonder if the fence might actually be part of the solution rather than a problem. I stood back to get a better overall view. I judged the distance from fence line to house to be about five feet. I'm not the greatest at estimating distances, but it didn't matter anyway. All that mattered was whether or not I thought I could leap from the top of the fence onto the roof.

With no other readily identifiable options, I decided I could.

As it turned out, I was only partially correct.

After scaling the fence and squatting atop it, all wobbly-like, like a drunken cat, I leapt towards the roof. This wasn't exactly a *Crouching Tiger, Hidden Dragon* move on my part. It was more Humpty Dumpty. I didn't jump because I was ready to, I jumped because if I didn't I'd have toppled off the narrow fence and all the king's horses and all the king's men would have laughed me out of the back alley.

Only half of me landed on target. The other half, meaning my lower torso and legs, missed the mark. As I flailed madly, trying to find purchase on something that would help me up, I could only hope that some good Samaritan wasn't witnessing my Mr. Bean moment and calling 9-1-1.

With a bit of scrambling and a nasty scrape on my knee oozing blood, I finally hoisted the rest of me onto the building. For a moment I lay there, on my back, looking up at the sky, wondering what I would have been doing today if I'd decided as a young man to become a farmer like my father. Would I be stranded on top of a stranger's roof, with a wounded knee, in a quest to find a hidden treasure? Probably not.

Inwardly I smiled. Good decision, Quant.

With a heave-ho, I rotated onto my stomach and regarded my situation. The pitch of the roof was gentle, and so I began to crawl. Before long, I reached the highest point, just where I wanted to be. After a short congratulatory speech, I maneuvered myself until I was straddling the peak like a sawhorse. I then laid myself flat out, and inched forward, until my head and arms were hanging over the peak right above the door. Only then did I allow myself to think about whether or not it was locked. This would be inconvenient to be sure. But, in my career as a PI, I'd yet to come across a locked door I couldn't get through one way or another.

Fortunately, I didn't need to call on my lock picking expertise this time. Using my fingernails as prying mechanisms, I urged the door and smiled in triumph as it stuttered open.

Edging even further over the roof's edge, I lowered my head down and peered inside.

Now, I don't know exactly what it was I was expecting to see. A gleeful woodland pixie, revealing the treasure's whereabouts, was too much to hope for, I suppose. But certainly, after all I'd done to get up there, I deserved something better than what I got: a big, empty, black space.

It was a disappointment to say the least. And then, things got worse.

"What are you doing up there, Mister?"

My gaze shifted from the black nothingness to the alley. At least the voice wasn't coming from the backyard. That would have been downright awkward.

"Aren't you afraid you're going to fall?"

The voice belonged to a young boy, maybe eight or nine. He had a ball under his left arm and was chewing a piece of gum that, by the way his jaw was moving, had to be the size of his fist.

"I'm just looking for something." I said the first thing that came to mind after "Shoo, boy, shoo."

"What are you looking for?"

Was I this inquisitive when I was a boy? Probably. However, I had preferred jawbreakers to globs of gum.

"Well, to tell the truth, I'm not quite sure." I swung the door back as far as it would go, allowing the kid to see that whatever it was that years and weather were supposed to have ingrained on it was nowhere to be found.

Instead, he said, "That's kinda cool."

"Huh?"

"That flower on the door. Did you do that?"

Uh, no.

I looked down at the door and couldn't see a thing. What was this kid talking about? Did he have x-ray vision or something? "You see a flower?"

"Yeah, right on the back of the door. Can't you?"

I examined the back side of the door. All I could see was a scarred piece of aged wood. No flower here.

"Okay. See you." And the kid was off.

Wait a second, I wanted to yell out: tell me more about the flower! But I was in no position to be doing any yelling or calling attention to myself.

Obviously, I needed to see the door from the kid's perspective. Up there I was looking at it upside-down and from way too close. Or maybe it was all the blood rushing to my head that kept me from seeing what he saw.

As I began creeping down the side of the roof, I quickly became aware of an unfortunate fact. There was no way I was going to get off the same way I got on. I couldn't jump off the roof onto the narrow top edge of the fence. Instead, I did what I needed to: I dropped off the roof, landing ungracefully on my ass on the strip of ground between Trounce House and its protective fence. I was now formally trespassing in the owner's yard. Until then I'd only been on fence tops and roofs. Certainly fence tops and roofs were considered public property? But, with no time to debate the issue, I hurriedly hoisted myself up and over the fence into the back alley.

After catching my breath and brushing myself off, I walked over to about the same spot where the boy had been standing. I turned my head up and stared at the door too high, which I'd left open.

I couldn't believe my eyes. The kid was right. There, etched on the wood—by years and weather, I was guessing—was a perfect replica of a flower.

"Hallelujah," I whispered to myself with as much reverence as if I'd just spotted the image of Santa Claus in the clouds on Christmas Eve. "I found it. I actually found it." I was smiling like a fool.

Even though I'm no horticulturist—or whatever you call flower specialists—there was little doubt in my mind that the flower on the door was a lily. I admired my lily for several seconds. Very cool.

What wasn't cool, however, was that I was going to have to crawl back up on that roof to secure the door the way it was when I'd first found it. Not only was it rude not to, I didn't want to help out anyone else who might be chasing the same clues as I was.

And there was one more thing that wasn't very cool. The first two verses of Walter Angel's treasure map had led me to a next location. But a flower carved on a door? What could that have to do with "Now to fame's portrait in a frame"? Unfortunately, I had no idea.

Chapter 5

Late Sunday evening, I found Sereena Orion Smith in her back-yard. She was sitting in a gazebo that would have looked at home on any southern plantation. To complete the picture, she sipped a mint julep while reading a Winston Churchill biography. She was wearing a diaphanous lounging outfit that seemed to be made of summer flower petals. A gentle sonata played over a set of invisible speakers and the air was soft. I almost hated to disturb her. But I needed her help.

She poured me a drink from a waiting pitcher while I found a comfortable spot amongst the colourful cushions on the bench next to hers. The sun had just set and flickering candles illuminated our perfect cocoon.

"Of course I'll watch over Barbra and Brutus," she responded to my request without hesitation.

The next favour was going to be a little tougher. "Would it be okay if they stayed at your house, rather than you coming over to check on them?" I knew this was an imposition. Sereena was on good terms with my schnauzers, but she wasn't in the habit of hosting house guests, human, canine, or otherwise. This was why, if I was planning to be away for longer than a night or two, I had the dogs stay with Errall. "It won't be for long."

"Of course. You know I'd do anything for you, Russell…within reason." Sereena's eyes narrowed with suspicion. "But you just came home. Why away again so soon? And why do you want none of us in your house while you're gone?"

I did my best to explain the last twenty-four hours since I'd returned from Hawaii, right up to finding the flower etching. The basic message was: my home is no longer safe for me or my dogs or dogsitters.

She nodded and sipped as I spoke, and when I was done, she laid a gentle hand on my thigh and asked, "Have you put disinfectant on that knee?"

I glanced down at the angry looking scrape I'd gotten at Trounce House. "Sure." I hadn't.

Wordlessly laying her drink aside, Sereena left me to go inside. A few minutes later she was back with a few things, and began ministering to my abrasion. I never could get away with telling my neighbour even the tiniest of lies.

"So you believe finding this treasure is the key to finding out why this man was killed?" she asked as she dabbed away.

"And by whom."

"The person in the white truck?"

"Possibly," I answered, then added, "I think so."

"So why not go after the truck? Why traipse around on this ridiculous treasure hunt?"

"How exciting would that be?" I responded with a little boy grin I knew she enjoyed. Then I sighed, and said, "Of course I'll go after the truck if I get a chance. But I never know when or where it'll show up. At least with the treasure map I have something solid—well, sort of solid—to go on."

"Well, I'm sorry to tell you that going into hiding from the white truck won't help you find it," she succinctly pointed out.

"That's true. But I have to leave something for the police to do. In the meantime, I need time to find this treasure without worrying about the white truck finding me first. It's not me they really want. It's the treasure. Since they're after me, they obviously don't have a copy of the map. Without that—or me—they're pretty much out of luck."

"And you have no idea what this thing is you're looking for?"

I shook my head. I knew it sounded bad. I was desperate to get my hands on something I couldn't identify. But sometimes a detective has nothing else to go on but faith.

"Stay in touch. Remember the wedding on Saturday."

"Of course. This will only take me a day or two. And being at the wedding for Anthony and Jared is a priority." I quickly added with an impish grin. "As is helping you."

"Are you all right, hon?"

Sereena was eyeing my wringing hands. There was nothing to see though. I'd taken the ring off.

"Right as rain."

"Where will you go?"

I'd already made the call.

The new and improved Ash House wouldn't be open to residents for another month or two, while the niceties and accoutrements and landscaping and general finishing-up-touches were completed. But I didn't need any of that. I just needed a roof over my head where no one would think to look for me. I couldn't stay at my house, my office, or any of my friend's houses (I had no idea how much White Truck Guy knew about me and my life). The new Ash House, vacant and a few kilometres out of town, was perfect.

When I'd called Ethan with my proposal that I move in for a day or two, he'd readily agreed. He actually liked the idea of having someone there. During the day it was busy enough with tradespeople and the like, but at night it was empty and secluded on its five-acre lot just south of the city limits. I wasn't sure if I was keen on the idea of playing live-in security guard, but turnabout is fair play, I suppose.

It was almost ten-thirty at night when I pulled into the yard. Although the newly paved driveway was lined with a charming parade of Victorian-style lamp posts, the power had obviously not yet been connected, as they sat dark. The only source of light came from the porch that wrapped around the three-storey, asymmetrical Queen Anne-style house with its fanciful towers and turrets. Jared and Ethan had done a masterful job of designing the place. It was immediately inviting and a feast for the eyes. I was hoping the porch light meant that Ethan had already arrived to hand over a set of keys.

I left the Mazda in a near-completed lot that would soon be used for visitor parking, and headed for the house with my sleeping bag and duffel. The path from the lot led me through an expanse of thick and gnarly prairie caragana that had been there long before the house. I appreciated the use of native vegetation, and the trail was made navigable by recently laid fieldstones, but the lights weren't working here either, so my progress was halting.

I made it only halfway before I stopped altogether. I cocked an ear.

I definitely heard something.

Why an unfamiliar noise in the dark would make me stop, rather than speed up, I don't know. Weird Quant gene, I guess.

I listened. Something was definitely rooting around in the underbrush. Human or beast? From far off I heard the unmistakable yowl of a lone coyote. Then several more answered back. I decided I didn't care to find out who or what was out there after all. I picked up the pace.

Happy to have reached the porch without incident, I tossed my stuff onto a wicker chair and turned to knock. That's when I saw the face peering out at me through the screen door.

"Who are you?" I said, a little louder than required.

"Damien."

Before I could react, Ethan's smiling face appeared behind the man.

"Russell, it *is* you. We thought we saw a set of lights pull into the yard. Welcome to Ash House!" And with that he threw open the door and his arms for a hug.

I hadn't actually seen Ethan for several weeks. Busy with work, avoiding temptation, that sort of thing. He looked good.

He'd cut his normally shaggy hair short. Suddenly scruffy Scooby Doo had become a sleek Great Dane. He was wearing cut-off jeans, which he filled out in all the right places, and an appropriately named muscle shirt. As we embraced, I could smell sweet sweat mixed with a light, orangey cologne.

"Sorry," he said with his ever-ready smile, "I'm a mess. We were working on the pool house today. Dirty work. Hey, you've met Damien, right?"

Wasn't that the name of the little devil kid from *The Omen*? "Uh, no. Not 'til just now."

Ethan flashed an embarrassed smile. "Oh, well, uh, Russell, Damien Janzen. Damien, Russell Quant."

As he made the introductions he placed an arm around the other man. International signal for: we're together. My heart plummeted to the soles of my feet. They're seeing each other. Something in my stomach curdled.

I shook hands and tried for a polite smile. Outside I was fine, inside I felt black and ugly, and I thought I might throw up on the newly planted potentilla bushes. Instead, I said, "Thanks for agreeing to this. And for meeting me here so late." I hadn't told him the exact reason, other than to say it had to do with work.

"Hey," Ethan said, "anything to help out the local gumshoe. Besides, we were here anyway. This place has got to be shipshape for Saturday."

"Yeah," Damien spoke up. "I think it's so cool that you're a detective and all."

I'd like to say he was trollish looking, or at least afflicted with a Shih Tzu under bite. But Damien was undeniably good looking...in an aging boy-bander kind of way. "Yeah," I agreed. "It is cool."

"Come on in," Ethan said as he stepped back to let me through. "How about we give you a quick tour before we take off for the night?" he said with obvious pride in his new home.

"Of course," I said, even though I wasn't sure I could bear to spend that much time with Ethan and his new boyfriend.

As we made our way through the large house, room by room, each carefully planned for the maximum comfort and ease of its eventual inhabitants, it was obvious to me that the place was going to be perfect. The first two floors had spacious suites for about a dozen residents, along with the requisite facilities, public spaces, a mini-gym, well-stocked library-gamesroom, and a movie screening room complete with comfy couches and a popcorn machine. The third floor was for Ethan and his daughter, Simon, but sadly no room for Damien. (I added that last bit myself). There were a great many superb features: charming nooks and crannies, and, befitting a Queen Anne house, wonderfully flamboyant touches. I made a note to set up a meeting with my financial planner and have him start planning to find a way to plop me into Ash House in my dotage.

Half an hour later the boys were headed back to the city and, I hoped, their respective homes. Left alone in the big empty space, I wandered around for a little longer on my own before deciding it was time to hit the sack. Without any beds in the place yet, I meant that literally.

It was almost midnight when I fell asleep on the back porch to the sound of a trillion crickets. I'd originally set up my sleeping bag in one of the bedrooms, but the night was so beautiful I couldn't resist. I needed something lovely and peaceful to assuage the muddle of emotions battling for dominance in my head. So many things were weighing on me. The murder of Walter Angel. The confusing treasure map. My engagement to Alex Canyon. Ethan Ash. Alex Canyon. Ethan Ash. And things weren't going to get better any time soon, for tomorrow morning I was doing something I'd been dreading for a long time. Saying a last goodbye to a friend.

Kelly Doell and I had attended the same small town high school. Years later, we reconnected in Saskatoon and became best friends. For many years, she and Errall lived the life of a typical lesbian couple. They met, they moved in together, they got a dog (Brutus), they pooled their k.d. lang CDs. Things were going swell for them. Errall was a workaholic lawyer and Kelly had found success as the owner of a popular craft gallery on Broadway that featured many of her own wood and pottery creations. Then cancer struck.

The disease took Kelly's breast and most of her inner glow. Eventually, she packed her bags and moved away. Ran away? We'd had little contact with her for years. And then, two years ago, she simply showed up again, and Errall took her in without a backward glance. Errall and I have had our issues over the years, but I'll always admire her for that. Of course, I have no real knowledge of what happened behind closed doors, but to all outside eyes, they once again became a devoted couple. We eventually learned that what had taken Kelly away from us in the first place— cancer—had brought her back. She'd come back home—back to Errall—to die. And a year ago, she did.

A container of ashes can be a great comfort, or a grim reminder of a loved one. Burial of a body in a casket isn't for everyone. But at least once it's done, it's done. It's not as if you bring the casket home with you, with the expectation of having it displayed on your mantle. A casket is left in the ground, and mourners are left with a lifetime of pictures and memories. But an urn of ashes demands to be dealt with. Somehow. Errall had been in agony for months, deciding what to do.

She moved the container from one room to another. First the living room. Then the bedroom. Even the kitchen. But nothing seemed right. Finally she realized Kelly wasn't meant to be bottled up in the house for the rest of eternity. She wanted to be free. And to do that, Errall would have to let her go. She would spread the ashes in the great outdoors that Kelly had loved so much.

The *Saskatoon Princess* riverboat departs from a dock behind the Mendel Art Gallery. When I met Errall there at seven on Monday morning, she looked better than I'd thought she would. She'd pulled it together for Kelly's farewell voyage.

Errall is an intense looking woman, with dark features, trim body, and more sharp edges than curves. She's beautiful in a Russian-ice-princess sort of way, with fiery cobalt eyes that could laser through granite. This morning, she'd bundled her tresses of near-black hair into a tidy bun at the nape of her neck, and wore all white. There wasn't a trace of makeup on her face, and I was startled at the difference it made. She was no longer the severe, powerful businesswoman, but a fresh-faced, outdoorsy girl.

Errall had chartered the passenger craft for our special trip. Normally it could hold up to thirty-five. Today it would be just the two of us. While I found a good spot to sit with my steaming Starbucks latte, she gave last minute—probably unnecessary—instructions to our captain (she was still Errall after all, fresh-faced or not). All he did was nod politely. He'd dealt with Erralls before.

"This'll take about an hour. That okay for you?" she asked as she took a seat next to mine. Her eyes were focussed on the water, not really paying attention to what my answer might be. So I didn't give her one. She knew it anyway.

The morning had that delightful nip that sometimes sneaks up as August matures. I was glad for the white cable-knit sweater I'd thrown over my shoulders at the last minute before I'd left the Ash House that morning. The forecast was for another scorcher of a day. But that would come later. After we'd said our goodbyes to Kelly. For now, the bracing cool felt just right.

"Why so early?" I asked as the boat pulled away from shore and headed for the first of four bridges we'd pass under.

"It was her favourite time of day," Errall explained, still looking away. "She loved nothing better than to get up early, especially in the summer when it's light out before five. Every morning, first thing she'd do is step outside, wearing nothing more than a T-shirt and panties, and take in a big gulp of fresh air. I think she preferred it to coffee." She chuckled at a memory. "You know, the whole time we had him, I don't think I took Brutus for a morning walk even once. They were such pals, you know. She'd put the harness on him and they'd go out for a run before I even woke up. She'd come back all rosy cheeked. Brutus would be excited and ready to eat. I'd give her a hug to warm her up. She'd feel all chilly and taut and strong." Errall pulled in a draft of air. "And she'd smell so...so wonderful. I loved the smell of her in the morning."

We were quiet for a while.

"How did you finally decide to do this here on the river?"

"That was the problem," she said, turning to face me. "I couldn't decide. No one place seemed right. But then I thought about the river. The Meewasin trail next to it was her favourite place to run. I thought about how the river flows through the city, through the province, and beyond. If I leave her here, it'll take her with it. On and on and on.

"We once rented canoes and did the trip from Cranberry Flats back into the city. She was like a kid, she absolutely loved it. Now, in a way, she'll always be on a canoe trip. Every so often, if I'm feeling bad or missing her, I can look at the river and pretend she's passing by, waving and laughing that crazy laugh of hers."

I nodded. "Why now?"

"You're just full of questions this morning." But by the way she said it, I knew she wasn't irritated, as she often is with me. She needed to talk about this. "It's the wedding. Anthony and Jared getting married this week is such a joyous thing, so positive and life-affirming and happy. I just...I wanted to remember Kelly in that same way. I don't want this to be a sad thing. I've been sad enough. We all have. Spreading Kelly's ashes so close to the wedding was the best way I could think of to make this a good thing. She loved those guys so much. She would have loved being part of all the wedding hoopla. And now, in a way, she is. I would have done this the morning of the wedding if I could have, but I thought today might be better."

"I get it." And I did.

"But you're wondering why I didn't gather a big gang of friends and family."

I was.

"Our families, our friends," she began, "that's who the funeral was for. Today...well, today is something different. I wanted today to be about her and me, and you too. You were her best friend."

"After you, that is," I said.

She gave me a grateful nod. "After me," she whispered.

I gazed out at our beautiful, peaceful surroundings and felt the cool, fresh air kiss my skin. "I like it," I said. "I think it's perfect."

Errall shot me a glance and I detected a mischievous glint. "Now, of course, when it's time for me to spread your ashes, I'll arrange for a parade, with bubble machines and dancing majorettes."

I grinned. "I'd appreciate that."

She smiled. "I'm grateful you're here, Russell. I don't know that I could have done this all alone."

"Of course you could have."

"Mmmm, yes, I suppose so. But, well, this feels better."

The shadow of a second bridge fell across us, and we both sat back to enjoy the view.

It was still early when we finished on the river. Errall went to PWC. I, still hiding out from my white truck shadow, did not. Instead, I made a pit stop at the Y to work off the knot of tension that seemed to be building up on my shoulders like a barnacle. Afterwards, I decided to head back to Ash House for lunch and to consider my next move.

Driving into the yard, I was surprised to see the place a beehive of activity. Outside the newly constructed house, landscapers and paving stone installers plied their trades, while inside, through the series of large windowpanes, I could see painters and finishers working on final touches. Delivery trucks ferried furniture and mattresses and box springs and all matters of goods needed to begin a new household. The driver of a rusty half-ton truck was busily unloading a cord of wood in one corner of the multi-car garage, and another was dumping topsoil on the driveway. I stepped out of my vehicle and spied Ethan on a second floor balcony, assembling a patio set. What had happened to my private oasis?

In the kitchen I helped myself to a diet Pepsi from an industrial-sized refrigerator, and filled a bowl with Fibre 1 cereal (the honey nut cluster type, not the hamster food type). Thinking I'd dine alfresco, I opened the kitchen door to the backyard and nearly took a nosedive off the precipice that greeted me. I noted the pile of lumber sitting where the deck should have been, and reminded myself that I'd promised to help with its construction on Wednesday. Alternatively, I had two days to come down with the flu.

I used the plank that was in use in lieu of steps, and made my way to ground level. I found a relatively quiet spot next to the still empty, kidney-shaped swimming pool, and settled in for some good eats and hopefully some good thinking.

As I chomped away on my dry cereal, I studied my new best friend: the treasure map. I was stuck. I'd found the lily engraved behind the "door too high" at the Trounce house. But now what?

The last line of the verse was: Now to fame's portrait in a frame. I needed to find something famous in a frame. After the *Saskatoon Princess* returned to dock that morning, I'd snuck into the Mendel Art Gallery to see if, by some extraordinary stroke of luck, they had a picture of a famous lily somewhere in their collection. They didn't. There was a rather dashing poppy, and some good-looking daisies, but no lily.

I'd only been working on this thing for a day, but I couldn't help feeling anxious. I was halfway through the poem, but I felt like I was in a race to get to the end before White Truck Guy found me. How long could I successfully elude him? This was a small city after all. And I wasn't keen on staying away from home, my office, and my pooches for much longer. I'd already been gone long enough in Hawaii. Then again, my luggage was still on vacation, so why shouldn't I be?

I began to wonder if I was doing the right thing. Maybe I should leave this up to the police. It would be easy to wash my hands of the whole thing, enjoy the rest of the week and the celebratory atmosphere of the upcoming wedding of my two good friends. I'd handed over the treasure map and the clues I'd figured out so far. Maybe the treasure had nothing to do with the murder at all. Maybe the white truck was just a coincidence. Maybe my house was broken into by some random neighbourhood hoodlums.

I gave my head a good shake. Even I didn't believe myself. Walter Angel had slipped that treasure map into my pocket for a reason. He must have guessed he was in danger when he landed in Saskatoon. The poor man must have known there was a chance something would happen to him, or the map. So he trusted me with its safekeeping. And then, something did happen to him. The worst thing. He lost his life. And now I was left with his treasured possession. What did he expect me to do with it? Did he give it to me for safekeeping? Or did he want me to use it to find the treasure—whatever it was—before someone else did? That had to be the answer. I was sure of it. And I was also sure that once I did find the treasure, this game would change. There'd be no turning back then.

...fame's portrait in a frame.

What was so famous about a lily on an old wooden door?

"Russell!" a singsong voice called out.

I turned and saw a blur of little girl rushing headlong in my direction.

Simon Ash. Ethan's daughter.

Simon collided into me for a bear hug, and we nearly ended up on the ground. But the chair held, and Simon giggled over the near calamity. The kid and I get along like gangbusters. Not having had many kids in my life, I treat her like I treat everyone else. Within reason, of course. She might as well be a very short thirty-year-old as far as I'm concerned, and she responds well to that. At twelve, Simon was approaching that delicate and sometimes complicated age between little girl and young woman. She didn't quite know whether she should be playing dress-up or going dress-shopping at the mall.

Simon was the biological daughter of Ethan's sister, Sarah. Sarah was a single mother at eighteen and was tragically killed in a car accident before Simon was a year old. The grandparents became guardians, but it was soon obvious that the real parent was Ethan. By time Simon was three, Ethan was her legally adopted dad.

Fortunately for Simon, many caregivers in addition to Ethan had eased the sad loss of her mother a little. She had lived most of her young life in Ash House, where residents regularly claimed her as their own honorary grandchild. From what I could tell, although the little girl could never replace her mother, the experience of growing up in that kind of environment did wondrous things for her. She'd lost a parent, but gained an entire fleet of protectors who loved and cared for her. And Ethan, well, he was just over the moon about her. She was always his topmost priority.

"Would you like to see my room? It's the first one all done. I'm ready to move in. I can hardly wait."

Ethan was now outside, shirtless, playing around with a sprinkler head. I watched as the device spritzed him with water. He gambolled away like a frisky calf, grinning from ear to ear, and then circled back around, as if it were mighty prey he could sneak up on. I could watch that all day. It was time for me to leave.

"I would love to," I told Simon, taking her offered hand.

She led me into the house through the garage. We climbed a back set of stairs to the third floor, the private residence for Simon and her dad. Traipsing down a generous hallway that led off a spacious living area, I was enthralled by the stunning prairie view through a series of large picture windows along the way.

Simon opened a door and with great pride introduced me to her room. It was, I'd think, a twelve-year-old girly girl's paradise. Lots of pretty things, and frilly things, and pillows, and soft places to sit, all in mellow pinks and beige. I was betting the room would have to be redone in a couple of years. But for now, it was perfect.

As the tour progressed, I noticed an open laptop on her work desk—pink, of course.

"Simon, I like your computer," I said, fingering one edge.

"Thank you. Daddy lets me use it for homework and stuff. I'm not usually allowed to keep it in my room. He likes to keep an eye on things. He wanted me to bring it along while we're out here working on the house, just in case one of us needs to use it. His is back at the old Ash House."

"You have a wireless connection working out here already?"

"Of course. Would you like to use it?" she kindly offered.

"Could I?" I felt like a kid asking to borrow a friend's new skateboard. Not being to able to get to my computer at home or the office was like having an arm chopped off.

"Sure. As long as you promise not to go on any porno sites," she said sweetly. "I think Daddy has those blocked anyway."

I stared at her while attempting to dislodge my tongue from my throat. There was that not-a-girl-not-quite-a-young-woman thing that was so…disarming. "Uh, sure, I promise."

"Okay. I'm going to go check on how they're doing with the doghouse."

"You're getting a dog?"

"Two, I think. I haven't decided yet. Daddy says that studies show that elderly people respond well to having pets around. I will too, I think. I'm going to get the kind that live inside the house, but they should have someplace to go when they're outside too, don't you think? How are your dogs?"

"They're pretty good. I'll tell them you asked about them."

She giggled. "Don't be silly. Do you like my hair today?"

Simon had Ethan's—and her mother's?—silky brown locks. She'd obviously taken some care to put them into a French braid. Or had Ethan done it for her?

"It's killer."

"Thanks." And with that the little girl was gone to play doggie house contractor.

I sat down at Simon's desk. The pink surroundings and not-quite-adult size desk and chair made me feel a little like a bear in a twink bar. But I got over it. I tapped a few keys and connected to the Internet. I had work to do, and I had some ideas I wanted to follow up on.

With the cursor in the browser, I typed "famous lily." I reviewed the first ten websites that came up and found nothing that struck me as helpful. Then I tried "portrait of a lily." This too got me nowhere. A few "lily" permutations later, brilliance struck. Of course! I typed in "Saskatchewan flower." The first site listed confirmed what I'd thought. The official flower of Saskatchewan is the western red lily. That's a pretty good claim to fame for a lily. This had to be it. I tried several more search parameters, including "western red lily portrait," "western red lily picture," and "famous western red lily."

For the next several minutes I did plenty of reading and viewing of pretty pictures. Nothing slapped me in the face as a clue to where to go to find "fame's portrait in a frame." Things were going nowhere fast.

I began to wonder if "Saskatchewan" and "western red" were too broad for my needs. This was a local treasure hunt after all. My hopes not particularly high, I typed in "Saskatoon lily."

In a flash, a slew of new sites were put on offer to me.

And that was how I met the Saskatoon Lily.

From various hits I was able to piece together a quick biography of a woman I'd never heard of before. Now I have to admit, I'm not as up on my 1920s, female, track and field Olympians as I could be. But the news of one from Saskatoon was rather astonishing.

It turned out that Ethel Mary Catherwood was not actually from Saskatoon (or even born in Canada for that matter, she later revealed). But she most definitely lived here as a youngster. Her time in Saskatoon marked the beginning of a meteoric rise to fame as a celebrated athlete. Apparently, as a young girl, Ethel excelled at baseball, basketball, and track and field, but it was her ability to jump that catapulted her (pun intended) to unexpected heights of glory.

Ethel Catherwood was one of a group of seven Canadian women who competed at the 1928 Summer Olympics in Amsterdam (the first Olympics to allow female competitors in athletics). Blessed not only with athletic aptitude but great beauty too, there was considerable focus on her physical attributes during the Games, earning her the nickname "Saskatoon Lily." A *New York Times* correspondent dubbed her the "prettiest girl athlete" at the Olympics. Backing up enormous promise with performance, Ethel took home the world's first ever gold medal awarded to a female high jumper.

I did a bit more checking and found out that our hometown heroine still held the title as the only Canadian female athlete to have won an individual gold medal in an Olympic track and field event. In one snarky article I came across, the reporter even went so far as to call it the "Catherwood Curse." At least as of the date of the 2004 article, every time a Canadian hopeful tried to end the decades of women's track and field Olympic drought, she failed miserably.

After Ethel's triumphant return from the Olympics, she was so widely admired for her athletic prowess and great beauty, she was offered a movie contract. And that's when things began to turn sour for the pretty young woman.

Scandal reigned. Ethel declined the movie offer. The media unveiled a secret marriage. The Olympian ran off and filed for a quickie divorce in Reno. She hurriedly married again. Pregnancy rumours swirled. It was all too much for a prudish public. In the nineteen twenties and thirties, people demanded a more virginal type than their Olympic darling was turning out to be. Canada resolutely shunned Ethel Catherwood.

Fleeing to the U. S., Ethel unsuccessfully tried to compete once more in the 1932 Olympics, this time as an American. The press hounded her every move, treating her like a Britney Spears who could jump and throw a ball, focusing on her missteps more than her skill. Viper-like, Ethel struck back with a vengeance. She scorned everything and everyone that had brought her fame and glory in the first place. She was unabashedly contemptuous of Canada. She claimed to hate sports of any kind. She rebuffed all interviews, often in the most colourful, unladylike language. She claimed to have sold all her medals and trophies. Ethel was pissed.

What a pip, I thought to myself.

After digging a bit further, I discovered Ethel Catherwood had died in 1987, alone and unknown, in Grass Valley, California, of bone cancer. She was 79.

Growing weary from the computer screen, I stood up, stretched, and walked over to the bay window. My eyes did a sweep of the developing property. Freshly laid squares of sod were being sprinkled. New flowerbeds, carved into the slightly scooped out backyard, were awaiting mulch. A workman was attaching the diving board to the swimming pool. The place was taking shape at a speedy clip. It had to: in five days, it would be the scene of a wedding.

Far off to one side of the yard, I spotted a bunch of lilies. How apropos. Their vivid orange faces were pointed up, drinking in the sun. Ethan or one of the landscapers must have planted them in full bloom.

I pulled the treasure map from my pocket and read the last line of the third stanza: Now to fame's portrait in a frame.

My mind began to tick. It was a very Jessica Fletcher moment. I love when that happens.

Rushing back to the desk, I speedily navigated through several Web pages. I'd just seen something...

Yes! There it was. I read the passage out loud: "In 1955, Ethel Catherwood was inducted into the Canada's Sports Hall of Fame, the Saskatchewan Sports Hall of Fame in 1966, and the Saskatoon Sports Hall of Fame in 1986." Fame in a frame.

Chapter 6

Canada's Sports Hall of Fame is probably in the East, Toronto or Ottawa likely, I though to myself as I sped down College Drive. The Saskatchewan Sports Hall of Fame is in Regina, nearly three hours away. But the Saskatoon Sports Hall of Fame is right here. And this was, after all, a Saskatoon treasure hunt, was it not? At least, that was my fervent hope on my jaunt to the Saskatoon Field House sports and recreation facility where the hall of fame is housed.

As I headed for my destination, I began to wonder about the original author of the treasure hunt. What was it Walter Angel had said again? A friend had given it to him. Glenda, was it? No. Maybe Helen? I was betting that whoever Helen was, she was intimately familiar with the history of Saskatoon. In particular, she had a keen interest in female pioneers: Baby Minnie, Margaret Marr, Ethel Catherwood. At least I hoped Ethel was on the list. I had still to prove my latest theory correct.

Who was Helen? And why had she put together this elaborate

treasure hunt in the first place? And, the most interesting question of all remained: what was the treasure? And what was Walter Angel going to do with it when he found it? I had to admit, the closer I got to the prize, the more excited I was becoming. I didn't know if I could give up the chase now, even if I had to. Was I becoming…a pirate?

Leaving the still dented and bruised RX-7 to cool its wheels in the parking lot, I dashed up the front sidewalk to the entrance of the Field House. Once through the glass doors, I was confronted by a reception desk.

"Sports Hall of Fame?" I asked the lady sitting there, looking bored.

Her head tilted right. And there, just past the desk, beneath a red-flame-in-a-torch-holder logo, were walls and walls of framed, black and white photographs. As I approached the large display, I saw that the pictures were divided into three categories: athletes, teams, and builders. That would help. The athlete section ran along a wall that led up a set of stairs to a second storey. There were a lot of them, but it didn't take me long to find my quarry.

The likeness of Ethel Catherwood was so beguiling, I was sure almost anyone would be drawn to it, whether they were looking for her or not. True to her press, Ethel was an uncommon beauty. Her photo further distinguished itself by being the only one where the athlete was wearing long dangling earrings and a high, ruffled collar that looked like Persian lamb, or fur, or some kind of luxurious fabric I was unfamiliar with. She could have stepped out of a 1920s jazz club, with her bobbed hair, puckered lips, and perfect complexion. Ethel stared into the camera as if daring the viewer to deny her loveliness. After a tumultuous life of great highs and lows, this is where she'd ended up, as a photo on a wall. But unlike some of her neighbours, Ethel Catherwood did not appear lost in time, an unmoving representation of something long gone and forgotten. I could see life in her eyes. I was willing to bet her spirit and spunk had been great companions to her in spite of her travails. At least, I hoped so.

I pulled out the treasure map. On to verse four.

Beneath the lonely trio
Where consumption did reside,
Nicknamesake toiled to foil
Then died.

Reciting the words in my head, I climbed the stairs to the second floor. This allowed me a bird's-eye view of the entire collection of photographs. I searched for a lonely trio. Somewhere there had to be three pictures all alone.

No such luck.

To the right of the facilities entrance was a small café. Consumption? Was the poem talking about consuming food or drink? Consumption resides in a café!

I ran down the stairs and into the cafeteria. It seemed to be closed for business, but the wide open front invited access. I slowly made my way around the room. There were more photographs here. I studied each one. Maybe it wasn't a trio of pictures I was looking for, but a trio of people *in* a picture. Or maybe it was a trio of something else all together.

Forty minutes later, I was growing tired and irritated at my lack of success. I'd scoured the cafeteria from top to bottom. I studied the walls and halls of fame until my eyes hurt. Maybe I was wrong about Ethel. As I'd fretted early on, one wrong move in this hunt, and I'd quickly find myself in a pie shop without a fork. For the umpteenth time, I returned to Ethel and stared at her likeness a bit more, hoping for inspiration.

None came. My eyes began wandering, admiring the faces of the many Saskatoon athletes who'd accomplished admirable sporting feats. One in particular caught my attention. On the left, two photos over from Ethel, was another female sports superstar. Her name: Lily Comstock. Ethel's nickname was the Saskatoon Lily. Could Lily Comstock be the *nicknamesake* who toiled to foil? Nicknamesake. Was that even a word?

"Are you looking for someone in particular?" The woman from the front desk had come up behind me.

"This woman," I said, pointing at Lily's photograph. "Do you know anything about her?"

"Oh yes. I'm a bit of a buff on our local sports heroes. Ask me anything and either I'll know the answer or I can find it out for you. I was quite a curler myself when I was younger. I did pretty well in broomball, too."

I nodded politely, then repeated my question.

"I love the female athletes from a few decades ago the best, I have to admit. Their stories always seem so dramatic, don't you think? All the things they had to go through to do what they did. Lily Comstock's was a sad story, though. She really was a hero. In more ways than one."

"How's that?"

"She was certainly considered a sports hero by a lot of people. That's why she's on the wall, of course. She was one of the best, if not *the* best softball player in the province in her day. She helped her teams win tons of championships. I think she even played a season with the All-American Girls League in the States. Quite something for that day."

"For sure. What happened to her?"

"Oh well, she knew she couldn't play sports forever. And she never got married. So she trained as a nurse. Ended up working at the San."

In a movie, this would be the place for dirge-like chords of music. I knew what the San was. Most Saskatonians do. Even though the imposing building above the shores of the South Saskatchewan River was condemned and demolished in the late 1980s, its dark past lingers on.

The Saskatoon tuberculosis sanatorium—the San—was built in 1925 as part of Canada's battle against an ancient malady. Tuberculosis was a cruel and cunning disease. It often masqueraded as some other ailment and long defied treatment beyond simple bedrest and sunshine. Those caring for the sick ran the risk of being infected themselves. Finally, antibiotics and sulpha drugs arrived to save the day, and many lives. Nurses and doctors were vaccinated and most, remarkably, stayed healthy. Some did not. Lily Comstock had been one of those.

"The last patient wasn't discharged from the San until 1978, you know," the receptionist told me as she concluded her story.

I wanted to hug her. It all made sense to me now.

I knew that tuberculosis had once been thought to be a disease of punishment. It was the leading cause of death in the mid 1600s, so you could see how they might think that. More important to my case, I also knew, thanks to Anthony and Uncle Lawrence dragging me to see *Les Mis*, that tuberculosis was known as...drum roll...consumption.

The lonely trio I was looking for wasn't here at the Sports Hall of Fame at all. It was at the San site, where nicknamesake—Lily Comstock—toiled to foil the disease, but ended up dying of it herself.

The San site is a little corner of dead space in the not-so-aptly named Holiday Park area of Saskatoon. It's a picturesque place, alongside the South Saskatchewan River, with plenty of towering spruce and rolling lawn. Picturesque and abandoned.

Somebody should do something with this land, I thought to myself as I pulled up to the stanchions that blocked vehicular access at the end of Avenue K. The lot had remained untouched since the main building was pulled down more than two decades ago. Despite the place's obvious beauty, no developer had swooped in and gobbled it up for a high-rise apartment building or condo complex. Too many people had lost their lives on this site. Enough time had not yet passed.

I stepped from my car and saw the beginning of a long, graceful driveway that curved into the property beyond a bluff of trees. It was overgrown with grass and weeds, the pavement cracked and in some places gone altogether. It was as if the city tore down the building, then turned its face and ran. The politicians must have guessed that nothing they could do would exorcise the ghosts that lived here.

A sign near the blocked entrance displayed an eerie black and white picture of the massive sanatorium. A brief written account next to the picture told of the thousands who had died here during the TB epidemic. I shuddered.

On foot, I followed the crumbling driveway into the site. I felt a chill. Looking up, I saw that the sky had grown overcast. How fitting.

As I slowly made my way up the road, I had visions of 1930s cars, with their narrow tires and bug-eye headlights, motoring up the curved drive, pulling up to the front doors of the Sanatorium. With muted thunks of car doors and trunks, they'd discharge loved ones and their belongings. There'd be tearful farewells. How many were last goodbyes? I could see wheelchairs being pushed along the paths of the sprawling grounds by nurses in their starched, white caps and dark capes, thick blankets resting on patients' knees, even on the warm days. I recalled once seeing an extraordinary sepia-tinted photograph of this place. There were twenty, maybe thirty men, sitting on folding chairs placed in a semi-circle on the lawn in front of the San. They were an orchestra, playing for the gravely ill, watching from bedroom windows and balconies. It reminded me of the scene from *Titanic*, where musicians played for the doomed, an offering of beauty to the ill-fated.

After walking through the empty park once, I retraced my steps to the black and white picture at the entrance. I studied it for signs of a lonely trio. There were three buildings in the picture. Without the mature trees and background cityscape of today, they certainly did look lonely, plopped there like three toadstools on a vast stretch of barren prairie. Looking closer, I noticed there *were* trees there after all. They were quite short, saplings at most, obviously planted in hope of one day providing shelter and beauty. I tried to match the saplings in the photo to the behemoths that stood before me now. But something was off. I noticed a loop in the road that didn't appear in the photograph. Maybe it had been added later? Or maybe I just couldn't see it because of the angle the photo was taken from.

I looked carefully. At the centre of the loop was a solitary tree. It was perhaps the tallest spruce on the entire site. I shrugged. Despite its awesome height, it looked like any other tree. But when my eyes travelled up its trunk, twenty-five or thirty feet, I noticed something strange. It was one tree, but there were *three* tops.

The lonely trio.

I let out a whoop of delight and ran to the tree. According to the treasure map, there was something beneath it, and I wanted it bad.

Surveying the base of the mighty spruce, I jumped at the sound of a ringing noise coming up behind me. I turned and saw four boys, about ten, racing toward me on their bikes. I waited, not sure what was about to happen.

Laughing about something ten-year-old boys find funny— which could be pretty much anything—the kids whizzed by without giving me a second look. I let out a pent up breath. I was getting paranoid. I was in a public park in the middle of the day, I told myself. There aren't bad guys waiting behind every rock ready to pounce.

I was about to get back to my task when I heard a lawn mower engine gun up. I stepped back a few feet and looked around. The owner of the house at the edge of the site had decided to get some yard work done. Then up a path that came from the riverbank, an elderly couple appeared, meandering at a snail's pace. Suddenly, my lonely trio wasn't so lonely anymore. Above me, I saw the clouds were still threatening, and selfishly hoped they would scare off my new friends.

I glanced about to make sure no one was eyeing me up. The couple, it seemed, had enough to worry about putting one foot in front of the other, the house owner was intent on his lawn cutting, and the boys were long gone. If I was going to make a move, I had to time it right. Now was the time.

I dropped to the ground, wincing as my scraped knee hit the rough surface. The boughs of the tree were thick and hung low to the ground, effectively hiding its base. After one last furtive look around, I made like a pig after truffles, and dove beneath the tree.

Although most of the branches gave way to my bulk, the sturdier limbs managed to poke and prod me in delicate spots. Long desiccated needles buried themselves in my hair and tickled as they trickled down the back of my T-shirt. It was dark down there. The ground smelled of peat, the soil rich and moist to the touch. Easy to bury something in. I scratched around a bit with my fingers but came up empty-handed. It was clear this was going to take a more concerted effort. I needed tools. Tools and privacy.

I crawled out from under the branches and brushed myself off.

The elderly couple had settled on a bench, watching me. I smiled, waved, and walked nonchalantly back to my car.

I chose Saigon Rose for dinner, craving a hot bowl of Vietnamese beef rice noodle soup with a side of crispy spring rolls. As I wiped the last drops of broth from my chin, I called Sereena on my cell to check on Barbra and Brutus. They were doing fine. Then it was time for my requested presence at an event I could not remember happening before in the seven or eight years since I'd been running my PI business out of PWC: a tenants meeting. The four of us, Errall, Beverly, Alberta, and I, seemed to have gotten along quite nicely without one. Basically, Errall made the rules, and we followed them. And paid our rent on time. Otherwise Errall got grumpy. And a grumpy Errall was an Errall to be avoided. Still, the meeting had been called, with no explanation or agenda proffered.

We were meeting in Beverly's office, which was, by far, the coziest of the bunch. Mine was nice enough, with a great view of the river, but it was the smallest. Alberta's was bigger, but simply had no room for the four of us. She kept the place crammed with trunks and wardrobes and heavy pieces of furniture with no discernible use. There was lots of draped fabric, overstuffed pillows littered every inch of free floor space, and it smelled of patchouli. Errall's was the largest, and certainly the most business friendly, in a stark, austere kind of way. It was a place you sat up straight and talked serious talk while someone took notes. Beverly however, had taken pains to make her office a comforting space for her clients. It was like a fifty-year-old soccer mom's living room, complete with comfortable but not too soft places to sit, handy places to put your drink (or your feet) and pleasant, never outlandish or outrageous or even too-bright, pieces of art and doodads. It was a gentle, calming place. I felt serene just walking in.

"Hi, Russell," Beverly greeted me in her velvety tones. "Welcome back from Hawaii. I haven't seen much of you around here since you got back." She was wearing a summer green blouse and skirt set, with mauve earrings and necklace, and a wheat-coloured belt.

I didn't have a chance to respond because Alberta, seated on a recliner, piped up with, "He's so obviously hiding something."

I glared at her. Say what you want about psychics—as I often do myself—but over the years I'd experienced Alberta pulling a few very suspicious rabbits out of her outlandish hat. Rabbits I couldn't explain. I'd long ago decided the best way to deal with it was not to try. Alberta is also what one might describe as "fashion forward," or, more succinctly put, a nutty dresser. Today she was rocking a red-and-white striped, Cat-in-the-Hat hat. Over an every-colour-of-the-garden patterned shift of a dress, she'd thrown a jacket that was vaguely Michael Jackson-ish. A fine match for her chunky-heeled leather boots. And, as was her style, everything was just a little too tight for her generous figure. Yet somehow, seeing it all right there in front of me, I couldn't imagine her wearing anything else.

"Am not," I shot back.

"Are too," she countered, at the same time stifling a yawn with her hand, which nicely showed off turquoise nail polish.

"Are you bored?" I asked, accepting a cup of green tea from Beverly and sitting down next to my aura-seeing fellow tenant.

"What's this meeting about, anyway?" she asked. "I don't usually get up this early."

I checked my watch. "It's eight p.m.," I informed her. "And should a psychic have to ask what a meeting is about?"

"Hi, everyone," Errall called out in a chipper voice as she swept into the office. She was still wearing the white outfit from that morning, but was now madeup in full businesswoman war paint. "Thanks for coming. I know it was kind of short notice."

"What's this all about?" Alberta wanted to know.

"Can I get you anything?" Beverly offered. "Tea? Glass of water? I have a few muffins and a bagel or two left from today. I could warm one up."

"No. But thanks."

Errall was being polite. And...nice. Sure signs of the Apocalypse. I was getting worried.

She and Beverly took to their seats. We were all within two or three feet of one another in a rough circle.

"As you know," Errall began without preamble, "I've had a tough couple of years. First Kelly leaving. A few bad relationships. Then Kelly coming back. Then Kelly dying."

We all murmured our sympathy and empathy.

"But if you knew Kelly, which you all did, you knew that the one thing she was excited about was life. She wouldn't want me to dwell in this state of...of misery. And neither do I. So I want to move on."

"You're so right about that, Errall," Beverly cooed. "I'm thrilled to hear you say it."

I could see Alberta's eyes narrowing. Did she know something before the rest of us did? From the look on her face, I hoped not.

"So I've made a few decisions," Errall kept on in a light voice. "And one of them will affect all of you. Which is why I called this meeting."

I wasn't a psychic, but something in my gut told me I wasn't going to like what was coming.

"I have decided," she began, a sharp smile cutting her fine features, "to leave my law practice."

Oh. Well. That wasn't so bad. Was it?

"Errall," Beverly said. "I'm surprised. You love the law. You love the work you do."

"That's true. But I work too many hours. And the work is always so serious. People in trouble. People arguing with one another. People wanting to stick it to someone else. Kelly always said all that negativity was going to start wearing me down sooner or later. She was right."

But Errall thrived on negativity. She had it every morning with milk and a cup of coffee.

"It's high time I started having fun in my life."

Fun? Errall Strane? I didn't know if I'd ever quite put the two together before. Nor, for that matter, had she. I sat, dumbfounded, looking at the woman in front of me. I wondered who this creature was, and what she'd done with Errall.

"What will you do with your time?" Beverly asked.

"Here it comes," Alberta drawled, her voice low and cautionary.

"I'm opening a clothing store!" she announced. "For business-women. It's a niche long ignored in this city. If a woman wants to look cute and pretty for a party, there are stores for that. If you need a gown for a banquet, there are stores for that. If you want to hide those few extra pounds, there are stores for that. If you get pregnant, or go to the beach, or take up jogging, there are stores for all those things. But if you are a serious business person, and you don't want to look like Jane Hathaway from *The Beverly Hillbillies*, there is nowhere to go in Saskatoon. Now there will be. Right here."

Ding dong.

"Right here?" Beverly repeated, her delicate voice admirably modulated.

"At PWC. Isn't it perfect? It's a return to the rich history of this building."

History, yes. Rich, I wasn't so sure about that. PWC stood for Professional Womyn's Centre. Yes, Womyn with a "y." It was orig-inally conceived to be a place where female entrepreneurs would run their businesses in an estrogen-fuelled environment. For a few years during the 80s the concept was actually a minor success, but eventually it degraded into a caricature of itself. Businesses failed and the building fell into disrepair. Errall purchased and refur-bished it, and eventually ended up with us four as her tenants.

"You don't mean just your office," Alberta stated, already knowing the answer. "Do you?"

Errall looked at each of us in turn. "No," she quietly con-firmed.

I heard Beverly's breathing quicken. She was distressed. As was I. Over the years, we'd become much more than people who happen to work in the same building. We'd become friends...family. I'd attended Beverly's daughter's high school graduation in June. I once babysat Alberta's pet ferret (never again). I'd have to begin taking vitamin C tablets without daily injections of our receptionist Lily's sunny smile. And, not to get mercenary here, but with things hopping in old Toon town, down-town rents had skyrocketed. Finding another spot just like the one I had for the same price would be near impossible. I didn't kid myself. I knew Errall had been giving us a break. She could have charged us much more than she did. I loved my little office with its tiny balcony overlooking Riverside Park and the river. I had it set up just the way I liked it. This sucked! It was horrible news no matter how you looked at it.

"How long do we have?" Alberta asked, as if we'd just been given a really bad diagnosis from our family doctor.

Errall swallowed hard and looked away. "Three months."

Chapter 7

It felt right to be back in the bleak pit of the San site. It matched my mood. Hearing that I had three months to find someplace else to base my PI practice was a shock. I was mad and sad and hurt and worried, all at the same time. An ideal time to go treasure hunting in the dark.

Garden shovel, trowel, and work gloves in hand, dressed in Cary-Grant-*To-Catch-a-Thief* black, I strode confidently toward the lonely trio tree. Walter Angel's poet hid something under this tree and I was going to find it.

I scoured the night landscape around me for any would-be gawkers. All I saw were the shapes of trees outlined against a charcoal background. Perfect. I dropped to the ground and crawled under the tree. There was no right way to do this as far as I could tell, so I just started digging. I wasn't expecting this thing—whatever it was—to be too deep. Whoever had buried it in the first place couldn't have gotten a spade under here. I was betting they'd just want it deep enough to keep it safe from the elements and wildlife.

Ten minutes later, I was rewarded with a satisfying clunk.

I'd hit something metal with my shovel. Barely containing my excitement, I began scooping away dirt with my hands. I cleared a moat-like ridge around something square, about ten centimetres by ten centimeters by ten centimetres. Given my awkward position under the tree, I couldn't actually see it, but I knew it was some kind of box. I wriggled it free, gently lifted it from the hole, and set it aside.

Spruce trees don't like to have their roots exposed. So, even though I'd only made a shallow gap in the earth, I pushed all the dirt right back in and trowelled it over so it looked much the way it had before. I wasn't just being a tree hugger. I had other potential treasure hunters in mind too. There was no guarantee I had the only map. As far as I knew, someone else with a copy of the treasure map could have been on their way to the lonely trio at that very moment. I didn't plan to give away any hints that I'd been here, or of what I'd found.

Satisfied that I'd covered my tracks, I slipped out from under the heavy branches. I sat on my haunches and regarded my find. I'd done good; it felt good. What came next, however, did not.

"You wanna hand that over, mister, eh?" a weaselly voice said.

Of course.

I tried to see who was talking, but it was difficult in the dark. He was just another outline against charcoal. I peered closer and caught a glimpse of something I'd rather not have seen. The moon had caught it just right. A steely glint was being reflected off the sharp edge of a knife.

This was not good. It was the middle of the night. I was not far from a part of town renowned for its nasty elements. If you had a death wish or felt like getting stabbed one night, there really wasn't a better place to be in Saskatoon. To be fair to Holiday Park, the real bad area was a few blocks north of here. This guy was obviously migrating south, like some kind of badass duck.

"Suppose I don't want to?" It couldn't hurt to ask. At the same time, I told myself it also wouldn't hurt to carry my gun every once in a while. It would come in handy at times like this.

The guy actually laughed. "Then my brother over there will take it from ya. How'd you like that, eh?"

Not much. So there were two of them. And indeed, I heard a grunt of agreement from behind me.

"So what is it you want? Money? How about my watch?"

The guy laughed again. He was having a pretty good time. "Sure, man, we'll take those too. But we really want what you got there in your hand. That thing you just dug up."

Curious. Why would they want the box? They didn't even know what was in it. Then again, neither did I, and here I was about to give up my favourite Calvin Klein watch and sixty bucks in cash just to keep it.

"Take the watch," I said. "This box is just some junk I found."

"Yeah, well, whatever, mister. We want that junk. You know what they say, eh? One dude's junk is another dude's treasure. And some dude wants your junk, man. So we're here to get it for 'im. Now hand it over already." His voice turned meaner. "Or do you want us to cut you up some first?"

My ears began to quiver. "Did you say another dude wants this junk? Did someone tell you to come get this from me?"

"Yeah, so what?"

"Yeah, so what?" the other, quieter brother, spoke up, although not with a very original contribution to the conversation.

"Who is this guy?"

"Like I know, eh. Come on, we don't have all night, right."

"Where are you going to meet him? Where are you supposed to hand over the box to him? Do you have a meeting place? Or a phone number? Are you supposed to call him when you have it? I'll pay you for whatever you can tell me."

More laughter. "With what? We're gonna take your wallet, mister."

That would have been kind of funny…in other circumstances.

"Besides, got nothing like that happening. He's just right over there, eh."

What! My eyes grew to owl-size. I spun my head around, but saw nothing. I really needed to invest in night-vision goggles.

"I can see you!" I screamed out the lie, letting it out before I'd really thought through a plan. Then again, any plan that didn't involve my getting sliced and diced by these hooligans was all right by me.

"Hey! What you doing, man?" the knife guy yelped.

"Was he driving a white truck, a Ford?"

"What?"

"What's his name? How much did he pay you? If you let me go *right now,* I'll pay you double whatever he's paying you!"

"Police! Put your hands up!"

Did I say that? Who said that?

After that, things started to happen very fast. And I still couldn't see a thing.

The boys, wisely deciding to take advantage of the cover of night, took the "put your hands up" thing as their cue to take a powder.

"Hold it right there!" the authoritative voice rang out. "Police!"

I heard running feet. Then nothing. Then one set of footsteps running back in my direction. Uh oh. By this time, I'd gotten to my feet and was doing a little I'm-not-quite-sure-what-to-do dance.

"What the hell are you doing?" Darren Kirsch shouted at me when he got close enough so I could see the veins pulsing at his temples. "Why did you tell them you could see me? Did you miss that day at the police academy when they talked about sneaking up on criminals?"

Oops. "Darren." I like to call him that when I'm trying to make nice. This wasn't really my fault, but I still felt bad. "I wasn't talking about you when I said, 'I can see you.' I was talking about the guy who paid those idiots to steal my box."

Kirsch exhaled big. "You'll have to do a little better than that, Quant."

"Yeah," I said, feeling a bit sheepish. "I know."

And then, Darren Kirsch did the unexpected. He said, "Beer?"

He was already sitting at a rooftop table, nursing a pint of something manly, when I arrived at O'Shea's Irish pub downtown.

"What is that?" I asked as I plunked myself down in the chair opposite his.

He told the waitress who'd followed me what he was having and she went off to get me one too. I like samesies.

"Good spot," I commented. Our table was street side, with a great view looking down at all the action of 2nd Avenue and beyond.

"You ever been here before?" he asked with a cocked eyebrow.

That's just like him. Thinking that just because I'm gay, I'd never been to an Irish pub before. He probably thought I favoured martini lounges and wine bars instead. I stared him straight in the eye and told him: "Uh, nope."

He smiled and took a healthy slug of his sudsy cold drink. Mine arrived and I did the same.

"Well, consider this my contribution to your drinking education."

Fair enough. "Listen, I'm sorry about back there. I was desperate. Those guys were about to knife me if I didn't give them what they wanted. When I found out that someone hired them, and that person was nearby, I took a shot. Either I'd get the distraction I needed, or I'd convince them to let me go after him. In a sense," I said in a vaguely accusatory tone, "you're the one who screwed up a good thing by running up like that, guns blazing, like some kind of supercop."

Supercop choked a little on his drink. Then he spoke. "First of all, Quant, my guns were not blazing. I did not discharge my firearm. And second of all, from what I saw, you were down on your knees, crying, and about to get yourself filleted. All I did wa…"

I didn't let him finish. "I was *not* crying!"

"Okay, maybe not," he relented. "But the rest is true."

"Well, maybe. We'll never know. How the hell did you end up at the San site anyway? Have you been following me?"

He gave me a sneer. "I didn't think there was any reason to. When you gave me the treasure map, I thought you agreed this was now a police matter."

"When someone rams my car, tries to break into my house, scares my dogs, and follows me around wherever I go, I make it my business," I rebutted in my tough guy voice. "So if you weren't following me, how'd you find me?"

"I didn't find *you*, Quant. I was hoping to find whoever it is who's after this…this thing, this treasure. You told me about what you found at Trounce House. That led me to the San site. Then I…"

"Wait, wait, wait, wait!" I stopped him, one hand up in the air, the other covering his beer. I didn't want him distracted by fermented hops. "*You* figured out the lily clue *and* the San site clue all by yourself?"

He shook his head and used his forefinger and thumb to pick my hand off his beer stein. "You act like you're the only one in the world with the title 'detective.' And mine is backed up with significant training, education, and the resources of an entire police department."

For a moment I sat there speechless, properly chastised.

I looked into Kirsch's eyes and I knew. "Your wife figured it out, didn't she?"

"Friggin' hell, Quant! How did you know?"

I couldn't help myself. I almost pissed myself laughing. And Darren laughed right along with me.

"Apparently Treena did a paper on Catherwood when she was in university. She was a bit of a jock herself back then."

Before she started spewing out Kirsch kids like a baby-vending machine, I was about to say, but held back. Treena and Darren had enough kids to have their home qualify as a hamlet. Had they never heard about condoms?

"And from there it was easy for her. She's so damn smart, that wife of mine. It scares me some of the things she knows.

"Unlike you, obviously, I figured there might be somebody else who had this map. And if that was true, they'd be looking for the same thing I was. I thought it couldn't hurt to stake out the San site for a coupla days to see who came digging around." He shook his head in mock disgust as he added, "And lookee who I found rootin' around in the dirt."

I let the comment slide. I was too busy trying to figure things out. "What I want to know is, how did White Truck Guy know where to find me?"

"You think that's who hired those guys?"

"Of course. Who else? What I don't get is *how* he found me. I've been so careful about getting him off my back. I'm not staying at my place. I'm not going to…oh."

"What?"

"I was about to say I'm not going to the office. But guess where I was earlier tonight."

"At PWC."

"Yup. He must have been hanging around hoping I'd show. And he was right. Damn! I should have noticed." I'd screwed up.

"Yeah, well, it's hard to keep your guard up twenty-four seven," Kirsch said, in a rare display of empathy. "Now hand it over."

This was what I was afraid of. The waitress came by and I ordered another two beers to delay what I knew was coming next.

"Quant, I want whatever it was you dug up from under that tree."

"And I want us to work together. This is the last clue. Two heads have got to be better than one. And by two, I mean me and Treena. You can watch."

Darren's eyes darkened. "You are perilously close to having your ass thrown in a cell for interfering with an active police investigation."

"If it's so active," I shot back, "why were you out there all alone tonight? Is it SPS policy to send its officers on dangerous stakeouts by themselves?" I knew Darren Kirsch. He was working a hunch. A hunch he wouldn't devote expensive and already strained manpower to until he was sure about it.

"Just show me what you got."

I had been a good boy. I'd brought the box with me. And I hadn't even peeked on my way to the bar. Nah, that's not true. I totally peeked. And I hadn't liked what I saw. That's why I was willing to hand it over. I needed help.

Darren received the box and set it down carefully in front of him. What? Did he expect it contained a bomb or something?

"So what's in it?" he asked.

I shrugged and waggled my head back and forth and did

whatever body movements seemed appropriate to convey the lie. "I dunno."

His eyebrows shot for his hairline. "What do you take me for?" And with that he loosened the tin's lid and pulled it off.

Popcorn. It was a tin full of popcorn.

Kirsch slowly upended the container and let the popcorn slide out onto the table in front of us. I'd already done that in my car. There were probably a few stray kernels left on the passenger seat. There was nothing in the box but popped corn.

"What the hell is this?"

I shook my head again. This time I was telling the truth. "I dunno."

"Jee-zus! This is crazyass shit! What does this mean?"

"Well, I do have one unsettling idea."

"What's that?" Kirsch asked.

"I've heard that some companies use real popcorn—instead of those Styrofoam ones—as packing material. It's more biodegradable."

"So what does that have to do with all this? You th...ooooooohhhhh. Shit. You think someone got to the box before we did?"

I nodded. "Yup. And all we're left with is the packing material."

I fell asleep on the cab ride back to Ash House. It had been a full day. Bit of an emotional roller coaster too. Everything from the early morning boat ride with Errall to spread Kelly's ashes, to finding out I was being evicted from PWC, to digging around in dirt and being threatened at knifepoint. So it was little surprise that, having ended up at an Irish pub with Darren Kirsch, that I said an exuberant yes to several "for the road" shots. And this was *after* we'd downed our third beer and started telling raucous jokes. As far as I was concerned, I had my reasons for over-imbibing. I don't know what Darren's excuse was. But I have to say, I'd never seen him laugh so much and so easily. Lots of beer does that to a guy, I suppose.

As the taxi was pulling into the yard—better lit now than it was last night (the workmen had been busy)—I saw someone getting into the only vehicle left in the parking lot. It was Ethan. First guy there in the morning, last to leave at night. He was burning the candle at both ends with this project.

I was short about five bucks for my fare. Those shots weren't going cheap. And who carries cash anymore? Besides, I hadn't really anticipated being in need of the services of a taxi that night.

While the cabbie scowled and growled at me, Ethan, having gotten out of his vehicle, slowly approached. I gave him a lopsided grin, wiped sleep from my eyes, and tried to act like I wasn't a bit looped. "Uh, hey, Ethan, buddy, you wouldn't happen to have five dollars on you, would you?"

Ethan paid the cabbie, sending him off with a nice tip.

"It's a little pricey coming out here in a taxi," I commented, frowning as I listened to my voice. In my head everything sounded just right, but when the words came through my lips they were slurred and maybe a bit pitiful sounding.

"Yeah," he agreed, kindly ignoring my altered speech patterns. "We're thinking of offering a scheduled shuttle service for the residents. It was one of Jared's many good ideas. That guy should be running a conglomerate or something. He really knows what he's doing."

"Yeah, he's great. Hey, I'll pay you back the five tomorrow." I didn't want him thinking I was a deadbeat.

He grinned. "No worries. Consider it a down payment on having you out here watching the place at night. The way I see it, I owe you."

"How's it all going?" I asked.

Smooth question, Quant. I knew Ethan probably had as long and tiring a day as I'd had. No doubt he just wanted to go home; maybe right into the arms of Damien the devil boy. I didn't think that was a good idea.

"It's a lot of work, but oh man, it's exciting. They got the pool running today," he answered, his enthusiasm as bright and vigorous as if he hadn't just put in a sixteen-hour day. "And it's got this great fountain attachment. It floats in the pool and shoots water up in a plume about fifteen feet into the air. I thought it'd be great during the wedding reception. And the new dishes came today. That's what I was doing tonight. Trying to find space for them in the kitchen cupboards. Do you have any idea how many dishes you need for fourteen people?"

"Fourteen?" I made a meek guess.

"Rhetorical question," he told me.

I knew that.

"Are you okay? You look a little bleary eyed? Do you n...oh, wait a sec...the cab...I get it." He chuckled. "You're soused, Mr. Quant. And on a Monday night!"

I gave him a sloppy smile, although I didn't mean for it to appear that way. "Not soused. Just a little happy."

He smiled back, then moved in to throw an arm around my shoulders. "Well, Mr. Happy, how about I help you into the house? There still aren't a lot of lights working. I wouldn't want there to be an accident before the place is even open."

Although I could see perfectly well, I allowed Ethan to guide me toward the house, up the steps, inside the front door, and down the hall to one of the future resident's rooms. The sensation of his body so close to mine was thoroughly enjoyable. I could feel the bunched up muscles of his arm as it held me upright. The sinewy firmness of his torso moulded into mine like it was meant to be there. Again his musky scent, compliments of a hard day's sweat mixed with tangy cologne, played in my nose like a pheromone. I'd never had the occasion to be so intimately near the man before. And if I'd been sober, I'd have had the good sense to be disturbed by what it was doing to me.

Ethan directed me to sit down on a fully madeup bed. The room was dim; the only light a faint shaft from the hallway. Even in my state and the diminished light, I was astonished to see how much had changed in just one day. Yesterday this room had been bare as a jail cell. Now it looked almost lived in.

"This is really something," I said, admiring the deep, rich colours of the walls and matching drapery and bed linens. "You got a lot done today."

"Oh, all the rooms don't look like this," he admitted. "We're only shooting to get the public areas looking presentable for the wedding on Saturday. But I wanted at least one hospitable room for our first guest."

I looked up at him. He was standing so close. "You mean me? You did all this for me?"

There was a two-second delay in his response. Not much, but I caught it. He answered, "Sure. Of course. We couldn't have you sleeping on the porch in a sleeping bag."

I'd enjoyed the sleeping bag on the porch, but I was warmed by his generosity. "Thank you," I whispered.

"You're welcome," he whispered back, his voice suddenly grown husky.

For a beat, there was only silence.

With a slow, deliberate movement, I reached for his hand.

When we touched, I felt explosions going off in the centre of my chest.

I ran my fingers up the length of the inside of his forearm, marvelling at how something so silkily smooth could feel so hard.

I could sense Ethan's body tense. An unidentifiable noise escaped his lips.

The next thing I knew, I had pulled myself up and we were nose to nose.

I touched his face. Cupping his jaw with my hand, I drew it closer. Our foreheads met and I whispered his name. For what seemed like forever, we stood there, breathing each other in. Heaving chest against heaving chest. Hip bone against hip bone. Muscled thigh against muscled thigh.

Our lips touched, gently. Our eyes were open. His brown ones mixed with my greens.

And then he was gone.

Chapter 8

Waking up with a gift-wrapped package on your tummy is pleasant. Realizing you can't quite remember the night before, is not.

It was actually the banging of hammers and deep voices that woke me up. The Ash House workmen were at it again. I gazed at an alarm clock next to the bed and was shocked to see it was almost ten a.m. I hadn't slept that late in a very long time. And it wasn't as if I'd had a ridiculous number of drinks. Yes, I'd drunk too much to drive home, but I wasn't smashed.

I shoved my body up into a half sitting position and tore open the present. I chuckled when I saw it. A large bottle of Aspirin.

There was a card.

Russell,
You'd think I was the one who'd had too much to drink, given how I acted. I hope the Aspirin helps. Unfortunately, there are no pills for being stupid.
Sorry.
Ethan

Now I remembered. It all came back to me. Vividly clear. Excruciatingly clear. Maybe I *had* been smashed.

I reread the note. What a guy. Taking the blame for something that was obviously my fault.

I was *that* guy. A drunken idiot. I'd made a fool of myself. And I had made things between my host and me uncomfortable. Too uncomfortable to stay. I had to get out of there. I jumped out of bed, called for a cab, and stuffed everything I'd brought with me into my duffle bag. I tidied the room, fixed the bed, and made a quick sweep of the room to make sure I'd left nothing behind. Maybe if I disappeared, I could pretend I'd never been there in the first place. Especially not last night. I ran a hand over my face and mess of hair. I'd have to shower and shave and brush my teeth at the gym. I would not come back here.

Anthony, Sereena, and I had long ago planned the mid-week get together for a pre-wedding meeting, to go over any possible last-minute wedding details. Silly, I know. As if with Anthony and Sereena, the two most organized and prepared people I knew, in charge, there'd be any element of the celebration, however minute, left undone. In reality, I expected lunch would be nothing more than one last pleasant gathering before my friend and mentor became a married man. Both Anthony and Jared had refused a bachelor party with the requisite stripping fireman. I was hoping we'd at least have a really cute waiter.

The Ivy is an urbane, LA-meets-Prairie restaurant and cocktail lounge in Saskatoon's warehouse district. The area had struggled for years to become more uptown chic than downtown ghetto, and by the looks of the place, success had arrived. After a brief work-out and hot shower at the Y, I'd found a handy parking spot across the street, and I entered the restaurant feeling much better than I had that morning. I was a bit underdressed for the well-heeled lunch crowd, but what can you expect when you're living out of a duffle bag?

Anthony and Sereena, meanwhile, had claimed the best table

in the house and looked every inch the sophisticated socialites who lunch. I joined them with the only things I had to offer: a killer smile and kisses on the cheeks.

At first I was having a perfectly lovely time. It wasn't until our main courses arrived that they hit me with the big one.

"So when were you planning to tell us?" This from Anthony.

My tongue grew thick and my mouth dry. Never has that sentence been uttered with something good coming after it.

"What do you mean?" I asked, wishing I were somewhere else.

"Alex called last night. Apologizing—again—that he can't be here for the wedding. Such a considerate, sweet man. Don't you think?"

Suddenly what had gone into my mouth as a perfect, oven-grilled ham and gruyere wrap perfumed with cinnamon and sweet petunia petals, became a meat and cheese hockey puck shooting goals against the walls of my stomach. "Of course," I croaked. "Alex is the best."

"Russell," Anthony eyed me over his chilled glass of rosé. "You put Jared and me in a most awkward position."

"Oh?" I glanced about, hoping I knew someone I could wave over to join us. But there was no one. I gazed over at Sereena, hoping for respite. She was studying me like a bug under a microscope, wondering whether she should squash me. Oh gawd, this wasn't going to be good.

"Nothing to tell us then?" Anthony asked. His Brit-flavoured voice was saucy, the heavy, serious kind of sauce that smothers game meat, not the light and restrained kind that subtly enhances subliminal flavours.

"Oh, you mean about the engagement?" I went for light-hearted coy.

No replies from either of my lunch mates. As I sat there, feeling like a bad little boy who forgot to mention to his parents that he'd just failed math, I realized that seldom was I ever solely in the company of these two. Anthony and Sereena, both such important people in my life. Both so potent. Both so intense.

It was too much. I had the urge to run for my life.

But lunch was far from over. The next best thing was to lie. I turned to Anthony and said, "I didn't want to steal your and Jared's thunder. I couldn't announce my engagement the same week as your wedding. This week is about the two of you. Not me and Alex."

"I was just wondering," Sereena asked, the words ominously sweet as they fell off her tart tongue, "exactly which turnip truck you think the two of us just fell off?"

"The one in front," I tried for cutesy. Which of course never works with these two.

"What happened, Russell?" Sereena asked in her most dulcet of tones.

And suddenly it just poured out. "So there we were in Hawaii. We were having such a great time. We were playing in the water. Sitting on the beach. Eating, drinking, and generally being merry and gay. And suddenly, out of nowhere, he's got this ring in his hand, and he's asking me to marry him. In a restaurant. With all these people watching us. I felt like I was on the final episode of *The Bachelor*, with a million people tuning in, hoping for a happy ending that I alone was responsible for. It all happened so fast. We'd never talked about this. He's never even hinted he wanted to get married. But there he was. With this ring. And all those eyes watching us. I didn't feel like it was about what I wanted at all. I didn't have time to think. I was just...stunned."

"So you said yes," Anthony said.

"I had to! What else could I do?"

"Could you have said no?"

It was such a simple question, powerful in its bluntness, it struck me dumb.

Anthony laid a hand over mine. "What is it, puppy? What is it?"

"We can see you're in love," Sereena stated, "but not with Alex Canyon."

With the effort it took to budge my head in reluctant agreement, I'm sure I could have moved a mountain.

"It's Ethan," Anthony said it as if he was revealing the obvious. "You're in love with Ethan."

I nodded.

"How long have you known?"

This I could answer with words. "From the first time I saw him."

Anthony smiled with sparkling eyes. "That's a wonderful answer. I'm so happy for you, m'boy. I can see it in you too. You are truly in love." He patted my hand and added, "And it's about damn time too."

"And Alex?" Sereena wondered, not unkindly.

My heart flip-flopped. "I don't know. I just don't know. When I'm with him it feels so good. I'm worried."

"About what?"

"That I feel this way about Ethan only because Alex isn't around. What if Alex lived here? What if we were together every day? Maybe I would never have developed these feelings for Ethan."

Sereena's lively eyes were warm and non-judgmental as she regarded me. "You've told me the long-distance arrangement worked for you. That you enjoyed having both your independence and a boyfriend at the same time. Has that changed?"

"It's true. It did work. It does work."

"Maybe you believe 'marriage' would be something different than that? That if you get married you'd have to give up your independence, and, in a way, having a 'boyfriend'?"

"No. It's not that. I don't think it's that." Now I was getting confused.

"So if Alex said that after the wedding he'd spend all his time in Saskatoon, that there'd be no more traipsing around the world, would that change your feelings for Ethan?"

I had to admit that it would not.

"And to be completely accurate," Anthony said, "from what I can see, you and Ethan haven't spent much more time together over the past couple of years than you and Alex have, even though he does live in the same city."

"That's true."

"Do you love Alex?"

"I think I do. It's jus…"

"Do you love Ethan?"

"Yes."

"There's your answer."

"No. It's not that simple. I feel something different when I'm with Alex."

"Russell," Sereena spoke softly, "I can tell you exactly what that something different is."

Thank goodness. I really needed to know. "What?" I almost shouted it.

"Less love."

I was crestfallen. And I knew without a doubt, that she was right.

I did love two men. But I loved one more, and in many more ways, than the other. But how can you fall in love with someone you're not in a relationship with? Alex and I were a couple. We were getting to know each other very well. We were figuring out all the little ins and outs of what made each other work. I knew how to make him feel good. He did the same for me. I knew his favourite colour, how he liked his steak done, what kind of movies made him cry (no kind!), how he liked to spend a day off. I knew this man. But Ethan. What did I know about him? I knew he liked to laugh. I knew he was a caregiver. He was a parent. He was a hard worker. But what really made him tick? What side of the bed did he like to sleep on? Was he hotdog or hamburger? Pop or rock? Mandals or flip-flops?

There was one more very important and undeniable thing: Ethan was taken.

Alex loved me. He gave me a ring for Van Cleef and Arpels's sake. Sex was great. The feel of his hand caressing my skin still gave me chills. And he wanted to make a life with me. He'd offered me his. All I had to do was give him mine. Yet I was about to throw it all away for someone I'd never even been on a date with. Someone who could have no desire for me whatsoever. Someone who might wear black socks with sandals. The decision should have been a no-brainer.

So why wasn't it?

"What will you do?" Sereena wanted to know.

I had nothing to tell her.

I had a lot of thinking to do and nowhere to do it. I couldn't go home or to work, just in case White Truck would be there. And I certainly couldn't go back to Ash House. Not after lunch with Anthony and Sereena. Not after last night.

I hadn't told Anthony and Sereena about the kiss. I didn't know what it meant. Other than that alcohol truly does lower inhibitions. And that Ethan Ash's touch had set my skin on fire.

I sat in the parking lot of The Ivy for a long time, letting my thoughts wander. This seemed to get me nowhere, and blasting rays of sun on my already hot head weren't helping. I needed to cool off. I needed distraction. There was one perfect spot. I used my cellphone to find what I was looking for, then sped off.

The lineup for snacks at the downtown movie theatre was sparse. Good sign. I wasn't even sure what was playing; probably some summer blockbuster with things blowing up. I didn't care.

"What can I get for you?" the greasy-haired attendant with a painful looking cheek piercing asked me as I bellied up to the counter.

"Can I get a..."

She gave me a strange look. I didn't blame her. I had simply stopped talking and moving. I'm sure it must have looked as if my batteries had just conked out.

But it was way better than that. I had it!

"Nothing, thanks!" I told her with plenty more enthusiasm than the situation called for. I handed my ticket to a teen coming through the entrance, and raced out of the complex, back to my car.

For the second time that afternoon, I purchased a movie ticket. This time for the first showing of a second-run movie at the Roxy. A few blocks on the wrong side of Idylwyld Drive, the old movie house is a curious place. Built just before the Depression, the Roxy is famous for its unique and fanciful interior, reminiscent of a

Spanish village. The larger of the two theatres boasts built-in balconies, whimsical towers, and charming window boxes overflowing with fake flowers. The ceiling is dark blue, with twinkling lights set into plaster, an eternal starry night. It was the starry night that did it for me. That and the popcorn.

When the concession attendant at the other movie place had asked me what I wanted, the first thing that was going to come out of my mouth was what most people say when asked the same question: popcorn.

Popcorn!

Ever since I'd found it, I'd been stumped by the popcorn in the tin buried under the tree at the San site. Why popcorn? Maybe I was wrong to think it was simply packing material. What if the popcorn itself was the clue? Using the old word association game, you say popcorn, I think movies. I repeated the last stanza of the treasure map poem in my head.

And finally it does hide,
Below sparkling sky,
Within a golden urn
Treasure you will find.

I wasn't sure about the golden urn, but I knew of a movie theatre with a sparkling sky: The Roxy.

It was worth a try. If I was wrong, all it would cost me was the price of admission...well, two admissions. But as soon as I entered the darkened cavern of the theatre, I knew I was right. In an alcove above the exit near the stage, below the twinkle-lights-in-plaster sky, was a golden urn. I was ecstatic with my discovery. If I was reading the poem correctly, what I was after was in that urn! I'd finally made it to the end of the treasure hunt!

However, one big problem remained. How the heck was I supposed to scale the faux Spanish wall, climb into the alcove, reach into the urn, and claim my prize, all without being seen? Even if I waited until the lights were lowered and the show began, regardless of how good the movie up on the screen was, I was betting my unusual behaviour would surely attract some unwanted attention.

Or would it? Sunk deep in my seat, I swivelled my head to study the other patrons in the theatre. There weren't any. Fortunately, matinees on warm summer Tuesday afternoons are not hot ticket events.

By the time the lights dimmed and the reels began to roll, only three other people had arrived to join me in the massive, dark space. Two were teenage girls who were too excessively engrossed in their own selves to pay me much attention. The third was a woman who sat front and centre with an extra large bag of popcorn, a bag of gummi bears, and a super-sized drink the size of a pail. I was hoping her location would not only keep me out of her line of sight, but meant she was there for the movie and couldn't care less about what was happening behind and just to the right of her.

Next, I put my brain to work on how I was going to get to the urn. The bottom edge of the alcove had to be fifteen to twenty feet off the ground. Now, if I were Indiana Jones or Zorro, this wouldn't be an issue. But I was fresh out of whips and ropes and mighty steeds on whose back I could stand on. I needed something a little less swashbuckling and a little more efficient: a ladder. I needed a ladder.

Pink Panther-like, I snuck out of the theatre to check the hallway. Certainly a place like this would have ladders all over the place.

Not so.

I returned to the theatre, this time taking a seat near the rear. It struck me that if I couldn't come at this thing from the bottom, perhaps I could from the top. I studied the space, front to back, looking for an easy way—I'd even take a not-so-easy way—to make my way up to the Spanish villa rooftop. But that too seemed impossible. And even if I could get up there and make it to the alcove, by leaping rooftop to rooftop (which looks pretty simple in all those James Bond movies), I saw that the distance from roof line to urn would be simply too great for me to reach down and grab whatever was inside. I'd have to hop down into the alcove from the roof, but then I'd be stuck there, with no conceivable way to get away, unless I suddenly developed the powers of Spider-Man. I slunk low into my seat, dejected. So close, yet so far. I had to wonder if I was making a big mistake. If I couldn't get to the urn, how could anyone else have done it? And if no one else could get to the urn, that meant the treasure wasn't in it.

I mulled that over for a few unhappy minutes. But then I got over it. There could conceivably be a thousand…well, maybe not a thousand…but lots of ways that someone could have gotten something into that blasted urn. Perhaps they knew someone who worked at the theatre; maybe they had an accomplice with darn good aim. I'd probably never know. But what I *did* know was that I could not leave that theatre without finding out if there was anything in that golden urn.

The movie finally ended and the teenage and not-so-teenage girls left. The lights went up as the credits rolled. Panic set in. If I was going to do something, it had to be now, before the next batch of moviegoers and theatre clean-up crew came in. I was desperate.

I ran down the centre aisle of the theatre, stopping just below the alcove with its tantalizing golden urn. I stared up at it, wishing for about the millionth time in my life that I was Samantha from *Bewitched*. A simple wiggle of my nose would bring me my greatest desire, which at that moment was whatever was in that damn urn. Was that too much to ask? Apparently so.

Hastily devising a new plan, I scoured the area for something heavy enough, but not too heavy. I finally settled on my cellphone, which I hoped had just the right amount of heft. I was pretty good at baseball in high school, so my hopes were high. With one last look around to make sure the place was still deserted, I took aim, and pitched the phone at the golden urn.

It connected! As the phone came whizzing back down—somehow or other right into my waiting hands—I watched as the metallic-hued urn tipped and tottered.

"Fall, damn you, fall!" I encouraged.

Finally, with a clatter, the urn fell to its side.

I groaned. The thing was still up there! Fortunately, the floor of the alcove was less than even. As I caught my breath, the urn began to roll, ever closer to the edge of the alcove.

Closer. Closer. Closer.

And then it fell, straight into my arms. Only then did I remember to breathe.

I quickly set the vessel on the ground, and reached inside. I felt wisps of spiderwebs wash over my skin as I searched for my treasure. My fingers fell on something. A tube of some sort? I was right! I'd solved the treasure map! I pulled out my bounty. It was a spiral-bound notebook, rolled up and fastened with an elastic band. Not exactly gold bullion, but who was I to complain?

"Hey! What are you doing?" a voice rang out from the back of the theatre.

Run, baby, run!

Luckily the exit was right there. Without turning to see who was after me—I didn't want him to catch sight of my face—I smashed through the door and made like Sylvester after Tweety Bird. I made a beeline for the street and kept on going, never looking back. I was hoping that once my pursuer saw that I hadn't stolen the urn, he'd leave me be. But just in case, I ran for several blocks, whizzing by people on the sidewalk, crossing streets against the walk light, dodging traffic. For a while there, I pretended I was in some sort of heist caper and needed to get away from the bad guy. In this situation, however, I kinda was the bad guy. At least the Roxy folks would think so.

Finally, when I started not to recognize where I was, I stopped. Although my lungs felt as if they wanted to explode, I was too exhilarated to care. Running away was fun. Finding treasure was fun. Now all I had to do was circle back to get my car. I could only hope a legion of cops weren't waiting there for me.

They weren't.

When it seems you've got nowhere to go, there's usually one place left: home. For me, it was killing two birds with one stone (which I've always thought is a rather gruesome analogy). I'd spend time with my mother (who'd been complaining she hadn't seen enough of me lately), and I'd have a safe haven while I figured out what my treasure was, how it tied in to the murder of Walter Angel, and what to do with it.

Before making the forty-five minute drive to Mom's farm, I checked my home answering machine and whooped with joy when it told me that Air Canada was finally in possession of my luggage. Instead of risking a visit to the house for fresh clothing, I could recycle my Hawaii duds. I swung by the airport, picked up my bags, then headed for my childhood home on the range.

As the Mazda and I headed north, I couldn't help but feel a wee bit guilty. I'd promised Darren Kirsch that we'd work on the last verse of the clue together. And now I'd gone and done it alone, and taken the treasure out of town to boot. He'd be pissed. But it wouldn't be the first time. It wasn't as if he'd been big on the sharing-of-information thing in the past either. Then again, this détente could mean the beginning of a new era of improved communications between the two of us. A private eye needs a reliable contact in the police department. By the time I pulled up to Mom's place, I decided I would tell him what I had found. Just not right now.

Even though Mom's yard, five kilometres from Howell, the nearest town, is decked out with flowerbeds spilling over with stunning plants, a meticulously cared for lawn, and many pleasant sitting areas, it is for show only. Kind of like the good guest china that never gets used, not even for guests. In Mom's world, one only spent time outside for work, not pleasure. It wasn't always that way with her. I have many fond memories of family picnics from when I was a boy. Me, Mom and Dad, my brother Bill, and even sometimes my older sister Joanne, when she was around, would pack up a picnic basket, a baseball for tossing around, some blankets, and head out for a Sunday afternoon in the pasture. Somewhere along the line, I can't even remember when, all of that changed. There were no more picnics.

Now, the concept of eating outdoors is foreign to my mother, barbaric almost. Why eat outside when there is a perfectly good table and set of chairs inside, where you're close to the oven, there are no mosquitoes, and you don't risk sunburn? Once, when she was visiting me in the city, I'd taken her to Earl's deck for lunch. She'd sat through the meal looking decidedly ridiculous wearing my Maui Jim sunglasses (as she owns no sunglasses herself), wincing with displeasure each time a fly landed on her plate, and glowering at the navel ring prominently displayed by our well-tanned and toned server. It was a veeerrrry long lunch.

Mom is short, stocky, sixty-seven, and speaks with a heavy Ukrainian accent, replete with rolling r's and wailing oi's. She sports a tightly permed head of dark hair with occasional sprigs of white, horn-rimmed spectacles, a kindly face that bears a scowl just as well, and can most often be found wearing a dress, thick nylons, and black shoes with low, clunky heels (even when she's gardening).

When I'd called from the car and told her I was coming for a visit, she told me she'd have supper ready. Big surprise there. What she didn't tell me was that I wasn't the only visitor she'd be feeding that evening.

The first clue that something unusual was afoot was the rental car parked against Mom's house. The driver had pulled right up on the lawn and had knocked over a planter of pink geraniums without bothering to set it right. The trunk was left open, as if the car's occupant couldn't be bothered to slam it shut after retrieving whatever it was they'd wanted. I parked on the spit of gravel meant for the purpose and got my bag out of my own trunk. I strolled up to the car and took a casual gander inside. The back seat looked as if a family of beavers had moved in several months earlier. On the front seat and the floor were strewn a collection of candy bar wrappers (Oh Henry! and Eat-More), two full bottles of water, an empty cardboard coffee cup, a selection of pill bottles, and half a mickey of brandy.

Ahh. Now I knew.

My sister had landed.

I have two siblings. A younger brother, Bill, and a much older sister, Joanne. Bill is the most respectable, organized, prepared, controlled, solid kind of guy I've ever met. He'd had his entire life planned out in his head before he was twelve. He knew what he wanted to do for a living—be an accountant—where he wanted to live—Winnipeg, a province over—who he wanted to marry—a beautiful blonde with few career aspirations—and how many kids they'd have—four. He envisioned the salary he'd make, the suits he'd wear, the cars he'd drive, the house he'd live in, the vacations he'd take, the church he'd go to, the sports he'd play, the fishing he'd do. And now that he had all that, his new goal was to do the same for each of his children. Why leave anything up to chance?

My sister, however, was a whole other story. If I were to imagine someone the polar opposite of Bill, that would be Joanne. I was somewhere in the middle.

I rounded the house and there she was, sitting on the side door stoop. For a moment, before she caught sight of me, I was blasted into the past. How many times had I seen her sitting in that exact same spot, looking like a train wreck, smoking a cigarette or a doobie.

"You moving in?" she asked, noting my luggage but showing no surprise at seeing me.

Mom must have told her I was coming. Why I didn't get the same warning, I didn't know. I smiled at my sister. I'd forgotten how her voice sounded like fifty miles of rutted, gravel road.

"Just visiting for a couple days," I said as I came closer.

I did the math and realized that my sister was nearly fifty years old. If having a sibling that age made me feel old, I wondered what it felt like to her. Then again, I guessed she probably didn't care. She looked every year of her age and then some. Always had.

A life of glut, with plenty of bad times offsetting the good, can't help but show on a person who's lived through it. With my neighbour Sereena, every drug-filled night, doomed relationship, and life taken too early, appeared on the planes of her life-hewn face. Yet somehow, an inner beauty, a sprightly spirit, an indefinable aura, shone through, making her almost painfully stunning. It helped that she'd been a beautiful woman to start with. But so had my sister. Pictures of her when she was in the bloom of young womanhood showed a healthy looking Joni Mitchell type, with shiny blonde hair, large eyes, rounded cheekbones, thick lips, and skin that glowed. But no longer. Life had exacted a toll, and the price was as obvious as a tag hanging from her nose.

She reached up to me. In her hand was a dark skinned cigarillo. I marvelled at the contrast of her beautiful French tips stained bronze by tobacco. Joanne liked the good things in life, and with equal fervour, lusted after the bad.

"No thanks. I don't smoke." I hadn't for years.

"No one does anymore," she commented, taking in a drag of smoke and holding it for a count of five.

"And you? Are you here for a visit?"

She laughed. It was maybe the only thing left of her that was pretty.

Or maybe...maybe she still sang? She must. It was the only way I ever knew of that she supported herself. Or tried to. When I was young, people would tell me: "She sings like a wounded bird." I had no idea what that meant. I hadn't heard her sing in years. Her voice today certainly wasn't making melodic sounds.

"Oh Russ, why don't you just come out and ask what you really want to ask?"

No one called me Russ. Only Joanne. And that's the way it would stay, if I had anything to say about it.

"You want to know how long I'm staying. And why I'm here in the first place."

She was right. Joanne rarely came home. Even so, she and Mom managed to keep up a close relationship from what I could tell. They'd always had a special bond, often spending Christmas or other holidays together. I don't know how it worked out that way. Joanne rarely lived in the same city, never mind same apartment, for more than a year at a time. But I'd hear about an invitation, and the next thing I knew, Joanne had driven down and spirited Mom away to some resort or ski lodge or cabin in the woods she was looking after.

To me, it seemed like a crazy amount of driving for Joanne. But both women preferred driving to flying it seemed; Mom once explained that the long car trips were part of the visit. Joanne loved to drive. She said highway trips were the only time she had to really think. I couldn't begin to imagine what my sister thought about during those long hours.

Our (indoor) meal that night consisted of meatballs with a sweet-and-sour sauce made by mixing together barbecue sauce and Mom's homemade jam, a full roasted chicken, fried perogies with mushroom sauce, cabbage rolls in an onion-y tomato sauce, baby potatoes fresh from her garden in a cream sauce, and a salad without one store-bought ingredient except for the creamy Caesar dressing. As we ate, along with giving my arteries a good testing, Mom caught my sister and me up on local goings on—mostly who died, who was sickly, who missed church on Sunday, and whose garden wasn't doing so well this summer. For dessert there was zucchini cake.

After supper, Mom poured me a strong rye and Coke, and Joanne had the same (without the coke), and we settled in to play canasta for *three* hours. Mom also told me I should cut my hair, which I'd let grow long and a little wild for the summer. It had lightened from its usual sandy brown to near golden blond in Hawaii. I kind of liked it. So did Alex. Kay Quant neé Wistonchuk did not. Joanne was indifferent.

Begging off one last hand and a late-night snack, I escaped to my boyhood bedroom near on midnight. Closing the door behind me, I laid my head against it and, with eyes tightly closed, slowly sank to the ground. I felt a shudder run through me. This was waaaaay too surreal. Way too reminiscent of childhood. I half expected brother Bill to come banging on the door asking me to check the assumptions in the compound interest schedule he'd created to forecast the cash he'd have on hand in his weekly allowance bank account by the time he finished high school. What a dork.

I opened my eyes and the first thing I saw was my *Back to the Future* poster. I'd loved movies as a kid. Still do. They're like comfort food to me. Living where we did, I didn't get to see a lot of movies growing up, usually only when they finally ended up on TV. By the time I saw the first *Star Wars* movie, and thought it was the greatest thing since Nutella, the whole world had long ago seen it and moved on.

Under my schoolboy desk I spied Tim. Tim was a stuffed bear I'd won in one of those fishing pole games at a local school bazaar. It's where you pay a quarter or fifty cents, throw a mock fishing line over a bed sheet, and someone on the other side attaches a prize to your line. I remember being a little more excited than I should have been to win a bear at my age. But I'd never won any-thing before that. I leaned over and pulled Tim into my lap. I pet-ted his brown head, and thought: it's good to be home, far away from airport murderers and knife wielding maniacs. I felt safe.

A little googly from the rye, my eyes bobbed around the room, taking in all my stuff. Was it really my stuff anymore, I wondered? Or did it belong to a boy who no longer existed? I remembered many nights sitting on that same bed, thinking, trying to figure out who I was. Those were the days before every kid's room had a phone, a TV, a computer, all the things contrary to introspection. Even as a youngster, I knew very well that I was different from other boys. Or, at least, different from what TV and movies and books and school teachers and even my parents and siblings told me boys should be. Yet, I wasn't particularly worried about it. I found it curious, and spent many hours thinking about what "it" was and what it would mean for me and my future life. But some-how, I was confident everything would turn out okay in the end. Naïve? You bet. But isn't that what kids are supposed to be?

Pushing thoughts of childhood aside, I shtumped across the floor until I was sitting next to the shelf displaying my collection of *Star Wars* action figures. I pulled my duffle bag into my lap and dug out the notebook I'd found at The Roxy. This was my first opportunity to uncover the treasure I'd worked so hard to find. I hopped onto the bed, propping my *Dynasty* pillow (featuring Krystle and Alexis) behind me. As I pulled off the elastic band that bound the journal, I felt a mounting excitement. Inside was the buried treasure Walter Angel had more than likely died for. Now I had it. Now I was going to be in on the big secret.

I opened the notebook to the first page. My breath caught when I saw the name.

Chapter 9

Simon Durhuaghe—pronounced Dur-hay-hee—was someone almost everyone would claim to have heard of, especially in Canada, and most especially in Saskatchewan. He was, undeniably, the most prolific and famed author of literary fiction to come out of Saskatoon. He'd written twenty-nine novels, seven anthologies, countless other short stories, and even one Juno-nominated song, and the count was still on. He had to be seventy, but his star was still on the ascent. His most recent novel, *Down this Rutted Road*, had been released to great fanfare this past fall.

To say I was astonished to find that the treasure I'd uncovered was a Durhuaghe original, was an understatement. At least I presumed the work I held in my hands had never been published. The first line of the notebook read, in beautiful, loopy penmanship: The Journal of Simon Durhuaghe – July 17, 1979 to January 3, 1985.

Before reading any further, I did a quick scan of the notebook. Several pieces of loose-leaf and other miscellaneous papers were stuck between various pages. The journal entries themselves were in the same lovely handwriting as the heading, and varied in length from single cryptic sentences like: "Just as I expected" or "Only time will tell," to longer sections that went on for several paragraphs. Sometimes his notations appeared every day, then there'd be nothing for weeks, even months.

I decided I needed something stronger than a glass of water if I intended to get through the whole thing before morning. So I slipped out of my room and made my way back to the basement kitchen, the centre of the universe in Mom's farmhouse. Anything you wanted, there it would be. And, not surprisingly, there too was Mom, still awake, at the stove, patiently stirring something in a simmering pot.

"*Sonsyou,*" she greeted me. "You're not sleeping yet? How come, den? Are you hungry, mebbe? I feex you someting goot."

"Oh no, I'm still thinking I might explode from supper."

"Oh, don't say dat. You deedn't like? How come?"

"No, no, of course I liked it. I just ate too much of it. I'm not used to eating so much." Bit of a lie there. "And I'm kinda supposed to be dieting." That part was always true.

"Vhat for you diet? You're too skeenny. You seet, I feex some pie."

I held up my hands in a defensive gesture. I'd have to tuck and roll to get out of there without some kind of foodstuff shoved into my mouth. "I just have some reading to do and wanted some caffeine to help stay awake. I'll put on a pot of coffee. Or do you have diet Coke or something?"

And that's how I ended up with yet another rye and coke.

On my way back to my room, passing by the "good" upstairs living room I don't remember ever being in as a child, I heard a croak. It was Joanne, curled up in a recliner chair, under a blanket. Without air conditioning, the house was stifling hot, and I wondered how she could survive under there. Although the room was dark, I could still make out a half-empty bottle of Crown Royal on the coffee table next to the chair.

"Good night, Joanne," I quickly said, hoping to make a speedy getaway.

"C'mere, Russ."

Foiled. I entered the room and stood over her. I could just see the top of her head. Her hair was greasy and lay in dead strands across her skull. Alcohol oozed out of her pores. And not just from what she'd drunk today.

"You okay?" I asked.

"I drink too much." She rasped. "Guess you know that though, huh?"

I settled into a nearby chair and watched as two eyes appeared from below the edge of the quilt. Tired eyes. Glassy. Haunted. I didn't want to know what they'd seen.

"You're just like him, you know." Her words were only slightly slurred.

"What? Who? I'm just like who?"

"Dad."

"What do you mean?" Our dad died more than ten years ago. He was a big-boned, black-haired, blue-eyed Irishman with ruddy cheeks and a proper brogue. And as far as I remembered, in looks and every other way, we were not alike at all.

"Because at forty years old, you're all alone."

I sputtered a bit, then, "I'm thirty-eight! And what makes you think I'm alone? And what does that have to do with Dad? He wasn't alone. He had Mom and all of us."

"Oh grow up, Russ. You didn't even know Dad. You don't know what he was like."

Was that the first bottle of rye she'd drunk tonight? Couldn't be, because she was making no sense. "Of course I do. He was my dad." I knew I hadn't spent tons of time with him or anything. Our interests were different. He loved being in the fields and fixing machines. I did not. "He was a pretty good guy," I said. "He was around and stuff."

Joanne snorted and reached for a cigarillo.

"You can't smoke that in here."

She threw it on the rug and instead shakily poured herself another glass of rye. No mix. "You and I had different fathers. You didn't know him when he was your age now. I did."

That much was true. When Joanne was born, Mom was only eighteen, and Dad twenty-eight. Bill and I didn't come along for over a decade.

"What was so different then?"

Another derisive laugh. Another gulp of booze. "He was like you. Couldn't commit. Couldn't settle down. Mom could tell you. But she won't. I only know because I saw it. He barely noticed I was around, but I was smarter than he gave me credit for."

My face turned crimson. I did not want to hear what my ears were forcing into my head. "What are you telling me?"

"I'm telling you, brother dear, that our daddy screwed around all the time. Went hand in hand with his boozing. He'd be good for a month or so, then all of a sudden he'd come in from doing chores or whatever, and he'd be as soused as a sailor. He hid bottles in the machine shop. Mom would go looking for them, but he was pretty clever with his hiding spots.

"He'd drink up a storm, do some ranting and raving about bad crops, his inconsiderate wife, the lousy supper on the table, or whatever else he could think of to lay blame on, then he'd get in the half-ton and drive to town to drink some more at the beer parlour. It always amazed me that he never once ended up in a ditch or arrested for DUI. He had horseshoes up his ass, and I guess there weren't many cops patrolling the highway between the Quant farm and Howell in those days."

All I could do was shake my hurting head.

Joanne kept on. "I'd see Mom sit by the window waiting for him. She'd pretend to be shelling peas or reading her recipe books, but I knew better. While she was hoping and praying for his headlights to turn off the highway into the yard, I was wishing he'd never come home. I used to wish, Russ, that one day he'd drive off and we'd never have to see him again.

"The worst was when he wouldn't come home until morning. And the asshole would actually have the balls to yell at her, as if it were her fault that he got pissed and spent the night with some town whore."

It was too much. "Stop, Joanne, just stop," I said, getting up. "You're the one who's been drinking too much." There were so many thoughts in my head, but none were ready to come out. I pulled back, intending to walk away.

"At least I try to have relationships," she yapped on. "I know none of them have worked out all that well, but I try." For a fleeting second, I saw the pain of a hundred bad relationships flit across her face. I winced at the harshness of the sight. "I try hard. I get my heart broken, but I pick up the pieces and try again. Look at Bill. He got married as soon as he could, and he holds on to that woman so tight she is never getting away. But you, Russ, you just can't settle down. You can't pick one. You just pick and choose and have little tastes, as if people are nothing more than appetizers."

I was frozen in my spot, but the heat of my fuming soon thawed me out. What I couldn't decide was if I was mad at her or mad at myself.

Mad at her was easier. I whipped about and, feeling my tongue sharpen, began my verbal assault. "You don't know me. You don't know the first thing about me. And I don't know you. You left home before I was old enough to figure out what a sister was. Ever since then, all you do is parachute in whenever you feel like it, make your proclamations, tell your stories, drink our booze, then bugger off again, disappearing into a life you've never invited us into. And because of that, you don't have the right to sit there and judge me!"

She looked at me calmly through filmy eyes. She was unrattled, a woman used to confrontation. "Oh Russ, I'm not judging. I'm the last person alive to judge anyone. And I have tried, a little, to find out about what's going on with you. I've asked Mom about who you're seeing. But she never seems to know exactly what's going on. She mentioned you'd been seeing someone for the past couple of years, but he doesn't seem to be around much and you don't talk about him. Russ, you don't share much of your private life either."

"That's not true," I shot back. "Did you ever think that maybe Mom doesn't know about my private life because she's not interested, because she doesn't get involved in my life the way she does in yours?" This was a lie. And the truth of that struck me like a plank against the side of my head.

Over the last several years—especially since that first Christmas she spent with me in *my* home—Mom had changed.

She'd become a much bigger part of my life, and my life as a gay man. Hell, she'd even cooked for Alex when he was recovering from a gunshot wound. Was Joanne right? Had I been shutting Mom out of my relationship with Alex? Why would I do that? It wasn't right. I suddenly felt very guilty, and very sorry for Alex. He deserved much better than that. I vowed to make a change.

"All I'm doing is telling it like it is," Joanne said, her words becoming more obscured by the alcohol.

I wasn't quite ready to play nice. "According to you."

She chuckled. "Yup, according to me. You can believe me if you want. Or don't. Up to you. I only told you to help you. Maybe you can learn from the old man's mistakes. By the time you came around and were old enough to wipe your own snotty nose, the old guy had changed. Or maybe he just got too old to tomcat around. Or maybe Mom gave him an ultimatum finally, I dunno. By the time he was *your* father, he was different. I don't know if he was any better as a husband, but I think he at least paid some attention to you and Bill. That's all I'm saying."

Suddenly, from the room next door, we heard sounds of someone making enough noise to let us know she was there. Mom. Oh God, what had she heard?

"*Sonsyou, Donya*, vhat are you doing up for?" she said as she toddled into the room.

I looked at her and gave her the fakest smile known to mankind. She returned it, proving she was either the consummate actress, or hard of hearing.

"We're just talking," I said. "I've gotta get some work done, so good night."

Mom gave me a hug and kiss good night. Joanne buried herself deeper under her covers.

I returned to my room, sipping the drink Mom had made for me. The Coke had gone flat and tasted sickly sweet. I wouldn't drink it.

Settling back on my bed, journal in hand, I thought about what Joanne had revealed about my father. Even though married, he still couldn't commit to one partner. Was it true, or was she spouting the imaginings of an eleven-year-old girl who didn't get enough attention from her daddy? I'd probably never know.

I opened Simon Durhuaghe's journal and hoped I could wash it all away by focussing on what was inside it. I needn't have worried. The journal quickly absorbed my attention, like plush white carpet sucks up red wine.

Durhuaghe was highly regarded for good reason. Even in his own personal journals, where he could rightfully have held himself to a lower literary standard, he wrote in a polished and compelling style. Words flew from his pen in full bloom. The man knew how to make even the simplest anecdote into a great tale. His descriptions of people, places, and things were rich and full of life. Even more important, the content of the period covered by the journal was nothing short of sensationally dramatic. Within a few pages, I had a few guesses about who just might be driven to kill to get their hands on this notebook.

"Raw what?"

I shot Kirsch a "you big dummy" look as I laid out the light sushi lunch I'd picked up from Charlie's Seafood on the way back into Saskatoon. After Mom's meat extravaganza meals (breakfast was a doozy—who knew pork chops and pancakes went together?), I needed something that came from the sea.

I'd called the cop to join me for lunch at my place. It took some convincing of course, but the allure of getting in on my discovery at The Roxy was the tipping point in his decision. Sure, we'd had some laughs at the Irish pub the other night, but based on the tone of his voice when he heard mine at the other end of the phone line, I was thinking that would be a one-time thing. It was like we'd had a one-nighter and he was bashful to face me again, just in case I was expecting more. Straight guys can be such dolts.

"Just eat it," I said, pouring water and hot sake before settling down next to him at the umbrella-shaded bistro table.

We were in one of the private nooks in my backyard, the one that affords the most shade on a sweltering hot day like this one was. The umbrella, angled to block the sun's harshest rays, was a periwinkle blue. The result bathed our dining area in a lovely cool blush of colour. Barbra and Brutus, who'd somehow over the years formed an inappropriate attachment to the big cop, were curled up near his feet. I think they were also a little put out because I'd left them alone again so soon after returning from Hawaii, so they were playing favourites. They'd get over it by tomorrow.

"It's kinda nice back here," Kirsch commented as he took in the landscaping and watched two black-headed grosbeaks cooling off in a nearby bird bath. "Treena would love this."

I was about to say I'd have them over for a barbecue or something, but that might have sent the guy over the edge. That was what friends would do. And I certainly didn't want him thinking me untoward in my intentions for our relationship. So I stayed mum while I munched on a California roll.

"Let's hear it, Quant. I don't got all day to sit around eating fish food in wonderland."

That's more like it.

"The treasure was a journal," I told him. "The private diary of Simon Durhuaghe. Simon Durhuaghe is a writer who..."

"I know who Durhuaghe is, Quant. I just finished his latest book."

Oh. Now that was a surprise.

"So what's he say in this diary?" Kirsch frowned as he attempted to use chopsticks on a piece of spicy tuna roll. "Is there fish in this one?"

I nodded.

"Anything important?" He frowned as one chopstick clattered to the tabletop.

"You might say that." I was tired of seeing him struggle. The poor guy was going to starve. "Just use the fork I brought for you."

He glared at me. He picked up the fork and used it to point at an *unagi*. "Is there fish in this one?"

I nodded. He tossed down his fork in a huff.

"Apparently Durhuaghe had an affair."

The cop eyed up another piece of sushi. "Is there f...oh, to hell with it." Kirsch grabbed a Spider roll and tossed it into his mouth. He closed his eyes and scrunched up his face while he chewed.

"Huh," was all he said after a quick swallow. "When?"

"Thirty years ago."

Kirsch gave me a deadpan look. "Ah jeez. Big deal. So he had an affair thirty years ago. That ain't enough to get someone killed today."

I shrugged. I was inclined to agree. "Maybe, maybe not."

"I suppose the wife might not know about it. But still." He picked up the little bowl of pickled ginger I'd set out, sniffed it, assessed it as inedible, and set it back on the table. "Do we know who the affair was with?"

"Some girl named Sherry Klingskill."

"Oh yeah."

"There's more."

"Whazzat?"

"The girl, Sherry, was only eighteen at the time."

"Uh-huh." He sounded bored.

"And she was engaged to another man."

Kirsch sat up a little straighter. "Now that sounds a little more promising. So both Durhuaghe and the girl were married, or about to be. He would have been, what, in his forties? She's only a kid, about to get hitched to some fresh-faced college boy. Durhuaghe seduces her. It's a bit slimy, I suppose, but enough of a reason for murder? I dunno, Quant. I think it's a stretch, especially thirty years after the affair is over." He hesitated, then asked, "It's over, right?"

I shrugged my shoulders. "I don't know."

"What about the husband, do we know who he is?"

"No. Durhuaghe never mentions him by name. For that matter, he rarely used her name either. I only found it out because of the letters. From the girl to Durhuaghe. She signed each one, 'Love, Sherry Klingskill'."

"Kind of formal, wouldn't you say? It feels more like correspondence between two people who don't know each other very well, or a young person writing to an older person. Are you sure they were having an affair? Maybe she was just an adoring fan."

"Wait until you read the letters. And the journal. Those two were having sex, no doubt about it. She was in love with him, I think. But I don't think he felt the same. In the journal Durhuaghe mostly refers to Sherry as 'WSG' and her fiancé as 'ESG'."

"Very espionage-ish." Kirsch dipped a finger in the green blob of wasabi I'd squirted on his plate and winced when he tasted it. "What the hell?"

"It's like Japanese horseradish," I explained.

"Jee-suz." He pushed the plate away. "The acronyms, do you know what they stand for?"

Fortunately, Durhuaghe, always the meticulous journaller, had spelled them out. "Sherry, WSG, was the 'west side girl' marrying ESG, an 'east side guy'."

Kirsch caught on quickly to the references to the oft hotly disputed socio-economic discrepancies between the older, less-affluent west side of Saskatoon with its crumbling neighbourhoods and higher crime rate, and the newer, more prosperous east side with its ritzy suburbs and big box retail outlet malls. "So the girl from the wrong side of the tracks landed herself a fancy boyfriend with a trust fund."

"Sounds like it."

"I still don't get how this leads to a corpse at the Saskatoon airport."

"Neither do I, but it certainly gives us some interesting new clues and suspects."

Kirsch gave me one of those looks that keep me from adding him to my Christmas card list. "Us? There is no us, Quant. *You* are going to turn the notebook over to *me*, and that's the end of *us*. Got it?"

I feigned alarm. "I thought we were working on this together?"

"Kind of like how you and I worked together to figure out the last clue? Kind of like how we found this diary together?"

I knew my lone wolf actions would nip me in the ass.

I'd already made a copy of everything I'd found in the urn, so I could afford to be gracious and agreeable. "Of course." I handed over the journal.

Kirsch stood up from his chair. "I gotta go. I need to get me some real lunch on the way back downtown. Thanks for the raw food and hot green goop, Quant."

"No problem. I knew you'd enjoy it."

"Are you staying here at your house again? I thought you were living somewhere else until this got figured out. Or have you decided the stuff with the white truck and the break-in were coincidences after all?"

"Nope. But I'm done being run out of my own home and office," I told him as I followed him down the side of the house to the front where his car was parked on the street. "So I've sent a message." I pointed to the front door of my house.

Kirsch stopped and stared in amazement. He let out a low whistle.

I'd posted a sign. In big letters I'd written: I FOUND IT. I HID IT. NOT HERE.

"There's another just like it on the front door of PWC, too. Whoever was after me was only doing it because they knew I had the map. They either had to get the map away from me, or watch me until I led them to the treasure. Now that I've found it, and hidden it again, there's nothing left for them to get from me."

"Unless they decide to torture you until you tell them where it is," the cop responded darkly.

Good point. I shrugged.

"You dumb ass. That's what you want, isn't it? You're trying to drive them into the open with you as bait."

I grinned. "The treacherous life of a PI."

"Yeah," Kirsch said. "Treacherous and short."

That afternoon I made good on my promise to help finish the new Ash House deck. Jared, at some point in his life having obtained the how-to-build-a-deck skill, was in charge. Fortunately for me, Ethan was busy elsewhere on the property. Less fortunately, his new boyfriend Damien was not. He was on our work crew, along with two carpentry-loving lesbians Jared had recruited. It was a big job, and we needed everybody we could find to get it done. Rails had already been cut and fit and support beams placed by Jared and the girls, but there was plenty of hammering things together that needed to be done to complete the structure. The wedding was now only two-and-a-half days away.

So for several hours I sportingly sweated and swore and swigged Gatorade. I also tried to perfect a hate-on for Damien, but I couldn't. It turned out he was a pretty decent guy, and handy with a hammer. My plans to "accidentally" bury him alive under the deck were ultimately dispensed with.

By the end of the day, we had a pretty fine looking deck, and I was utterly exhausted. I turned down an invitation for beers and headed for my car and a long shower at home. It was only as I was leaving that I saw Ethan again. He was on the far side of the yard, attaching a latch to a gate. He gave me a hasty wave in the failing sunlight, then quickly turned away. Up until that moment, I'd thought I was the one avoiding him. I was thrown, and a little hurt, to realize he'd been avoiding me too.

Barely in the back door, I heard the insistent ring of the front doorbell. Unless it was someone delivering a tub of Cherry Garcia ice cream, I was not looking forward to seeing whoever was on the other side of the door. Barbra and Brutus accompanied me to check it out. They too were hoping for ice cream.

"See, I knew he'd be home," Alberta said over her shoulder.

Beverly was halfway down the front path, either coming or going, I couldn't tell.

"What a surprise," I said with little passion. I like my PWC co-tenants well enough, but I was not in the mood for company.

Alberta, resplendent in a puffy, off-white skirt that looked like a giant piece of popcorn, a black ruffled blouse that must have once belonged to an accordion player, and a barbershop quartet hat, stepped past me into the foyer. "Hello doggies! I brought you something!" she announced with enough enthusiasm to give a sideshow barker a run for his money. She distributed biscuits to my equally enthusiastic canines.

"I'm sorry about this, Russell," Beverly said as she approached the front door. "I told her we should wait for tomorrow. It's so late. It's just that we've been at the office until now, getting ourselves all worked up over this. We decided we had to talk to you. It won't take long. I promise."

"Of course, come in," I said, surprised by the stress I heard in the psychologist's normally mellifluous voice. "You'll have to excuse me though. I was helping with the Ash House deck and I'm all dirty and sweaty."

"Mmm mmm, I like that!" this from Alberta who'd taken herself into the kitchen.

The rest of us followed. While we got ourselves settled around the kitchen island, Alberta snooped in the refrigerator. After some consideration of the options, she pulled out a pitcher of milk and a strawberry and rhubarb pie Mom had sent back with me.

"Russell, it's this Errall thing," Alberta said as she searched for a knife to slice the pie. "We have to make her see reason and change her mind about turning PWC into a *women's dress shop*. Of all things, how she came up with that hare-brained scheme, I'll never know. I mean, she dresses like a mortician!" This from the woman wearing popcorn.

There was no use fighting it. I pulled out plates and forks and poured the milk.

"Russell, what do you think?" Beverly asked, sincere worry painted on her pretty face. "Do you think she's doing the right thing?"

"Of course she's not doing the right thing!" Alberta exclaimed. "She's gone gaga over everything that's happened to her this past year, Kelly's death being top of the list. Yes, it's sad. Yes, take some time off. Yes, go sit on a beach for a couple months if you have to. Yes, get laid by women of questionable morals. But don't change your whole life to the point that it's unrecognizable from what it was before. Makes no sense. Beverly, you know this. It's your thing. This could be a case study in one of those textbooks you're so fond of. Am I right? Do you want your pie heated?"

"No, thank you."

Alberta handed out slices of the pastry and plunked herself down. "Let me tell you, just in case it's not obvious to the whole world, Errall Strane is over compensating. It's typical. Happens all the time in cases like this. Right, Beverly? The death of someone close forces you to confront your own mortality. Do enough of that, and you begin thinking it's time to throw caution to the wind, do all those things you've always wanted to do."

"Is that wrong?" Beverly sagely questioned.

"It is when you're already doing what you always wanted to do. I've had these talks with Errall before. Here *and* in the spiritual world. She grooves on being a lawyer. She grooves on PWC the way it is. But she's lost control and gone gaga. Beverly, you can see it, right?" Alberta laid a multi-ringed hand on Beverly's arm, but did not wait for an answer. "She's grasping for something, anything, that she thinks will make her feel better, more alive, more excited about life. All because she's got fear in her, like a big red flashing light in her head, telling her she could lose it all any day now like Kelly did. I can see it all around her. Every time she passes by, my skin shifts because of the negative energy of terror radiating from her aura." Alberta shivered and made a "brrrrr" sound to make her point.

"What she's forgotten is that the law and PWC can do that for her again; they can revitalize her. If only she gives it some time. This whole idea of selling shmatte to businesswomen is just a bunch of bull doo-doo."

"Alberta," Beverly broke into the psychic's soliloquy with a gentle but firm tone in her voice. "I think it's important that we try to look at this from a perspective outside of the fact that Errall's decision means we're going to have to move our businesses out of PWC. We need to consider what's best for Errall. Whether or not we think it's the right plan, maybe we need to respect her decision. What do you think, Russell?"

The ruffles on Alberta's blouse stiffened with her indignation. "I'm not just saying this because I'm going to lose my office. You know that. To tell you the truth, I rarely use that office for work. Most of my clients prefer the atmosphere of my home rather than a sterile, downtown office environment. It's a little less, shall we say, corporate."

I nearly choked on my pie. I'd never been to Alberta's house, but I couldn't imagine an office less "corporate" looking that the one Alberta resided in at PWC.

"I stay at PWC for several excellent reasons," Alberta continued, holding up her pudgy hand, preparing to count them off. "I stay because it's a good place to store my stuff. I stay because my aura enjoys having a place to exist other than home. I stay because I believe it's healthy for a psychic to take in new vibes on a regular basis. And mostly," she stopped there, having reached the ring finger on her counting hand, for a meaningful pause and to give Beverly and I pointed looks, "I stay because of you. I love you, and you, and even Errall most days. And," she held up her pinkie finger to indicate a fifth reason, "without all of you and PWC, I wouldn't have anyone to have an office Christmas party with.

"Russell, I know you agree with me. I know you think this is wrong."

"Maybe Russell doesn't agree with you, Alberta," Beverly contended. "He also had a close relationship with Kelly, and Errall too, for that matter. He may think starting over is the best thing for her."

"I am getting so sick of everyone getting on the starting over bandwagon as soon as things get a little rough," Alberta responded. "Russell, you know what I'm talking about. It never lasts. Remember when Kelly left town? Nobody was happy about that. Quite the opposite. She really pissed off a lot of people. But she wanted to 'start over.' But she came back, didn't she? When things got even rougher, she knew where to go. She came back to what she knew.

"Then Jared decided to leave Anthony because his face got all screwed up. He wanted to do guess what? 'Start over'."

I stared wide-eyed at Alberta. I didn't think anyone else knew about that. Damn psychic.

"Well bah humbug to that!" Alberta exclaimed. "Now they're getting married on Saturday. You see? When people really need help, when they really figure out what life is all about, they see as clear as day that what they already have in their lives is most often the best thing for them. Just like keeping PWC the way it is, and staying a lawyer is what is best for Errall Strane. I promise you," her voice fell an octave into foreboding, "if she does this thing, she'll wake up one day and regret it. She'll miss being a lawyer. She'll miss PWC. And she'll miss us."

"Oh, Alberta," Beverly let out a heavy sigh. "Despite all your furor and feather flapping, you may be right." She gave me an apologetic glance. "But I promised Russell we wouldn't keep him long."

"Good pie," Alberta said, with a lick of her lips.

The two women headed for the front door.

"Thanks for the talk, Russell," Beverly said. "We knew you'd help us get some clarity on the matter. I guess the next step is for one of us to talk to Errall."

"Russell will do it of course," Alberta said, petting the dogs and kissing their snouts. "You're so good about handling her."

"I don't know if she wants to be handled," Beverly said as they made their way out the door and down the walk.

"I think that's exactly what she needs right now," Alberta responded.

I shut the door. Had I actually said anything the whole time they were there? I was too tired to remember.

I had never understood what they meant when people said, "I used muscles I didn't even know I had," until the morning after the marathon day of deck building. I woke up Thursday morning with yowling spots of pain spread quite liberally over my entire body, some in places "I didn't even know I had." Fortunately my plans for the day did not consist of anything too physical. First I checked the bookshelves in my den and found two Simon Durhuaghe books. I'd purchased both with good intentions, but when push comes to shove and I just want to relax with a good book, I generally choose genre fiction over serious literature.

After a light breakfast, heavy on the fruit, I collected the Durhuaghe books, his journal, my laptop, a fresh pad of paper, the schnauzers, and a glass of iced tea, and headed for the backyard.

I set up behind a froth of Russian sage and ray flower near the back of the property, where Beta grapevine and Virginia creeper had taken over a wrought iron gazebo. The result was a covered area I treated like an outdoor living room for the few months each year that prairie weather made it possible. I'd filled the space with outdoor couches and comfy chairs, and strung it with cheerful patio lanterns. The sun was already baking the yard, and mid-summer bloomers filled the air with a drowsy scent. For the first while I just sat there, petting Barbra's head, watching Brutus sniff things. I sipped my drink and tried to organize my thoughts. Thoughts about Alex and Ethan and Errall and Walter Angel and Simon Durhuaghe. To be a good detective, you had to learn to compartmentalize. Today could not be about me. I needed to push my boy troubles aside. And Errall too.

I began to focus on Walter Angel. The discovery of the journal and its damning contents made me reconsider the little old man I'd met on the plane. First off, I had to consider the question: why does anyone want to find hidden treasure? Personal gain, of course. But gold coins and rubies were not what Angel had been seeking. He'd wanted this notebook. Why? What could he possibly gain from the secrets it held?

I could think of only one thing. Money. Blackmail money. Even though he didn't have it in his possession—yet—Walter Angel must already have known what was written in the journal, and how he could exploit it. But that led to a lot of other questions. Who was this Helen who gave him the treasure map in the first place? Did she give it to him? Or did he take it? Either way, why did she bother creating the thing in the first place? Assuming she wanted him to have it, why didn't she just tell him where the journal was? To hide the notebook and create the treasure map would have taken an awful lot of time and effort. It was almost as if she hoped no one would find it. Ever. But if that was true, why not hide it and forget about it? Or burn it? Why the map?

I had few answers, but there was one thing I was quite certain of. The map was important. Someone had murdered Walter Angel because of it.

I grabbed the pad of paper and started writing down names. Suspects.

Helen (maker of the treasure map)—who is she?
Simon Durhuaghe
Simon Durhuaghe's wife?
Sherry Klingskill—where is she?
Sherry Klingskill's fiancé (husband?)

White Truck Guy—who is he?

Other? Someone unrelated to the map?

I liked the last option the least. I put aside the pad and replaced it with my laptop. Without a last name, there wasn't much I could find out about Helen. But I could do a little investigating into the life of Simon Durhuaghe. I tapped a few buttons and I was on my way.

Durhuaghe had an official Web site of course. Those are always good for some basic factual information. I found out the author was seventy-one. He still kept a house in Saskatoon, but spent most of his time in a place he had bought many years ago in south-west Nova Scotia. He was born in small town Saskatchewan and was educated at the University of Saskatchewan. A *Quill & Quire* reviewer once referred to him as a "god of words," a moniker that stuck and was repeated by others many times over the years. He received the Order of Canada in 1987. He had been married to the same woman, Olivia, for more than fifty years. His latest tome, *Down this Rutted Road,* was being considered for numerous presti-gious literary prizes and awards. The best news of all, however, came from the Web site's events calendar. Durhuaghe was in town. He was scheduled to do a reading at McNally Robinson bookstore that very night. I planned to be there.

In the meantime, I decided to try finding out a little something about the wife. Spurned spouses are always good suspects. I returned to the browser and typed in Olivia Durhuaghe. Most mentions of her name were little more than that, noted in articles about her husband. Disappointed, and debating a fresh glass of iced tea, I typed in the name Sherry Klingskill.

Suddenly the computer came to life.

I sat up straighter and stared at the list of sites that Google popped up. My eyes were pulled into the screen like planets to the sun.

"Holy shit," I said, not quite believing what I was seeing, not quite believing who Simon Durhuaghe's one-time teenage girl-friend had become.

Chapter 10

By the time I arrived at the bookstore, the place was packed. It was only seven-thirty p.m. and the guy wasn't slated to read until eight, but every seat in the Prairie Ink restaurant, where readings are held, was taken. I took in the size of the crowd with awe. Spending time with a good book is one of my favourite activities, but I'd never attended an author reading before. By the looks of things, it was a pretty popular thing to do. Or maybe it was just that Durhuaghe was a member of that pantheon of literary celebrity that commands a crowd no matter where or when they appear. Regardless, McNally Robinson was the place to be that night in Saskatoon, bubbling over with the heady excitement of rabid readers. Who knew?

I looked around for something to lean on, in lieu of a seat, and caught sight of two hands wildly waving in the air. One belonged to my sister, Joanne, the other to my mother. They were seated on folding chairs in one of the overflow sections behind a half wall, from where latecomers could still get a decent view of the performance area. What on earth were they doing here? As far as I knew, the only things my mother ever read were recipe books and Harlequin romances. She thought no one knew about the Harlequins, but I'd found her stash with great titillation one Christmas when I was eleven and searching for gifts.

I wedged myself into the tight spot, past a serious-looking librarian type and an old fellow in a wheelchair, with an oxygen tank, thick glasses, and a hearing aid in each ear. I plopped into the waiting chair next to Joanne, and leaned across her to give Mom a quick kiss hello.

"Dat chair vas supposed to be for Auntie Mary, but she decided she couldn't come because her feet hurt," Mom announced in a louder voice than I'd hoped for.

Raising my eyebrows at Joanne, I asked, "What are you doing here?"

"Simon Durhuaghe? Are you kidding? I wouldn't miss this for the world. He's a fu...he's a real genius. Can I smoke in here?"

I shot her a you've-got-to-be-kidding glower.

"Besides, I thought it would do Mom good to have a night out on the town. It's so fu...it's so dull sitting around doing nothing on that farm every day. You really should get her to go out more. See," she said, nodding her head in the direction of our mother, who had begun a conversation about beets with the young man sitting next to her. "She loves this. She loves meeting new people."

"She goes out," I told my sister, already feeling a little peeved with her for making general pronouncements about Mom's well-being. She was acting like Saint Joanne, come to meet the needs of the desperately wanting. In a few days she'd have disappeared in a puff of smoke, and then who would be left to take Mom to readings? Me, that's who. Not her. Me. Not that I wouldn't take Mom to readings, if that's what she really wanted to do.

"Vhat kind book ees dis?" Mom, finished with her beet story, leaned over to ask us.

"This one is called *Down this Rutted Road*," Joanne informed her. "It's a multigenerational study of a family who pass through life watching their male offspring suffer an ever worsening mental deficiency, yet grow from a developing ability to love those who care for them. It's an exceptional read. You should try it, Mom."

"Oh, vell, I don't know..."

"Come on," Joanne said, grabbing Mom's arm. "I'll take you to the bathroom before the reading starts. And while you're in the can, I'll get you a copy. He'll even sign it for you after."

"Oh, vell," Mom uttered, not quite sure what to say to that. "I should go to the batroom."

"Russ, you'll watch our seats, okay? They're like vultures around here. Guard them with your life."

And off they went.

The man who'd heard all about beets from my mother gave me an empathetic smile. I smiled at him and sat back to wait for whatever would come next.

After spending a full day researching the writer on the Internet, re-reading the telling entries in his diary, and grazing through the two Durhuaghe novels I had on hand, *The Archbishop's Son* and *Coming by It Easy*, I fancied myself somewhat of a Durhuaghe specialist. I hoped there'd be a quiz at the end of the reading that night. At the least, there would surely be a question and answer session. Of course, I had questions the author probably didn't want to answer.

Before leaving the house, I'd remembered to adjust the suspect list I'd come up with earlier. I scratched off Sherry Klingskill's name and replaced it with Sherry Fisher. Below that, I added another name: Cantor Fisher, and in brackets I noted: (Mayor of Saskatoon).

Yup, Simon Durhuaghe's west side girl had indeed landed herself an important east side guy, one who would one day become mayor of our fine city. Cantor Fisher's obvious wealth had come from the profits of a family dynasty that included a province-wide string of drugstores, a "homemade" burger franchise, and all the wildly successful subsidiary business ventures that went along with them. Probably bored with counting money, he had entered politics, first as a city councillor, then, following an unexpected landslide three years ago, becoming the top guy at City Hall. There'd been nothing particularly wrong with the incumbent candidate. He was tried and true, free of controversy, and ultimately a big snooze. He'd simply been around a term too long. Pundits claimed the people were bored. They were looking for a younger, dynamic leader to match the good times forecast for the city and province as a whole. Cantor Fisher fit the bill.

A good match for her husband's pizzazz, Sherry Fisher had been the most visible and verbal mayoral candidate's wife in recent memory. The public seemed to respond well to her. She was gregarious and devoted to good causes, particularly "helping the children." She added an extra bit of sparkle to a normally dowdy public office. Cantor and Sherry Fisher were touted as a breath of fresh air.

I think I voted for the other guy.

As I waited for my sister and mother to return, and fended off a couple of aggressive would-be chair squatters, I scoured the room for any sign of the mayor's glamorous wife. Wouldn't that be a corker? But of course, she was nowhere to be seen. What I did spot, however, were several cliques of giggly young women, the type you'd expect to see offstage at a rock concert, waiting to throw their panties at someone like that guy from Guns N' Roses. What were they doing here? Durhuaghe must really be some kind of hound dog to still attract such young groupies. How did he do it?

According to Durhuaghe's diary, the affair with Sherry hadn't lasted all that long, ending sometime before her twentieth birthday. (Perhaps she'd gotten a little too long in the tooth for him?) In my online research, I was surprised to find not even a single mention or hint of the affair with Sherry, nor, for that matter, with any other girl, teenaged, engaged or otherwise. By all accounts, the Durhuaghes were a long-loving, devoted couple. Then again, this was the world of CanLit, not Hollywood. The *Star Phoenix* and *Globe & Mail* weren't competing with Perez Hilton for juicy gossip.

Eventually Joanne and Mom came back, my mother the proud (ish) owner of a brand new Simon Durhuaghe novel. I suspected she'd use it as a doorstop. At ten minutes after eight, the crowd suddenly grew hushed. The bookstore events coordinator, an attractive young woman with a pixie face behind serious eyewear, stepped behind a microphone set up in the far corner of the room.

She looked a bit nervous and awed by the size of the crowd. After a few fawning minutes—you'd swear she was in the presence of a deity—she invited the man of the hour to the mic to a thrush of rousing applause. Even my mother clapped as if Durhuaghe was her long-lost son.

At seventy-one, Durhuaghe was still a mighty handsome and virile looking man. He was tall, with a bit of a stoop—either a mark of age or the sign of someone who spends too many hours hunched over a computer—and rangy looking. On his broad, bony frame he wore a simple navy jacket over a white shirt, and a pair of well-worn jeans. His hair was a shock of unkempt silver, longish, parted on the side. He had a habit of continually pushing aside stray locks that regularly fell over his brow. His eyes were such a startling grey, I could see them from as far away as I was. Although he smiled at the audience, the eyes did not follow suit, and his unique laugh, low and throaty with a quivering cadence, was as irregular as its appearance.

When the man finally began to speak, you could have heard a sequin drop. They were eating him up. For the first fifteen minutes, all he did was talk. Not even necessarily about the new novel, but rather random experiences he'd had as an author over the past fifty years. It was interesting stuff. Eventually, he did turn to his latest book. He opened it to a pre-planned page and began. His voice projected well in the large room, his enunciation was clear and precise. He was quite obviously a practiced reader. A professional at work.

Twenty minutes later, Durhuaghe softly closed his book. He gazed at the assembled fans, some smiling, some wiping away tears, as they applauded his undisputed talent. I saw on his face that this was a man used to the admiration of others. Mom clapped too, but a little less enthusiastically than before. In his reading, he'd made a few explicitly sexual references that would not have gone over too well with her.

It was after ten by the time I, wanting to be the last, made it to the front of the book signing line. Joanne, using the "my mother can't stand too long" bit, got through much quicker, then took Mom home. As I stepped forward and handed Durhuaghe my book, I had to give the guy credit. He had patiently signed books and chatted with his readers for over an hour, yet I noticed no perceptible flagging of energy or willingness.

"I really enjoyed your reading," I told him truthfully. His was the kind of book I could listen to. Read the whole thing? I wasn't sure about that.

"Thank you. And to whom shall I make this out?" he asked politely as he opened the book to the title page.

"Russell Quant, Private Detective," I said, watching for his reaction.

"Well," he responded with a faint smile, "that's quite a title you have there." And that was it. He began signing the book as I'd requested.

"Mr. Durhuaghe, I know it's been a long evening for you, but I wonder if I might have a word with you in private about a case I'm on."

Now he stopped signing. He looked up at me with those cool, eagle eyes. "Oh? What type of case?"

"Murder," I said, going for shock. I wanted this guy's attention.

"Well," he said, once more lowering pen to paper, preparing to continue with his signature. "That's very interesting. But I don't know anything about murder. I write literary books, Mr. Quant, not murder mysteries," he informed me with barely camouflaged disdain for the genre.

"Oh, I don't mean that," I quickly clarified. "This is about a real murder. One that happened quite recently, in Saskatoon. One that you may be involved in. Indirectly of course." I added the last with a cheap smile.

He lay down his pen and sat back in his chair. "Oh, and how is that? You've certainly piqued my interest now. Who was it that was murdered?"

"Walter Angel. He was murdered at the Saskatoon airport."

His face remained the same. I could detect no telltale sign of recognition. Or guilt. Then again, I didn't know Mr. Durhuaghe too well yet.

"I've only recently returned to the city," he said. "But, now that you mention it, I think I may have seen something on that in the papers."

He was right. The *Star Phoenix* had been running daily stories, sometimes more than one. The paper recounted the shocking killing at the airport, complete with photos of the murder scene, and printed unrevealing statements from the Saskatoon Police Service spokesperson, airport officials, and anyone else who cared to offer an opinion.

"I fail to see, however, why you would think that I'm somehow involved, indirectly or otherwise."

"How about if I buy you a coffee and fill you in?" It was a little awkward standing there, him sitting under a spotlight at a table covered with books. There wasn't anyone left behind me in the line, but several fans were milling about the room, probably hoping for a chance to speak with their favourite author in private. Maybe they wanted to pitch book ideas, or get his opinion on a manuscript they'd written. I had no idea if that sort of thing really happened to writers. But from what I could see, Durhuaghe certainly had some hangers-on. A few I'd classify as definite literary groupie types, and of course there was the contingent of young women I'd noticed earlier.

"How about you fill me in right here and now." His voice sounded mocking, then took on a steelier tone. "As you said, it's been a long night."

It wasn't ideal, but looked to be the best I was going to get. So I went for it.

"At the time of his murder, Walter Angel had something in his possession that led to information about your past." He either already knew about the treasure map, or if not, I didn't intend to tell him. "This information, Mr. Durhuaghe, was the kind I suspect you might not want brought to the public's attention."

Durhuaghe stood to his mighty height and gave a dismissive wave with his hand. "Oh who cares about any of that? The past is past. It's dreary. It's old news and it's tired news. There's nothing worse." He began to pack up his things.

"Do you know the specific information I'm referring to?"

He released a practiced chuckle. "Of course not. I've done more stupid things in my life, Mr. Quant, than you could ever dream up of. And I forget most of them quicker than I do them. Now, if that's everything…?"

"This is about Sherry Klingskill, now Sherry Fisher, the mayor's wife? About the 'time' you spent together when she was *much* younger." I'm nothing if not tactful. Well, sometimes.

The man's face changed. His eyes grew even colder and the skin at his jowls drew tight as he clenched his jaw. He leaned into me and placed a long finger on my chest. "Rumour and innuendo are dangerous things, Mr. Quant. And be they fact or fiction, you're talking about a time long ago, long over, long forgotten. You'd be wise to forget it too." He pulled back. "I fully admit I've done many foolish things in my life. But I've nothing to hide. From you or from anyone else. Now, young man, I think I've put on a good show tonight. I've earned a glass of scotch and an embrace from my loving wife, who is waiting for me at home. So I know you'll understand if I leave you now to claim my reward."

And with that, he stalked off, his shoulders noticeably more stooped than at the start of the evening.

I looked down at the book he'd been signing for me. He'd written: For Russell Quant, Private Detective. But no signature. Now I'd have to buy the damn thing.

After shelling out $34.95, I headed for the parking lot. Even though I'd left the top down, I still locked the Mazda's doors, which also activates the car's security system. I was just about to unlock the driver's side door when I heard a "Hey, you!" behind me. I turned and found a tough looking woman, in her mid forties, approaching me.

"What was all that fuss about?" she asked between puffs of her Player's Light. She had the pinched lips and smoke-deterring winced eyes of a longtime smoker.

"Excuse me?"

"In there." Her head did a little backward bob, indicating the bookstore behind her. "You were talking to Mr. Durhuaghe in there. It didn't look like fun and games to me. He left kinda upset."

"He told you that? He told you he was upset?"

"No," she said with a sarcastic drawl. "I got eyes, don't I? I could tell. Usually he stops to talk if you look like you want to. This time he didn't. You upset him with whatever you were talking to him about."

"I'm sorry, who are you exactly? Are you his manager or something?"

She wagged her head back and forth. "I'm just like everybody else that was here tonight. I love Mr. Durhuaghe's books. I have a personally signed first edition of every one. Well, except for *Phoenix Rising*, that's a second printing, but that's on account of I was in the hospital when the book first came out. I couldn't make it to the book launch. But the next time he was in town I still got him to sign the book I did buy. He said he noticed I wasn't there, at the launch." She let out a raspy little laugh at that. "I'm not sure if that's true or not, there're so many people at these things. But that's what he said, anyway."

I was quite confused about why I was having a conversation with this woman. Maybe it was an all-us-rabid-fans-should-be-best-friends-for-life thing. "Okay, well, good night then."

"Hey!" she barked. "You never answered my question. What was all that about in there? Why were you upsetting Mr. Durhuaghe? After all he does for us, and all he gave of himself tonight, don't you think he deserves a little more respect than that?"

I'd had it. I was tired too. "What I talked to Durhuaghe about is none of your business. I'm going home now."

"I just made it my business." She tossed her cigarette on the ground, grinding it out with a hefty boot, and immediately lit another.

Then it struck me. I wondered if she drove a white Ford truck. "What's your name by the way?"

"Stella. And just so you know, if you bother Mr. Durhuaghe again, you'll have to answer to Stella. Got it?" She pointed at me to make her point. Her fingers were short and thick with nails that were badly chewed.

I looked at her as if I thought she might be crazy. Which I did.

She blew some air out of her nose—bull-like—then stomped away. I watched her get into a blue half-ton. I memorized the licence plate number. I hadn't gotten too far with Durhuaghe tonight, but the evening hadn't been a complete waste. I had a brand new suspect to add to my list: Stella (deranged fan?).

It was too nice a morning to eat inside. I loaded a tray with cereal, a carafe of coffee, coffee cup, and the newspaper and hauled everything to the deck. As I ratcheted up the umbrella over the table, several moths, disturbed from their evening resting spot, fluttered away. Barbra and Brutus, having already had their breakfast, dogged off to patrol the yard, no doubt checking to see whether anything interesting had taken up residence during the night.

The sun was shining, but there was just enough of the previous night's dampening coolness tincturing the air to require long sleeves. I brought the coffee cup to my lips and savoured the hot liquid as it passed over my tongue like a fluid wake-up call. There is nothing quite as tasty as that first sip of hot, aromatic coffee on a beautiful day. For a few minutes I sat back and, well, smelled the roses. From my cushioned chair, I undertook an inventory of my flowerbeds, potted plants, bird baths, and Zeus, the four-foot cement fountain in the shape of a male nymph that was a focal point of the yard. The sound of splashing water never fails to relax me. It reminds me of pleasant days spent on sandy beaches in tropical locales, sipping drinks with fruit juices and lots of rum, the smell of sunblock, and the catch-of-the-day grilling over an open pit.

I'm a big believer in doing whatever you can to make home a holiday paradise. Why should we indulge in all that good stuff only when we're away? So, in the summertime, I treat my backyard like a vacation destination. As I sat there, I knew that in a few months I'd be shovelling a path through drifts of snow to get from back door to garage, my nose and ear tips growing redder by the minute, and I'd recall the sound of Zeus and the feel of this morning's sun on my skin, and feel a little brighter.

It would have been a good day to stay exactly where I was. After all, this wasn't a real case I was on. No one was paying me to find Walter Angel's murderer. Tomorrow was Anthony and Jared's wedding. Certainly I could focus more on that than a case that wasn't one. But no, I couldn't leave this half done. Not that Darren Kirsch and the Saskatoon police force weren't capable of figuring this out on their own. But I was on to something. I could smell it, as sure as the petunias in my backyard. I wanted to be the one to open that final door and see who was behind it. That is truly one of the most exhilarating parts of my job: revealing the bad guy. Walter Angel deserved that.

Upon returning from overseeing her realm, satisfied all was safe and secure from intruders (i.e. pesky cats), Barbra settled near my feet. I'd obviously been forgiven for abandoning her. Brutus was still at it, however, standing stock-still at the back of the yard, quizzically staring at the butterflies and dragonflies dancing for his pleasure. Spoon in hand, I started in on my Fibre 1 and the paper. It wasn't until I reached Section D, the classifieds, that I came upon something of interest: the obituaries. My eyes devoured the first one:

Angel – Walter Dustin, was tragically taken from us on Saturday, August 10 at the age of 64. Walter was born and raised in Rosetown, Saskatchewan. Shortly after graduating high school he moved to Saskatoon where he attended the University of Saskatchewan. As a young man, Walter travelled extensively during his tenure as a cruise ship entertainer, singing and dancing his way around the world. Eventually, Walter returned to Saskatoon where he pursued a career as an archivist. He spent the last twenty years at the University of Saskatchewan Archives, most recently as head archivist. Walter was predeceased by his parents, Liv and Herman Angel, brother Lewis, and sister Angela. He is survived by his husband, Sven Henckell, and their beloved Pomeranians: Liesl, Friedrich, Louisa, Kurt, Brigitta, Marta, and Gretl. As per Walter's wishes, there will be no funeral service. His ashes will be returned to the sea, which he loved so dearly in his youth.

I was disappointed to find there would be no funeral. It sounds flippant and a bit disrespectful, I know, but funerals are never-to-be-missed bonanzas in a detective's bag of tricks. Not only do you get most of the players in the game in one place at one time, but also you can tell a lot about people by how they react in the situation. As a bonus, it might surprise you to know how often a murderer shows up at his or her victim's final service. This goes hand in hand with the familiar statistic that most killings are committed by someone known to the deceased.

There were two things of great interest to me in Walter Angel's obituary. The first was the identification of his spouse. The second was the fact that Angel was an archivist. That set the bells in my head to clanging. Irritating, but I was grateful, for this was the sound of fresh new leads. I downed the rest of my breakfast with zeal, made a few phone calls, told the pooches to guard the house, and then I was off. I had a lot to do today.

Reginald Cenyk was one of those baby-faced guys who would always look at least ten years younger than he really was. Flaming red hair, fair, smooth skin, and lots of freckles helped. Or hurt, depending on how you looked at it. I'm sure as a younger man, Reginald had cursed his youthful complexion and features, wanting to be handsome instead of pleasant-looking, rugged instead of delicate. Now, appearing a fresh-faced forty, but probably closer to fifty, the new University of Saskatchewan head archivist seemed as comfortable in his own pasty white skin as he was ever bound to.

A tight smile had greeted me when I, directed by an archives technician, entered Reginald Cenyk's on-campus office. He sat behind a desk and, after introductions, invited me to sit across from him. He was wearing a short-sleeved shirt that showed off skinny freckled arms.

In my opening gambit, telling the man who I was and why I was there, I lied and embellished as little as I could. It felt good. If he assumed that I was more formally related to the police investigation than I really was, it was none of my fault. For the most part.

"I appreciate your willingness to talk to me today," I began. It's always a good idea to grease the wheel with a nice spritz of syco-phancy. "I understand you've taken over the role of head archivist since Mr. Angel's death, so I'm sure you must be extremely busy."

"Er, well, yes. I have, however, been employed here for over a dozen years." His voice was quiet, and squeaked a bit at the begin-ning and end of each sentence. "During that time, Walter and I shared many of the archives's duties and responsibilities. Much of what I do today is the same as before."

"Which is exactly what I'm fascinated by. I have to admit, I've never met an archivist before. I know so little about what you do."

I could detect the thin man's chest puff up just a tad. "Well, I like to tell people to think of us as the university's memory. We keep track of and manage all information having to do with the history of the university, and really the province as a whole."

"So you keep records of who taught at the university, campus clubs and activities over the years, that sort of thing?"

"Oh, it's a great deal more than that, Mr. Quant. Our records cover every college, department, unit, and campus organization that make up the University of Saskatchewan. I know many con-sider the university to be something greater than the sum of its parts. I believe it is the parts that make it great. Here at the archives is where those parts live on." Cenyk leaned in a little closer as he warmed to his topic. "We have the *private* papers of many of our past, and even some present, faculty members, and those of alum-ni. We've had many very interesting people pass through the halls of these greystone buildings over the years, Mr. Quant.

"We also work on special projects here at the archives. For example, quite recently we began collecting the histories and memorabilia of alumnus who served during wartime. Fascinating material. We also maintain a great number of virtual exhibits and digital collections. It's all very exciting. There is a listing on our website if you're interested in taking a look."

"So for instance, as an alumni of the University of Saskatchewan, I could donate my papers to you?" Not that I real-ly wanted to, but I was leading him to where I wanted to end up.

Cenyk hesitated briefly, giving the suggestion sincere thought, before responding. "By all means. As a Saskatchewan detective, people might be very interested to learn about your life and the cases you've been on. There aren't too many of you around, I wouldn't think. Obviously there would be some sensitive and privileged information included in your records, but we could deal with that in our donor agreement by way of specified access restrictions."

I was surprised, and, I have to say, a little flattered. Now who was spritzing the sycophancy? "Well, that certainly would clear up some storage space in the ol' garage."

He didn't laugh.

I moved on. "So the university archives hold the records of anyone famous who's lived in Saskatchewan?"

The man shook his head, a dismayed look on his face. "Unfortunately not. The decision of if, when, and where to donate one's papers is, of course, completely up to the individual. As an institution we do solicit certain people and organizations, in the hope they would consider using us as the safekeeping repository for their information. With certain high profile collections, a competitive environment can arise in the pursuit of obtaining physical ownership and other rights. Obviously, the more famous the individual, the more competition.

"In an effort to appease different organizations and meet loyalty obligations, there have been cases where a set of records is divided up amongst several archives, locally, provincially, and even nationally. As I'm sure you can appreciate, as archivists, most of us prefer that a collection remain intact at one location."

"What about someone like, say, Simon Durhuaghe? Are his papers here?"

Again the archivist hesitated. I guess my transition wasn't as seamless as I'd hoped.

He began typing on the computer keyboard in front of him, his eyes fastened to the screen. "Well, let me double-check, but I'm quite certain...yes, there it is. We do hold an extensive and, I believe, *complete* set of Simon Durhuaghe's papers. According to the finding aid, we have draft manuscripts and galleys for most of his early novels, including first editions of those published at the time of the donation. We have short story compilations, including drafts and final edited copies. We hold various research materials and notes, travel and book tour itineraries, as well as personal and professional correspondence and journals. It looks to be quite a comprehensive collection, a lot of material. We're lucky to have it."

"So how exactly does this work? Did he just drop a bunch of boxes off one day?"

"Oh no," Cenyk responded, taken aback by the idea. He referred to his screen again. "In the case of Mr. Durhuaghe, this was a solicited donation. We obtained the material ten years ago. If I recall correctly, Mr. Durhuaghe was happy to make the donation but, like many of our busier donors, didn't want the responsibility of sorting through and organizing the material."

"So he *did* just drop it off."

The man's face coloured slightly. "I suppose you might say that, yes. It would have been up to the archivist or archives technician, whoever happened to be assigned to the initial accessioning, to process the material."

"Accessioning?"

"That's the first step in processing a donation. A control number is assigned and some basic data is recorded. Then the material is arranged and described, assuming the donor hasn't already created some sort of filing system. If they have, we try to maintain that order as much as possible. But, I must say, that is rarely the case.

"At this stage we do appraisal and weeding; separating material having long-term value from that which doesn't. Once this is done, and we know what we are keeping, physical processing is undertaken. We store documents in acid-free file folders, boxes, or whatever other container is required given the type of material being handled. Finally, we create what we call a finding aid. The finding aid is a summary report of the full collection, along with a listing and brief description of each file or piece in the collection. If the donor requests a tax receipt, we also have an independent monetary appraisal carried out."

"Was a monetary appraisal carried out for Mr. Durhuaghe?"

There was a pause while Reginald considered whether or not he should answer my question. "I believe so," he finally said.

"Was it significant?"

"I'm not at liberty to say."

I had to try.

"You said Durhuaghe donated his papers ten years ago. So both you and Walter Angel were on staff at the time?"

"Yes."

"Was one of you assigned to this accessioning process for the Durhuaghe donation?"

He began tapping at keys again while he spoke. "It's quite possible. Oftentimes with a donation of this import and size, an archives technician might be responsible for the initial accessioning, but further processing would be undertaken by an archivist." More key tapping. Then he stopped. "From what I can tell here, most of the work on this file was done by neither Walter nor myself."

"Oh? Can you tell me who did it?"

I smiled at the answer. It was a name I'd heard before.

Chapter 11

Ten years earlier, Helen Crawford had been the senior archivist at the University of Saskatchewan Archives. Helen was the name mentioned by Walter Angel when he first told me about the treasure map. Was she the map's creator? Was she the one who started all this?

At the time Helen worked at the archives, Walter Angel was a fellow archivist, Reginald Cenyk an archives technician. The three were the only permanent staff. According to Reginald, five years ago Helen Crawford suddenly retired, leaving Walter the role of lead archivist, and Reginald a place as a full fledged archivist. With Walter's death, Reginald moved up the ladder once more, taking over as head archivist. As he described the events, I briefly toyed with the idea of Reginald Cenyk killing Walter Angel for his new job. But somehow it just didn't fit.

"So what you're telling me is that Helen Crawford had sole responsibility for the Durhuaghe archival material?"

Cenyk swivelled his computer screen so I could see the screen.

His finger moved down a column in a spreadsheet. The name that appeared over and over again was Crawford. "She signed off on every aspect of the processing," he confirmed. "Now, that's not to say that one of us, or maybe another part-time staff member—we sometimes have summer students or grant employees—didn't help her, but she did have primary responsibility. Which doesn't surprise me."

"Oh? Why do you say that?"

"Helen was a stickler for detail. Rules and regulations were her best friends—as they should be for an archivist. There was no way she would have let just anyone touch the Durhuaghe papers. She'd have taken great pride in obtaining the rights to them for the U of S archives, and overseeing the processing herself. Not that she didn't do a lot of processing herself anyway, but this would have been a special case. She was a bit quirky in some ways, but she was very good at what she did."

"Reginald, you've already been a great help today." My tone turned serious. "But I need to ask for your expertise on one more issue of concern. I hope I can count on your discretion."

His pale blue eyes widened as he nodded.

"Reginald," I began, even glancing to the side for would-be eavesdroppers, "would you know if something had been stolen from the archives?"

This time the slight man remained speechless for several seconds. After a dry gulp, he said: "I don't know for sure. I hope I would. Do you think something has been taken from the archives? Something from the Durhuaghe collection? Is that it?"

I nodded. "Could you find out, Reginald?"

He considered this. "It would depend on when it was taken. If it disappeared before the finding aid was created, I don't know how we'd ever know. The only way would be for the donor to proclaim it missing. If the piece was stolen after the donation was processed, the chance of discovery would be much greater. Depending on what it was, of course."

"What do you mean?"

"Well, if it was a specific file or book or document that was significant enough to be listed on the finding aid, or as part of the monetary valuation, we could confirm if it was missing quite easily. Otherwise, we'd have to rely on the memory of the processing archivist or other practical methods, like checking missing entries in documents filed in chronological or date order."

"You mean like letters or journals?"

"Exactly. If someone left us their diaries, for instance, we could check for gaps in date chronology. Or maybe certain material is footnoted in one file, but is missing when the referenced document is checked."

"I see."

"Mr. Quant, what exactly is it that you think is missing? And who do you think took it?"

I wasn't prepared to take the archivist into my full confidence just yet. But I needed his help. What needed to be done sounded like a lot of paper shuffling for someone who didn't know what they were doing—me—but less shuffling for someone who did. "I'm not sure yet, Reginald. But I was wondering if you could help me find out."

"Me? How?"

"I need you to look through the Durhuaghe archives. See if you can find evidence of anything missing. And more important, evidence of who might have taken it."

Another gulp. "That could take a lot of time."

That wasn't what I wanted to hear.

I left with Reginald's promise that he'd try to do some digging, but no guarantee he'd find anything. It was better than nothing.

Childhelp Saskatchewan was one of Sherry Fisher's favourite projects. The jury was out on whether the mayor's wife had started the children's advocacy group to actually help kids, or to raise her own profile. Part of the problem was the group's spokesperson: Sherry herself. When questioned by the media, she had difficulty exactly putting into words what it was Childhelp actually did. As far as I could tell, it had something to do with helping kids who needed help. Yup, it was that concise.

Despite a rather vague mandate, the charity's fundraisers were glittering affairs. They always took place in fancy hotel ballrooms with gourmet menus, pricey drinks, and not-too-shabby entertainment. They were also poorly attended, mostly by mayoral toadies who either had no choice or wanted to curry favour with the big guy. Still, according to press releases following each of these shindigs, the tally of donation dollars was always impressive. Rumour on the street was that most of the funds came from the mayor himself, through various holding companies and whathaveyous, supporting his wife's philanthropic hobby. Nothing wrong with that, I suppose. After all, didn't we all want to help all those help-needing kids who needed helping?

Today's event was a luncheon at the Saskatoon hotel nicknamed "the castle on the river," otherwise known as the Delta Bessborough. With its rich carpeting, reclaimed millwork, and detailed trimmings, the hotel's elegant Adam Ballroom is one the city's most sought-after banquet rooms for weddings and big bashes of every ilk. So of course, that was where the Childhelp luncheon was being held.

I'd seen the advertisement in that morning's paper. It was the perfect way for me to get in front of Sherry Fisher and find out what she knew about Walter Angel. The only problem was that the same ad loudly proclaimed the event "sold out by popular demand." I cattily wondered how far back that set the mayor this time. To solve my dilemma, I called on another woman I know, one inestimably more powerful than any mayor's wife.

Walking into a room with Sereena Orion Smith on your arm is unlike any other experience. The woman is the enigmatic embodiment of exotic yet damaged beauty combined with magnetic allure. People are drawn to her, yet fearful at the same time. She is a lovely but carnivorous flower that begs to be smelled. Many stare and try for a smile. Others simply frown. Few dare to approach unless they know her, then they do come up, and wait for her to bestow upon them the golden touch of her famed wit. When her light shines upon you, you feel like a star, and everybody wants to be a star.

"I'm not particularly interested," Sereena half-whispered into my ear as we stepped through the ballroom's foyer. "But for conversation's sake, why is it again that you had me procure tickets for this insipid lunch?"

"I need to speak with the mayor's wife. She might be involved in the case I'm working on."

"And you really think confronting the woman while she plays patron saint at her pet event is the best way to go?"

With a glint in my eye, I gave my shimmering companion a sidelong glance. "But when else would you have the opportunity to wear that outstanding outfit?"

Sereena had donned a rather short Vertigo scarf dress with long sleeves, graphically patterned in cobalt blue, sky blue, and white. Sky-high, black patent Dolce Vita shoes with a Bernardin day bag completed the get-up. Her legs looked as if they were on loan from Cyd Charisse. She wore her hair in an unusual-for-her simple pageboy. Her lipstick was stoplight red. A lady who lunches, Sereena-style.

"What? This little gardening smock?"

We stopped at the entry of the grand room. The Adam Ballroom can hold six hundred for a reception, four hundred for a banquet. Looking around, I estimated a crowd of less than a hundred. But Sherry had made the best of it. The room was done up beautifully in a summer garden theme, with racks of flowers and pretty wrought iron arbours and benches placed around splashing fountains. There was so much "stuff" in the room, there was barely enough space for the handful of tables needed to seat the paltry number of guests. She'd definitely made some kickass lemonade out of her lemons. In we went.

"Oh Sereena!" came a shrill greeting as we circulated amongst the flora.

Sereena rarely smiles, and she didn't do it now as we were overcome by the fluttering chiffon belonging to Miss Mabel Maplethrump, the event's coordinator and the mayor's personal secretary.

"I am *so* glad we were able to accommodate your late request for tickets for you and your escort. As you so well know, this event has been sold out for months, but I said to Mrs. Fisher—I called her personally, you know—I said we need to move heaven and earth to make this happen, we need to find room for Sereena Smith, of all people."

"All what people, Mabel?" Sereena asked, silky politeness over steel barbs.

"Oh you silly," Mabel trilled, all giggly like and not really understanding the question, or its pointed intent. She turned her vivaciousness on me and grabbed one of my arms with her chubby fingers. "And who is this? It's a great pleasure to meet you, Mr...?"

"Quant," I told her. "Russell Quant. I'm happy to be here, to support such a good cause."

Mabel's face and demeanor immediately morphed into more appropriate weighty gravity. "Oh yes, the children. We're all here for the children, aren't we?"

"Are any of them here?" Sereena asked.

Mabel glanced at her. "Who? Who is that, dear? Oh, you mean the children? Oh well no, they're all, well, you know, busy."

Sereena showed off a faint upturn of her lips. She didn't really mean to bust this poor woman's chops, only play with them a little.

"I'd like to say hello to Sherry," Sereena said. "I don't see her anywhere in this throng of people," she added generously. "Do you happen to know where she is?"

"Of course, of course. She was supposed to be at the door greeting guests, but was called away to the telephone. The dear is so busy, so involved, in so many worthwhile, ah, things. But she's always so good about making herself available for the children."

"Yes, yes, the children. And she would be where, exactly?"

Mabel rotated her roundish body to take in the room. There were a few people here and there, but generally not much was happening. Finally she hopped up a bit and proclaimed, "Oh there she is! See her? Just coming in from the foyer."

"Thank you, Mabel," Sereena said as she began pulling me away. "And thank you for all your hard work here today."

The woman beamed. "It's for the children."

Like repeating a toast, we left with a half-hearted chorus of: "For the children."

Sherry Fisher was standing at the entrance to the ballroom, a much younger woman by her side. They were speaking to one another in that awkward, stilted way you do when you're trying to look engaged but really hoping someone will come up and talk to you because that's why you're standing there in the first place and you have nothing left to say to the person next to you. Excellent.

The mayor's wife was a plain woman camouflaged by expensive decoration, like beautiful linen and sparkling flatware adorning a chrome and formica table. Her clothing, haircut, and acrylic nails were certainly expensive, but they couldn't hide the harsh, tough features that lay beneath. Maybe that's why the affair with Durhuaghe had ended when she was nineteen. Perhaps the rose's youthful bloom had already begun to show its fading petals. Her body was fit, but poorly proportioned, with too-wide shoulders over a hipless torso and shapeless legs. Her nose was bulbed at its tip, and her eyes heavy-lidded and set too close together. Her teeth, although whitened and straightened, were horsey, and her skin was leathery in a way that made me think biker chick rather than high society lady.

Her eyes flashed as we approached, giving each of us a quick appraisal before the requisite smile. "Sereena," she greeted my date. "Mabel told me you were coming. How nice to see you." I got the feeling she wasn't sure if it was.

"I'd like you to meet Russell Quant," Sereena said.

I stepped up and took the woman's hand. It was big and her grip firm. She gave me a look as if perhaps she knew me but wasn't sure.

"And let me introduce my daughter, Carleen." This was the woman standing next to her. Upon closer inspection, the daughter was older than I'd thought, likely bearing down on thirty. But she'd been fortunate to inherit few of her mother's coarse features, obviously favouring her father's end of the gene pool. "My husband and I are very proud of Carleen. She's just opened her own hair salon here in town. It's called Cutz."

"How clever," Sereena purred.

"Congratulations," I said shaking the pleasant looking young woman's hand. "How's business so far?"

"Pretty good," she answered brightly. "I really like cutting hair."

"Sereena," I said, turning to my friend. "Weren't you just saying the other day you were looking for someone new to cut your hair?"

Sereena gave me a heated look. Her hair was never "cut." It was styled, coiffed, designed, but never cut. She flew to Montreal monthly to meet with her long-term hair care professional, Pierre LaFlueg. In between, a Pierre LaFlueg trained associate who worked in Saskatoon, catered to her needs.

Sereena quickly figured out my ploy, and she and her hair took one for the team. "Yeeeeeeees. I suppose we could discuss your credentials, darling," she said, threading her arm through the young woman's and leading her away for a tête-à-tête.

"So, Mr. Quant, what is it you do?" Sherry asked, straightening the upturned collar of her bronze-metallic hued dress, which incidentally (or not?) matched her hair colour.

I didn't think the mayor's wife was particularly interested in my answer, but I imagine she was thrilled to have someone at her fundraiser who wasn't related, a childhood friend, or a member of her husband's staff.

"I'm a private investigator, Mrs. Fisher."

Her eyes grew flat as if she'd just heard some unhappy news. "I see," she said, looking over my shoulder.

"I find out things people want to keep hidden," I added for good measure.

Her mouse brown eyes fell on me with a decided thud. "I see." She fumbled a bit as she pulled a cellphone out of her purse.

"Usually things that happened a long time ago, maybe when they were very young."

She began to chew off the lipstick on her upper lip. "I see."

"Do you still have contact with Simon Durhuaghe, Mrs. Fisher?"

There was an icy silence, followed by some pretty erratic eye movement, then, "I don't know what you're talking about, Mr. Quant." She began to punch numbers on her phone.

Wow, what a believable response. "Do you know Walter Angel?"

Her brow creased and I could feel the waft of heat shimmering off her reddened cheeks. "I'd like you to leave right this minute. How dare you come to my fundraiser and start accusing me of things."

"I haven't accused you of anything." Yet. "I just wanted to know if you've been in recent contact with either of these men."

"Yes, Allan," she spoke tersely into the phone. "I want you to come to the ballroom right now." Pause. "By the front doors." Pause. "I need you to escort out a gentleman who shouldn't be here."

But I'd paid for a ticket. At least she called me a gentleman.

"That's fine, Mrs. Fisher," I said calmly. "I appreciate the escort, but I think I can make my own way out. Perhaps there's a better time for us to talk?"

She narrowed her eyes and her thin-lipped mouth grew mean. She whispered, "Fuck off."

See? I knew it. Biker chick.

I spent the rest of the afternoon in my office, basking in the glory of being the only person I knew to have ever been thrown out of a lunchtime fundraiser for "the children." PWC was quiet as a tomb. Ever since Errall's bombshell announcement that we were out on our butts in three months' time, an uneasy pall had fallen over the building's residents. Even the welcoming smile of Lily, our preternaturally cheerful receptionist was at half wattage. The doors to all the offices were resolutely shut as if none of us wanted to talk to the others. Fine by me. I had some thinking to do.

As I settled into the Muskoka chair on my balcony with a cup of coffee, I chewed over the idea that there was a very good chance my kindly murder victim, Walter Angel, wasn't such a nice old guy after all.

It was more than likely that, as one of the main archivists when Simon Durhuaghe donated his papers to the University of Saskatchewan, Angel would have known about the damning journal and personal letters from Sherry Klingskill-now-Fisher. Obviously Durhuaghe didn't know, or didn't remember, that this controversial material was part of what he'd absent-mindedly handed over.

He was one of the kings of CanLit, and certainly one of Saskatchewan's most famous sons-done-good, so the university had been bound to go after the Durhuaghe collection. The man himself probably didn't care one way or another. I could hear him saying, "Sure, take the stuff, and good riddance." He was probably thrilled to get rid of the piles of boxes cluttering his basement, and the tax receipt was probably welcome, too.

I could easily imagine that as the first to cull the material, Helen Crawford would have been the one to come across the evidence of Durhuaghe's dalliance with a young girl and his betrayal of his wife. She might have shared her shocking discovery with her colleague, Walter Angel. Then what? Did she begin blackmailing Durhuaghe? Is that why she hid the stuff? Is that why she created the treasure map? Maybe she wanted to be able to tell Durhuaghe that if anything ever happened to her, the documents were hidden someplace he'd never find. The only one who could find them would be the holder of the treasure map. Who had that been? A friend? Family member? Another colleague? Or had she simply hidden the map in a safety deposit box only to be opened upon her death?

Maybe Walter Angel's coming into possession of the map—for some reason as yet unknown to me—was a simple passing of the baton from one co-conspirator to another? Which made him complicit in the scheme. Perhaps he was getting a cut of the blackmail monies all along.

But why would Angel only be getting a copy of the map now? Why not ten years ago when the journal was first discovered and hidden? In any case, Walter had to have known the import of the treasure map. He'd flown all the way to Victoria to retrieve it. If indeed this was all about blackmail, it seemed certain Walter Angel was somehow involved in the whole scheme. And someone else knew it too. They had killed him for it.

Was it Durhuaghe himself? Trying to put an end to the hemorrhage of money he was paying out to keep a lid on his indiscretions?

Or was it Sherry Fisher? Desperate to keep her reputation as first lady of Saskatoon untarnished. A cruel media might decide to paint her as a wanton Lolita rather than the teenage victim of a much older sexual predator. Or was it both of them? Were the famous writer and the mayor's wife in cahoots? I thought back to the afternoon. She'd reached for her phone to contact her goons long before she had reason to really feel threatened by me. Had she been expecting me? Had Durhuaghe warned her?

And then one more possibility slid uncomfortably into my mind, like a slimy, sneaky, invading snake. An icy shiver shook my skin, from the tip of my toes to the base of my skull.

Had I stumbled upon a murder plotted by the mayor of Saskatoon?

Chapter 12

The rehearsal dinner is a longstanding tradition, held the evening before a wedding. Sereena Smith is anything but traditional, but she'd agreed to host the affair, as long as she controlled the content. She'd decided the Friday night event should be an homage to history's great lovers—of which Anthony and Jared were two—and that the meal, served in her yet-again newly redecorated home, would be a medieval feast. This meant costumes, eating meat without utensils, serving wenches, and mead, plenty of mead. The only part of the idea I wasn't keen on was the costumes. Where do you get them? They never fit right. And there was always someone wearing the same getup as you, and looking much better in it.

Fortunately, Sereena knew this about me. So when I pulled into my garage at the end of the day, there was a plastic wardrobe bag hanging on the door that led from the garage into the backyard.

Unfortunately, once inside and wiggling my way into the costume, I realized something my neighbour obviously didn't know about me: I am not big on showing off my genitalia in public. When at first I squeezed into the ballet tights for the Rudolf Nureyev costume she'd chosen for me, I assumed she'd either gotten the size wrong, or else my gym routine needed a major adjustment. But the tunic, which ended just above my hips, fit perfectly. As did the waist sash and slippers.

I studied myself in the bedroom's full-length mirror and winced. Even Barbra let out a sympathetic whimper. Brutus simply looked away, too embarrassed to say anything. I stared at the nether region just south of my midsection. Actually I was rather impressed with the seemingly gargantuan lump. What miracle material was this thing made of, I wondered? Could I have a new pair of wonderpants made of it?

I turned to the side and checked out my profile. Oh my. No way. Appropriate for a porn video or professional ice skating perhaps, but for a party? Uh-uh.

As I scurried to my walk-in closet to look for a spare Scarlett O'Hara costume I was sure I had in there somewhere, the doorbell rang. Wrapping a towel around my manifest man bump, I followed the dogs down the hall and into the foyer. When I opened the door, there stood two white haired men, one wearing a traditional Indian kurta.

"Who are you supposed to be?" I asked Anthony and Jared.

"Ismail Merchant and James Ivory," Anthony answered.

"You know," Jared said when I gave him a confused look. "They made *A Room with a View, Howards End, Maurice*. All those great movies. A lot of others too. They were together for forty-four years. It was either this or Raymond Burr and Robert Benevides."

"Raymond Burr?" I said, almost losing my towel. "*Ironside* was gay?"

"I liked him better as Perry Mason, but yeah. And he was Canadian, too."

I was a poorly informed gay man. "Next thing you know, you're going to tell me Doogie Howser is gay."

Jared cringed. "I need to get you a subscription to *Out*."

"Sereena asked us to collect you," Anthony said with a wicked smile on his handsome face. "And she instructed us that if what

179

you were wearing was anything less than-skin tight, we're to call immediately for reinforcements."

I threw down the towel. "Look at this!" I yowled. "I cannot be seen in public like this."

Jared grinned as lasciviously as his altered-but-oh-so-sweet face would allow. "I think I may be marrying the wrong guy," he growled as he eyed up my bottom half.

"That's it! I'm not going. Mary Poppins just made a pass at me." I turned and made tracks for the bedroom.

"I'm James Ivory!" Jared insisted, yanking me back by my waistcoat collar.

"Besides," Anthony insisted as he helped his fiancé guide me out the front door, "this isn't public. It's just a few friends. Half of them have seen you naked anyway."

"That's not true!" I protested.

And so the futile argument continued as we trekked the short distance to the house next door, the great Nureyev being dragged by two white-haired filmmakers.

Sereena has many passions. One of them is redecorating. I have seen her kitchen decked out in Greek village style, her bedroom in Asian chic, and her master bath in Egyptian splendour. Tonight, the large area that sometimes serves as her living room, sometimes her dining room and sometimes as a ballroom, had become a medieval banquet hall, complete with rough-hewn wooden furniture, brightly coloured royal standards, thick woven wall hangings, and sconces and floor torches alive with dancing flames. A large table, set for about twenty, dominated the centre of the room. It was laid with several ornate candelabras and a mixture of silver and gold goblets. No plates. No cutlery.

In deference to the happy, romantic occasion, the room was ablaze with hearts. Great big electric glowing hearts. About two dozen of them, ranging in size from a foot tall to one that was almost six feet. They were fashioned after the candy hearts we used to pass around (or, in my case, eat by the handful) on Valentine's Day when we were kids. Each bore a syrupy sweet saying, like "Be Mine," "I'm Yours," or "Cute Stuff." Every heart pulsed pastel—pink, green, yellow, and orange—throwing the room into a slightly amusement park-ish haze.

The couple of the hour having been whisked away by well-wishers the second we entered the wild scene, I looked around for more people I knew. Instead, I saw Edward VIII and Mrs. Simpson, Spencer Tracy and Katharine Hepburn, Anne Morrow and Charles Lindbergh, Kermit the Frog and Miss Piggy, and several other couples whose claim to romantic fame I couldn't quite figure out. For a moment my heart sank. Everyone here was in a couple. Except me.

Then Elizabeth Taylor came to my rescue.

"Where's Richard?" I asked Sereena, who, since I'd seen her at the Childhelp luncheon, had completely transformed herself into Liz Taylor, circa 1960s. Her head was piled high with mountainous, bouffant black hair, she wore plenty of eye makeup and loads of jewellery. The heaving bosom, though, was all her.

"I'm so dreadfully tired of him." Her nasal, sex kitten tone was perfect. "I'm in the mood for a senator this week."

With my hands strategically placed in front of me, I said, "Sereena, about this outfit…"

"Hello." We were joined by someone wearing a dowdy, brackish-hued outfit that might have been natty in the 1920s (probably the last time it saw an ironing board).

"Let me guess," I said as I appraised Errall's new look. "Alice B. Toklas."

"Close. Gertrude Stein. I don't really know much about the avante garde literary world, but they were the most famous lesbian lovers I could think of that I had the wardrobe for."

"You had *that* in your closet?"

"Long story." She gave my package an assessing stare, her right eyebrow raised high. "Who are you supposed to be? Jeff Stryker?"

"Who's that?"

"Famous gay porn star from the Eighties? Why don't you know that?"

Why don't I?

Sereena gave each of us a piece of paper. "Before the end of the evening I want you to return these to me."

I looked at the blank slip. "What's this?"

"I want you to write out a message for the newlyweds. Nothing lengthy required. We'll be entering them into the electric sign, along with the telegrams, e-mails, and well-wishes that have been pouring in from all over the world."

She pointed to a corner of the room where a road-sign-sized monitor sat. It was the kind that usually delivers messages like: "Reduce Speed—Construction Ahead" or "Traffic Reduced to One Lane" or "All Rose Bouquets 50% Off."

"That's a great idea, Sereena."

"Yes," she agreed. "It'll be set up on the lawn during the reception, and scroll through each message while we have our cocktails."

"Hi!"

Everyone looked at the new addition to our group. He was also wearing tights, but, unlike mine, his magnificently embroidered, laced tunic fell modestly to mid thigh. His sleeves were proudly puffy, as was his chest. It was Damien, looking very dashing, I suppose.

"Wow, that's quite the outfit," Errall commented.

"From the fifteen-hundreds," Damien said with a curt nod of his head, which was resplendent in a plumed hat. "The men were all about being fancy back then."

I shook my head. There he goes, I thought, showing off that he's smart as well as pretty. Gawd, I hate when that happens. "Who exactly are you supposed to be?" I asked.

He gave me a killer smile accompanied by an arched eyebrow. "Romeo Montague at your service," he announced with a bow and flourish of his arm.

Oh save it.

"Does that mean...?" Errall started off, quickly surveying the room until she found what she was looking for. She shrieked. We all turned to see what had elicited such a reaction.

"Oh my," Sereena commented dryly. "Juliet has certainly filled out."

Big, burly, bulky Ethan Ash was lumbering towards us, decked out as the pride of the Capulet family. His dress was crimson with gold brocade detailing, his hair a hip-length shaft of brown mess. There'd been an unsuccessful attempt at cosmetic application.

I couldn't quite tell from the set of Ethan's face whether he was mad, sad, or simply in shock to realize he'd never make even a half-decent drag queen. Many gay men, whether they actually ever plan to do it or not, assume—with no real evidence to support this—that throwing on a frock, a pair of stilettos, and applying some lipstick, will magically morph them into Marilyn Monroe, with the voice of Barbra and the wit of Bette (Midler or Davis, doesn't matter). They figure it's one of their unassailable rights as a homosexual. The fact that they have broad shoulders, hairy legs, a baritone, and have never told a joke in their lives doesn't dissuade them for a second. The result is often shockingly and hideously disappointing.

As the ungainly Juliet stepped into our circle, Damien fell to his knees and recited in a dramatic voice, "What's in a name? That which we call a rose, by any other name would smell as sweet. See, how she leans her cheek upon her hand! O, that I were a glove upon that hand, that I might touch that cheek! Good Night, good night! Parting is such sweet sorrow, that I shall say good night till it be morrow."

Oh, good, lord.

Errall, however, thought it quite the show of chivalry and gallantry. "Oh Romeo, where art my very own just like you?"

I was about to point out that he'd mixed up the quotes, taking the best bits from Acts I and II, not to mention one of Juliet's lines, but quickly concluded that it would be petty. And, in truth, I knew I was just mad because I wanted to be the man kneeling down before Ethan—ugly Juliet or not. Instead, I looked at him and smiled. We'd not talked since the night of the kiss. I knew I should apologize for it, but I really didn't want to. So I said nothing.

Ethan gave us his good-natured smile and said, "Does this dress make me look fat?"

We laughed. Damien explained how he'd come up with the idea of Romeo and Juliet, but at the last minute couldn't go through with wearing the dress. Ethan sportingly took on the role of Juliet, the gown meant for a smaller man, and the ill-conceived makeup job.

"Come with me," Sereena said as she pulled Ethan from our group. "We have a few minutes before the rehearsal begins. You're a girl in desperate need of a visit to the powder room."

Damien scurried after them.

"Does it seem weird to you," Errall remarked, "that Anthony and Jared are getting married tomorrow?"

I gave her a look. What was she getting at? "No, I don't think so. Why do you say that? Don't you think they should?"

"Of course I do. It's just that there's been such a rash of gay weddings. It's like a runaway train. I feel like it's taken over my social calendar for the last couple of years. Every weekend I'm going to a 'gay wedding.' And why do people call them that? They're just weddings, people, not *gay* weddings!

"I don't know," she continued with a sigh, "it just seems kind of weird. Imagine if all this time eating cornflakes was outlawed. Suddenly the law changes and everybody can eat cornflakes wherever they want, whenever they want. So they do, whether they really want to or not. I just wonder if half the people eating cornflakes are doing it before they've even had a chance to figure out if they like the damn things."

I gave Errall a sideways look. "Would you and Kelly have gotten married?"

"Hell yeah," she said without hesitation, then quickly laughed at herself. "It just seems so odd going to all these weddings at once, all our friends getting married at the same time. These are weddings that should have happened fifteen years ago. But here we are, heading into our forties, attending our first round of nuptials and getting hitched ourselves. How will we ever find the time to have kids, fool around, get divorced, and discover the joy of second marriages?"

I chuckled. For a moment we stood in comfortable silence, watching the people around us. I wondered if now, given her rare companionable mood, was a good time to bring up our concerns about the fate of PWC and Errall's future. "Errall, about this women's clothing store…"

"Oh yeah, yeah, yeah, I've been meaning to ask you," she said, her eyes glistening with excitement. "I've been trying out names for the shop. What do you think of Errall's Place?"

I flinched. "Are you offering country fries with your blue plate special?"

Her face hardened. "Okay. What about No Strane? I really like that one. You know, with my last name being Strane, no strain on your pocketbook, no strain garments…meaning they're affordable and fit well…get it?"

"Uh, yeah, I get it," I said, looking even less impressed.

"No?"

I shook my head.

"Then what great ideas do you have, Mr. Creative Gay Guy? What would you call the store? It has to have some kind of name."

"What about, Errall Strane, Attorney at Law?"

She made an unhappy sound and, glancing about, asked, "Can we smoke in here?"

In some ways, Errall was cut from the same cloth as my sister. "No. Errall, I think you're rushing things. Kelly has only been gone a year. You just spread her ashes this week! Give yourself time to settle into a new normal."

"Kee-rist, have you been reading self-help books again?"

"I'm not kidding around. I wonder…we've all been wondering if maybe you're being just a wee bit rash."

"'We? Meaning you, Dr. Phil, and the Amazing Kreskin?"

"Errall, of course Beverly and Alberta and I don't want to leave PWC. But we also care about you and what you're doing with your life. We'll leave in three months, hell, we'll leave right now if you want us to, but don't change PWC just yet. Don't give up your law practice. Don't rush into something you might regret. Just…just chill for a while."

"What makes you think you can tell me what to do?" Her piercing blues were flaming. "Then again, I suppose you of all people should know about regret."

"What do you mean by that?" Big mistake. I'd taken the bait.

"Tomorrow you're going to watch a man who you've lusted after for a decade, walk down the aisle with a man who has always looked out for you and been the best friend you ever had." Her words were heavy and spit out like nails meant to be driven into my chest. "Do you regret never telling either of them the truth? Don't you think it's about time you told Anthony that your friendship is a sham, because you're in love with Jared? And what about Keith?" she changed direction without hesitation. "Kelly told me all about you and him. Four years the two of you were together. From what I hear, you just walked away. Do you regret that?"

"We weren't ri..." I stuttered, but she wasn't letting me off the hook yet.

"And what about now, Russell? You're hiding an engagement with one man, while hanging around here giving puppy dog looks to another man, who you know very well is in love with someone else!"

The silence that followed the outburst was truly deafening. It felt like an explosion of nothingness in my ears. My cheeks burned with fury and embarrassment and surprise. How could she say these horrible things to me? Had I really betrayed my friendship with Anthony and Jared? Had I been unfair to Keith, my lover for almost four years when I was in my twenties? Was Ethan...in love?

Our eyes met and all the hurt and pain and fear we felt inside were communicated in that gaze, a look too potent to sustain for long. Seldom have I ever seen tough-as-nails Errall Strane cry. Today was no different, but as she stalked off, I saw the sharp blades of her thin back shudder.

The rehearsal went smoothly. Luckily there were enough jovial people about, behind which Errall and I could hide our misery. We both half-heartedly partook in the medieval feast. We both left early.

By the time I got home I was feeling black and blue all over, without anyone laying a finger on me.

Giving in to longing looks, I handed Barbra and Brutus each a ham-flavoured doggie treat (a favourite). I made myself a strong gin and tonic with a quarter of a fresh lime squeezed into it. We made the pilgrimage from kitchen to den and settled on the couch.

I was still wearing my Nureyev getup. Damned if the thing wasn't comfortable, especially once I sloughed off the tunic. Brutus slumped down on the floor next to the unlit fireplace, as if in wait for crisp fall weather. Barbra, a little more in tune with my mood, hopped onto the sofa and set her fuzzy head on my lap. Every now and then her rough tongue would dart from her mouth to lick my hand.

Errall and I had a long and stormy history of biting each other's head off. We were just that way with one another. Like two hungry locusts trying to be friends. Sometimes it ended badly. Like tonight. Usually the words we threw against each other meant nothing, other than that we were frustrated and needed someone to lash out at. Errall was going through a load of personal crap right now. Her acting like a bitch to me wasn't that difficult to figure out.

But I had to wonder if she was right about some of what she'd hurled at me. I'd made my peace with how I felt about Jared long ago. Anthony could not doubt that I loved him *and* Jared as friends. My attraction to my best friend's boyfriend was undeniable. It went deeper than his looks. Something about him pulled me to him. But all those feelings had come to a head five years ago when Jared and I had been abandoned in the middle of a killing winter blizzard. We had no idea where we were. He'd been wounded. We'd only barely found shelter before hypothermia could set in. We survived. We saved each other. It was during those desperately dark hours that we cemented our love for one another—as friends—for life. That friendship is the most important thing between me and Jared. Sure, I still think the guy is heart-tuggingly sweet and drop dead gorgeous, but my yearning for him is long over. In my heart, I knew I was truly thrilled that Anthony and Jared were getting married tomorrow.

And all that stuff about Keith, well, she knew nothing about that. The relationship was over ten years ago. I was young. Idealistic. A bit stupid, maybe. But what about Alex? And Ethan? I hated to admit Errall might be right in that case. My behaviour over the past week had been abominable. I hadn't returned Alex's call. I'd kissed Ethan. What was wrong with me?

I feared that this too, wasn't so difficult to figure out.

I had other problems to deal with as well. There was a murderer out there. And I had a feeling I was getting very close to finding out who it was. The closer I got, the more dangerous it became. But there was no turning back now. I'd volunteered for this job.

The ringing of my phone startled me. I checked my watch. Not yet eleven p.m. Probably Sereena wondering where I'd disappeared to. I set down my drink and reached for the phone.

"Hello."

"Mr. Quant?"

"Yes. Who is this?"

"It's Reginald Cenyk, from the university archives."

"Of course, hello." I hadn't recognized his voice. It sounded higher and even squeakier than before. And there was something else I could hear over the phone line. He sounded frightened.

"I did what you asked," he told me. "I've just finished going through the Durhuaghe collection."

"Oh gosh, Reginald, I'm sorry, I didn't mean for you to give up your Friday night to do this."

"I had to," he told me. "Once you told me you thought there might be something missing from our archives, I had to be sure. I take my position here and the reputation of the archives very seriously, Mr. Quant."

"Of course, I understand. Thank you." I waited a beat, and then asked, "Did you find anything?"

"I'm afraid I didn't find any indication of your missing journal or the letters. But…I did find something else. Something you might be interested in."

I got that great little tingly feeling detectives get when a seed of their investigation sprouts a clue. "What is it, Reginald?"

There was a deadly silence on the line. It lasted so long I worried he'd hung up. Then I heard: "I-I-I don't know if I should tell you."

"Why not? Of course you should tell me. This could have something to do with Walter Angel's murder. You knew Walter. He was your co-worker, your friend." I had no idea whether the two men had been friends or not, but it was worth a shot. "Why wouldn't you tell me?"

"I'm...I'm afraid. This involves some very...well, powerful people. I could get fired. Or worse."

"Reginald, where are you right now? Are you still at the archives? I can meet you there, or wherever you say. Right now. Tonight."

"No!" he exclaimed. "Not now! I can't do this right now."

"Okay, okay. When? Where? If you feel you're in danger, I can help you."

"Tomorrow maybe."

My heart sank. The clock was ticking. "I can meet you now," I offered again.

"Tomorrow," he insisted. "I need some time to think about this some more."

That's what I was worried about. I worried he'd think himself right out of talking to me. But the archivist was the one in control. All I could do was make it easy for him.

"Okay. Just name the time and place."

There was another silence while he considered this. Then he said, "Do you know the Impark parking lot on the corner of First Avenue and Twentieth Street?"

"The one across from the Galaxy Theatre?

"Yes. It's near where I live. It should be safe there. Meet me on the top level. Nobody should be able to see us up there. Park in the southeast corner. I'll find you."

"Yeah, sure. What time?"

"Midnight. Most of the movie traffic will be gone by then. Can you be there at midnight? If I don't show up it's because I think there's someone else around or something weird is going on...I can't lose my job over this ....I have to be sure."

This guy was freaking petrified. It made me wonder what exactly he'd found in those archives. "Yeah, for sure. I'll be there."

Midnight would be just when the party was getting going tomorrow night. I had no idea how I was going to slip away unnoticed from the wedding festivities, but I'd deal with that when the time came. "And don't worry. I'll be extra careful that no one follows me."

He hung up and I was left listening to a beep beep beep on the line, telling me I had a message. I hadn't bothered to check when I got home. I typed in my code and listened for the message:

"Mr. Quant, you have no idea who you're messing with. If you know what's good for you, you'll stay away from me, and my family, and my past. If you don't, I *will* make your life a living hell."

I knew the voice.

Sherry Fisher.

And then the power went out.

Oh crap. The woman meant business.

Chapter 13

I'd only managed a couple of hours of sleep. With my power turned off—by the mayor's wife?—my alarm clock was useless and I was afraid I'd sleep in. I couldn't afford to waste one minute today. Not only was I hot on the trail of a killer, but I was best man at the wedding of two of my best friends. That's a nice full day.

Shuffling into the kitchen, I was heartened to see flashing lights on every appliance with a digital clock. Power had been restored. After letting the dogs out back to do their morning ablutions and resetting clocks, I trundled out the front to retrieve my Saturday morning paper.

Not there.

That was odd. The paper was always at my front gate by six a.m., rain, shine, or blizzard. I stepped into the quiet street and scoured the front lawns of my neighbours. Mine was the only one without a paper.

"Hey Russell, g'morning!" a voice called.

It was Graham, a fireman who lives two doors down. Friendly

sort. Paper tucked under his arm, he was rolling his big, black garbage bin back to his garage. I waved a greeting as I headed over to collect my own. I let out a surprised grunt at the effort it took to move it. What the...?

It hadn't been emptied.

Leaving the trash container where it was, I fumed as I contemplated the exact wording of my call to the city's sanitation department. Grumbling my way back to the house, I stopped short at my front door. There was some kind of letter posted to it. I hadn't noticed it on my way out. I pulled it off and opened it. It was from the City of Saskatoon Animal Services Program:

This official Notice of Violation is issued for breach of Bylaw No. 7860 (The Animal Control Bylaw, 1999)

Offence: Failure to immediately remove a dog or cat's excrement (defecation) from public or private property other than the property of the dog or cat's owner [Section 13]

Penalty: $250

Even though my mouth was open, wide, I couldn't seem to catch a breath.

The power. My newspaper. My garbage. Now this.

Sherry Fisher.

This woman wasn't fooling around. And I had a feeling these were just warning shots. I stuck the ticket in my housecoat pocket. I didn't want Barbra or Brutus seeing it. They would be mortified to think anyone was accusing them of pooping where they weren't supposed to.

I marched into the house in full huff. Sure, I could empathize with Sherry Fisher's having been unhinged by my visit yesterday. At the least, I'd brought up memories that were likely very distressing to her. At the most, I was messing around in her garden of secrets and posed a threat to her carefully crafted public persona. If the mayor's wife was being blackmailed because of a decades-old teenage dalliance, I could manage some sympathy for her plight. But that didn't mean she had the right to wield the power of the mayor's office like a battering ram. If there's one thing I cannot abide, it's a bully. When I get pushed, I push back harder.

I decided to salvage the morning with pancakes. Indulgent, and a little time-consuming, but I needed something pleasant to offset the rotten start to the day. Not to mention that beating eggs and whipping batter felt pretty good about then.

When my feast was prepared, I stuck my nose outdoors and debated eating on the deck. The morning was surprisingly cool. (I hadn't noticed earlier because of my hot head.) Billowy clouds playing hide-and-seek with the sun were keeping the day from warming up. So instead, I took my food and coffee into my office and set up in front of the computer. It would be a working breakfast.

A couple of hours later, Sereena and I were in the backyard of the new Ash House. We were supposed to be putting finishing touches on the arbour beneath which Anthony and Jared would be wed, but mostly I was complaining about the curse of Sherry Fisher. Sereena seethed in sympathy as she artfully attached gladiolas and palm leaves to the metal structure. She too was not fond of bullies. When we (well, mostly she) finished, Sereena crossed something off a list and tilted her head up to study the sky.

"You look worried," I said, following her gaze.

Indeed, the sky did not look great. Anthony and Jared were on the wrong side of fate. It had been hot and sunny and windless for over a week. On the Saskatchewan prairie, that meant one thing. The polar opposite was on its way.

"I never worry," Sereena observed nonchalantly. "I simply adjust to what I can't change."

I doubted there was much Sereena couldn't change if she put her considerable mind and resources to it. But even she couldn't do much about a rainstorm on the day of an outdoor wedding.

I assessed the distressingly cool blue horizon, rumpled with threatening stratus clouds. "What do you think?"

"I think two wonderful men will get married today," she proclaimed.

I smiled. "Come hell or high water!"

"At this point, I'd prefer hell. Easier on the shoes."

"What's next?" I asked, trying to be peppy about wanting to help, at the same time itching to get away like a schoolboy wanting to ditch homework for the park. The time had come in my investigation into Walter Angel's death to make like a gopher. I needed to dig holes wherever I could, to see what lay beneath the surface of dirt.

"You need to get a trim."

"What?" I just had a haircut before I left for Hawaii. I ran my hands through my longer-than-usual, sun-blonded hair. I wasn't ready to abandon it quite yet. "I like my hair the way it is."

"A clean up couldn't hurt," Sereena suggested. "Perhaps you might try someplace new this time. I was thinking Cutz?"

Carleen Fisher's place? What was she talking about? Was this another one of Sereena's moments of caprice? Every now and again my neighbour discovered a new favourite person, place, or thing. Like the artist whom she'd insisted was modern day Picasso. The restaurant whose chef she'd thought was the Prairie's answer to Emeril Lagasse. She said everyone needed to buy their art or eat their food, or risk missing out on something quite extraordinary. She was usually right.

"You never know what you might find out," Sereena kept on, seemingly more interested in consulting her to-do list than in our conversation. "You know how these common hair salons and barbershops are such excellent breeding grounds for gossip."

I frowned at that. Sereena disliked gossip almost as much as she disliked too-sweet wine and potato chips. Both, she said, were a waste of time and natural resources. Something was up here.

"I've made an appointment for you." She consulted her watch. "If you hurry you can still make it."

Cutz was the hair salon equivalent to one of Carleen Fisher's mother's fundraisers. Stylish, expensive, and poorly attended. The business was in a high-rent spot just down the street from Anthony's menswear store, *gatt*, on downtown's 2nd Avenue. When I stepped inside, a wholesome young woman wearing trendy clothing that revealed a taut midsection and eagle tattoo greeted me. She gamely took my name and, as a first-time customer, had me fill in a questionnaire that asked a lot of questions I didn't know the answers to. In the blank spot after the query about which hair care products I used, I wrote: "the bottle on the shelf."

Carleen seemed genuinely happy to see me. But so would have been any of the client-less operators at the half-dozen empty stations spread throughout the spacious room. An assistant washed my hair with something fantastic smelling, then set me up at Carleen's station, in front of a huge, oval mirror. She brought me a steaming mug of fresh latte that could only have been brewed by something that was big and silver with many knobs and a foreign-sounding brand name. Cream coloured walls were adorned with original oils by local artists who I knew sold their stuff for plenty. Mayor Fisher had spared no expense on his little girl's business.

"So, what can we do for you today?" Carleen asked with admirable verve. "A little trim? Maybe you'd like to get rid of some of the grey?"

I was about to yank away the lightweight cutting cape from around my neck and stomp out of there, but common sense prevailed. My hair was blond. Not grey. Maybe the lighting was hitting me wrong. At thirty-eight I supposed there might be a tint-challenged strand or two in there somewhere, so I decided to forgive her.

Carleen continued to assess my hair like a gardener would a plot of unruly weeds. "There's a whole patch of it right here at the crown." This girl could not shut up to save her life. Unforgivable.

"Just a trim," I muttered.

"Oh, okay." She sounded disappointed.

Well, too bad. "No, not even a trim," I instructed. "Just give me a quick check for split ends. If you find one, chop it off, otherwise, just leave it as it is."

Why had Sereena forced me to come here?

I was thinking about that when one of the other stylists said something that sent Carleen into gales of laughter. Me, not so much. I wasn't in the mood.

But then, my ears began to tingle. Carleen's laugh…there was something about it. It was low and throaty with a quivering cadence. It was peculiar. Unique.

I'd heard it somewhere before.

But not from Carleen.

More laughter.

Then I had it. Could it be? She laughed again, and I was certain. I'd heard the exact same laugh two nights ago at Simon Durhuaghe's reading.

As I sat there considering this curious bit of information, I suddenly realized why Sereena had sent me here. She was too much of a lady to spread a rumour—even if it was to help me out—but she wasn't beyond putting me in the perfect position to come up with it myself. In this case, Carleen Fisher's salon chair.

Again Carleen cut loose. The likeness of the laughs was eerie. Sereena must have met Simon Durhuaghe at some point, and noticed the uncanny similarity when she met Carleen at the luncheon.

"Carleen," I began in a pleasant conversational tone. "Starting up a new business must be quite a challenge. Especially for someone so young."

"Oh, it's not that difficult really." Then, with yet another of her unusual laughs—the girl was really going to town—she added, "And I'm really not that young either. But thanks for saying so."

"Really? How old are you? Twenty? Twenty-one?" I know it's rude to ask a woman her age, but this was work.

"Twenty-eight," she told me proudly.

I quickly did the math in my head.

Bingo.

Sherry had ended her affair with Simon Durhuaghe when she was nineteen and newly married to Cantor Fisher. Her daughter, Carleen, was born when she was twenty. It could work. The mayor's daughter might have been fathered by another man. If that was true, the delicious question was: Who knew about it?

Saturday continued to be a test of my multi-tasking prowess. I had a lot to do and little time to do it in. After finishing up at Cutz and picking up my tux from the rental store, I tracked down the address of Simon Durhuaghe's Saskatoon residence.

When in town, the Durhuaghes lived in a charming, two-storey character house on Temperance Street with a wraparound porch and a beautiful front garden. Very nice. Very peaceful. Until I showed up, that is.

A lovely looking woman in her late sixties answered the front door. Her greying hair was gently teased into a soft corona that folded neatly into a discreet bun at the back of her head. She wore a plain but elegant dress under a thick cardigan.

"Hello," she greeted me with a genuine smile on her heart-shaped face.

"Hello. My name is Russell Quant. I was wondering if Mr. Durhuaghe is home?"

"Are you a friend of my husband's?" she asked, her words betraying a slight British accent.

I hesitated.

"Oh well," she said with twinkling eye, "never mind then. Do come in anyway."

I gave her a confused look.

Her laugh tinkled like a bell as she pulled back and motioned me in. "I'm Olivia Durhuaghe, Simon's wife. You see, my husband isn't the sort of man with many people in his life to call friend. Still, after all these years, I hold out hope that one of these days at least one will show up. Silly of me, I suppose."

I could immediately tell there was nothing silly about this woman. "Perhaps tomorrow?" I suggested with a small smile.

She gave me an appraising look, one that said she found my sense of humour acceptable, and replied, "Perhaps tomorrow. Now, Mr. Quant, what is it you're here to talk to my husband about?"

No, not silly at all. "I'm a private investigator," I told her. "I'm working on a case I'd like to discuss with him, if I may." I watched her closely for any telltale reaction. Maybe she knew something too. But there was nothing, other than keen curiosity and intellect, and a desire to protect her spouse from the unsavoury.

Her clever eyes surveyed me more closely. Then, decision

made, she turned and beckoned me to follow. I was led down a narrow hallway lined with countless framed photographs. She walked slowly—intentionally?—giving me opportunity to study the images. Some were obviously professional publicity shots used for book jackets and in magazines, but the majority were simple family photos, many in black and white, some very old. There were pictures of Simon and Olivia in groups, but most were of just the two of them, always looking like they were having the time of their life. On a beach. In a rowboat. In front of the Eiffel Tower. With a Boston terrier. At a circus. They showed a full life lived away from the public eye.

One photo in particular caught my attention. It was one of the smallest in the group, but pulled me in with its intensity. Standing side by side, in a playful pose, were Simon and Olivia, fifty years younger than they were today. Both were dressed in white for some social event, looking for all the world like a pair of screen idols. He, tall and strong and big boned, with a shock of black hair spilling over eyes so pale they were almost translucent. She, magnificent with dewy skin, rosebud mouth, and hair that seemed as if it would bounce if you just looked at it. The camera had caught them laughing, and gazing at one another with undisguised adoration. I was so taken by the image, I stopped following my hostess and found myself staring at it. When I was done, I saw that Olivia was waiting patiently for me at the end of the hall. She gave me a smile, then, without saying anything, turned and walked on.

We ended up in a back porch where a series of windows faced the backyard. Through them I could see Simon Durhuaghe pacing up and down a cement walkway, from the rear of the house to a small garden at the other end of the lot, then back again.

"I send him out there to smoke his pipe," Olivia told me as we watched her husband. "Ten years ago, I would have never considered asking him such a thing. Now, it would be foolish of me not too." She laid a pale hand on my arm. "Truth be told, I really don't mind the smell of truly fine pipe tobacco. Nevertheless, I send him out there whenever he decides to light up. Just because I can. Isn't it wonderful?"

I grinned. Olivia Durhuaghe was a formidable woman.

"Good luck with whatever it is you hope to learn from him, Mr. Quant."

I cocked an eyebrow at her.

"Simon is an impossible man," she told me. "Always has been. It's what makes him interesting to people. Although they'd hardly admit it."

"Any advice?"

"None," she said as she slowly walked away. "Do your best, young man."

The door groaned with age as I pushed it open. Durhuaghe looked up. For a moment I could see a struggle on his face as he tried to remember who I was. I figure it came to him at about the same time as the frown.

"What the hell do you want?" he growled, pushing aside a few strands of his thick, silver hair.

He was standing about halfway down the path. It didn't seem likely he was going to come to me, so I went to him. As I approached, I saw something different in the man. Here in his home environment, banished to his backyard to indulge his vice, Durhuaghe appeared less virile than I remembered. The stoop of his shoulders was more pronounced, the wrinkles deeper, the eyes less fiery.

Still, this was a man who did not suffer fools gladly, not one to waste time on idle chat. So I jumped right in. "Mr. Durhuaghe, I know you're hiding something about your involvement in Walter Angel's murder."

"Hells bells!" his crusty voice rang out. "That again? What about it?"

"I believe Walter Angel knew about your involvement with Sherry Klingskill."

"So what? I already told you, Mr....?"

"Quant. Russell Quant."

He huffed and puffed. "I already told you, Quant, all that mess is long forgotten. Barely a memory as far as I'm concerned. I don't know why anybody else would care about it. I surely don't."

"Someone might care about it because Sherry Klingskill is now Sherry Fisher, the wife of the mayor of Saskatoon." I'd mentioned this before at the bookstore, but I wanted to be sure he knew that I knew.

"I know that, for heaven's sake. What do you take me for? Some kind of imbecile? What about it? So I had a fling with some dolly who ended up marrying a politician? Who cares? Million years ago. Old news. Besides, this is the twenty-first century. This sort of thing happens every day to people much better known than me. Presidents, for crying out loud. Every second politician puts it where he shouldn't. Nobody cares. They still get elected." He was trying hard to be cavalier and offhand, but I wasn't buying it.

"Sherry Klingskill was very young when you had your affair, Mr. Durhuaghe. And she was engaged to and then married another man."

He exhaled a heavy cloud of smoke, along with a grunt. "Alleged affair."

"And," I hesitated for dramatic effect (just because I like to do that once in a while). "Sherry Fisher gave birth to a daughter just shy of nine months after your *alleged* affair ended." Based on the details in the journal and letters, and the ages of Sherry and her daughter, I couldn't be exactly sure of this math, but I was betting my bluff wasn't too far off the truth.

Durhuaghe seemed shaken for the first time. He bumbled a bit then spat out: "That's a load of hogwash, and you know it! All you're doing is spreading vicious lies, Mr. Quant. I was mostly a nobody at the time. That girl was after much bigger fish than me, let me tell you. Just because she was young, doesn't mean she was naïve or innocent or stupid. She knew what she was doing when she got engaged to the richest boy in town. And when it was time for her to get pregnant, she broke it off to do just that. Any child she had was his, not mine. If she tells you any different, she's a goddamned liar!"

Of course I couldn't prove a thing without a DNA test. A quick check of my pockets told me I was fresh out. But proof only counts in a court of law. My job was to get him there in the first place—if that's where he belonged.

"Walter Angel was blackmailing you, wasn't he?" I didn't know this for a fact either. But I was working a hunch that Angel knew what was in the journal and letters, even though he didn't have physical possession of them. "He worked for the University of Saskatchewan Archives. You donated your papers there ten years ago. He read the journal where you wrote about your affair with Sherry Klingskill. He either figured out who she was, or who her fiancé was, or that she had a child with you, or maybe all three, and decided to use the information against you. Isn't that right?

"You paid him off to keep it from the public. Especially in the year of an important book release. Publishers and agents don't appreciate controversy like that, do they? I know they say any publicity is good publicity, but a reputation as an old lecher who seduces young girls, and with a lovechild you've never supported, probably doesn't count at all, does it?"

"Stop it. Stop right there. I don't have to stand here and listen to this crap from you!"

"We could sit down."

He didn't seem to appreciate my sense of humour as much as his wife did.

"I had never heard of this Angel character until I saw his name in the papers when he was killed. Yes, I was stupid and sent my papers to the University without bothering to cull them myself. But as I told you, I'd forgotten about the whole mess years ago. I don't even remember writing about it. Out of sight, out of mind.

"I may very well have met this Angel chap back then. But in truth, I don't recall who I dealt with at the Archives. The whole deal was a bloody nuisance to me. They wanted my stuff. I gave it to them. End of story.

"And Sherry, well, Sherry and I...well, it well may be true that we had a certain type of relationship when she was rather young." I detected a tremor in his voice. "I knew she was too damn young for me. But I was a world class cocksman in those days, Mr. Quant. I don't deny it. My wife doesn't either. So I've nothing to hide from her, if that's what you're thinking. That woman has stuck by me through thick and thin. She is a saint, and the love of my life. Always was. Always will be. I never deserved a woman like her, but she's put up with the worst of me."

If that was true—and I was inclined to believe it was—it wasn't his wife he was trying to keep his past from. But there was still the public, the daughter he had never met, maybe even the mayor of Saskatoon.

"Mr. Durhuaghe, this whole thing has gone too far. Your secrets are no longer safe. Someone has committed murder because of them. I think it could be you. And if I think so, so will the police."

"No! I would never do such thing! Never! But..." He checked himself there and busied himself puffing his pipe.

"What?" I pushed. "What is it?"

He exhaled deeply. My eyes fell to the pipe in his right hand. It was shaking.

"Blackmail." His voice was so low I could barely hear the word as it passed through his lips.

So there it was. "Walter Angel *had* been blackmailing you?" I said to confirm my suspicions.

He looked up then, his forceful grey eyes on mine. "I don't see how that would be possible, Mr. Quant."

Huh? "What do you mean?"

"I *am* being blackmailed," he admitted. "But it didn't begin until after Mr. Angel's death."

The details of the blackmail being perpetrated on Simon Durhuaghe were sparse. Either that or he just wasn't in the mood for sharing. Or he was hiding something. Fifteen minutes of verbal sparring didn't get me much. But I did manage to squeeze out of him that the threat came in the form of a letter with no postmark— so it had been hand-delivered to the mailbox on their porch—and clichéd letters cut from a magazine pasted on the page. When I asked to see it, Durhuaghe claimed he had tossed the thing. I pushed him, and he told me the letter simply said, "I know. You pay. I'll be in contact about how much and when." He said it hadn't worried him much.

That was it. It was time to leave.

I didn't want to bother Mrs. Durhuaghe again, and Durhuaghe himself wasn't the kind of host to see me out, so I skedaddled down the path that ran alongside the house. I was halfway down the front walk when I heard the voice.

"Did you get what you came for?"

I turned and walked slowly back toward the front porch, where Olivia Durhuaghe sat, knitting needles working on something that looked like a sweater.

"Excuse me?" I said from the first step up.

"Were you successful, Mr. Quant? Did Simon tell you anything worthwhile?"

I didn't know how to react to this. I went with a grin and said, "We talked."

"About that woman? About his dalliance with the mayor's wife?"

I stood stock-still, an uncomfortable look pasted on my face.

"Oh don't worry about all that, Mr. Quant," she said, eyes focussed on her handiwork. "My husband broke my heart a long time ago with that one." She looked up. "I've a different heart now. The part that broke, you see, I no longer need."

"Oh."

"Are you he?"

"Excuse me?" I seemed to be saying that a lot.

"Are you the blackmailer? Is that what this visit was about? Have you come for money? Or something else?"

"Oh, Mrs. Durhuaghe," I said, my voice quivering at the idea that she thought I was the bad guy. "No."

"It's all right if you are," she said, quite calmly. "I'd actually prefer it if you were. One likes to put a face to an enemy. It's somehow easier that way."

"No, Mrs. Durhuaghe. I am not the blackmailer."

"All right then, just thought I'd ask." She hesitated for a second, and then added. "I believe you, by the way."

"I'm glad."

"Me too. I rather like you," she declared, looking up at me. "I'd hate to have to think of you as the enemy. Because then, of course, there'd be all the messy business when I put an end to you and your shenanigans."

Suddenly Mrs. Durhuaghe's eyes appeared ten times more resolute and steely than those of her husband. It was obvious to me then. Although it was he who people both feared and worshipped, it was she who wielded the power and had the strength in this relationship.

We stared at one another for a moment. I knew one more thing. Olivia Durhuaghe had lied to me. She did not believe me when I said I wasn't the blackmailer. She only said so in her quest to protect her husband. Keep your friends close, keep your enemies closer. That was a saying meant for Olivia Durhuaghe.

I'd surmised that if Simon Durhuaghe was somehow involved in the murder of Walter Angel, he'd be a redoubtable foe to conquer. In that war, I'd yet to figure out on which side his wife would battle.

Chapter 14

I'd promised to contribute some sort of salad for the midday meal for the cast of thousands scurrying about Ash House preparing the property for the sunset wedding. I stopped by Colourful Mary's hoping to score something tasty and looking like I might have made it at home, but Marushka is a stickler for preparing every-thing from scratch. Apparently this means there isn't five pounds of potato salad sitting around in the cooler.

As I dashed off to Safeway, I had a sense of time being eaten up at rapid pace by one of those round heads from Pac-Man. The streets were packed with Saturday shoppers, and by the time I was on the short highway ride back out to Ash House, I was running late. I hate being late.

Screeching to a halt in front of the house, I retrieved the plastic bucket of Safeway potato salad from the trunk and dashed into the house to feed the starving masses. As it turned out, my salad was hardly missed, for my mother had arrived. And with my mother comes more food than most small towns can eat in one sitting.

The place was a hurricane. The forecast (not surprisingly) had failed to predict the surly clouds with spitting rain that showed up to stay by early afternoon. So, to accommodate the possibility of a cloudburst during the eight o'clock sunset ceremony, a massive white tent had been rented and was being hastily erected in the backyard. In case of wind, anything that wasn't already battened down was being secured or removed from the grounds. Garlands of flowers were being strung from posts to mark the pathway from the parking lot to the reception area. Inside a few carpenters, electricians, and painters were putting finishing touches (or rather, this-will-have-to-do-for-now touches) on various rooms. Several Molly Maids were doing their best to work around the throngs of workers and gathering family and friends.

In the kitchen, Mom was lording it over a buffet that had, in her presence, transformed from a submarine sandwich, chips, and *my* potato salad quickie lunch into a hot meal with sour cream slathered *perogies*, thick knots of Ukrainian sausage, mashed potatoes with gravy, farm fresh carrots and peas, and rice pudding and chocolate-zucchini loaf for dessert. How would anyone be able to go back to work after that? I surreptitiously slid my container of sad looking, store-bought potato salad into the refrigerator and helped myself.

Anthony and Jared were off somewhere getting massaged and facialled and in all other ways appropriately pampered. Ethan was doing his affable best to control the madhouse and its residents, dealing with each of the million-per-minute problems arising in the mayhem. Damien was nowhere to be seen. Sereena and Errall never moved from behind the desk in Ethan's office, taking and making calls, typing madly into a computer, printing things, and generally looking like two women in full control of running the world.

With no specific duties after lunch, I took my leave, telling myself I'd only be underfoot anyway. Besides, I had another visit to make. One I wasn't looking forward to.

I knew I was at the right place as soon as I knocked on the door of the Grosvenor Park house. Barking-a-plenty. I'd found the home of the *Sound of Music* dogs. And Walter Angel's widower, Sven Henckell.

It took a while for Sven to answer the door. When he did, I saw why. The short, shrivelled man had to be at least eighty-five. And not a particularly well-preserved eighty-five at that. He was thin, with flagging skin pale as a nun's belly. What was left of his hair was wispy and white. He wore thick glasses, two hearing aids, and walked with a cane. His brown slacks and faded blue, striped shirt looked about six sizes too big for him. The only thing that fit him were the corduroy slippers on his feet, around which scampered and yipped and hopped and tripped seven fluffy, fox-faced Pomeranians in a cornucopia of colours: red, orange, white, cream, brown, black, and even a near blue hue.

The old man stared at me for a few seconds, either trying to focus his eyes or deciding if he was supposed to know me or not. "Can I help you?" he finally asked, with no sign of the accent I'd expected with a name like Sven.

"Mr. Henckell, my name is Russell Quant. I met your husband, Walter. I just wanted to tell you how sorry I was to hear of his death."

"Yes," he said, his profound grief evident in the uttering of the single word.

"I know this must be a difficult time for you, but I was wondering if I could come in and speak with you for a few minutes?"

His eyes fell to the floor. "Well, girls and boys, what do you think? Should we ask the young man in?"

I gave the dogs a sweet and innocent smile that said, "you can trust me." Some of them moved forward to sniff at me, hopefully catching the friendly scent of Barbra and Brutus. One particularly snippy looking creature backed up and bared her fangs. Fortunately she made no noise as she did so, so it escaped Sven's clouded vision.

"Seems it's okay with them," Sven said, slooooooowly turning around and leading me and the pack inside.

The living room we entered was more unkempt then dirty.

There weren't stacks of magazines filling corners, uneaten food on crusty plates, or coffee stains on the carpet. But a fine layer of dust had settled over anything that hadn't recently been touched, pictures on the wall were askew, and one window blind was badly mangled. The room needed some attention, which the old man was obviously too unwell to provide. Or too short-sighted to notice.

Sven settled into a well-worn armchair that faced a TV. I chose the couch, as did five of the seven dogs. I gave my surroundings a closer once-over. Despite the general disarray, the room was pleasant enough. The furniture was middle of the road stock, nothing too old or too new, nothing too old-fashioned or too fancy. If Walter had been involved in a blackmail scheme, he certainly hadn't been using the proceeds on home redecoration. There were plenty of plants, several of which looked desperate for water. Around a corner I could make out one half of a dining table. On it were a box of cereal and two placemats.

"You wouldn't happen to have a lozenge, would you?" the man asked. "I seem to have gotten a bit of a sore throat over the last couple days, and I think we're all out."

I was immediately concerned. How old was this guy? How mobile was he? Could he get to a store on his own? Was anyone looking after him since he lost his husband?

I uselessly patted my empty pockets. "I'm sorry, I don't."

He shook his head and made a tsking sound with his tongue. "Wally did all the shopping. As you might have noticed, there is a small age difference between the two of us. Wally was only sixty-four. Still a youngster. He was going to retire next year, you know. I'm seventy-seven."

My eyes widened. Angel's husband was several years younger than I'd guessed. It was becoming apparent to me that there was something more at play in his physical deterioration than advancing age. Either Sven was not a well man or grief had taken a resounding toll in a very short time.

"That's thirteen years difference," he said. "Oh, the stories I could tell you. What a scandal our relationship caused amongst people when we first got together. He was only nineteen. I was thirty-two." He thought about this for a second, then said, "It seemed like a lot of years back then. And it does now too, I suppose. But not so much for everything in between. We had a good life together, me and Wally. For forty-five years. Not many people can say that, you know."

"No, they certainly can't." These two men had committed themselves to one another for over four decades in a time when it wasn't easy to be a gay couple, never mind a devoted gay couple. So what the hell was my problem? But now wasn't the time to think about that. I said, "I'm sure you must really miss Walter."

"Horribly, son," he admitted. "Just horribly. And so do the kids. Especially Brigitta and Gretl. They're the youngest. All they've done these last few days is sit and wait by the door. They've been expecting him to come home and laugh that honking laugh of his, which he used to do every day. They'd run and jump all over him, and lick him so much their tongues sometimes ended up his nose. It tickled him. And oh, he laughed, he loved that. They loved doing it too. They don't understand why he's not coming home."

"It sounds like you had a wonderful life together."

"He was not supposed to go first. I always thought of it as my one reward for being so much older, you know. I'd never have to see him go. This…this wasn't how it was meant to be."

I swallowed hard.

"It's so quiet now. Even with the girls and boys. So quiet."

"Mr. Henckell…"

"Call me Sven, if you can. It makes me feel young."

I smiled, but I wasn't sure he could see it. "Sven, I first met Walter a week ago. We were on the same flight, coming home from Vancouver."

"Actually he was in Victoria. That's where Helen was. He must have made a connection through Vancouver, I suppose. I didn't really pay much attention to his itinerary. Other than the date he was supposed to come home. I was sitting up waiting for him that night. For hours. I didn't know what had happened. I thought maybe I'd gotten the wrong day. I don't know how many times I checked the calendar to make sure I had the right one. Then they called..." He took such a deep breath, I could see his thin chest struggle with it. I debated leaving. Maybe it was too soon to have this talk with him. But then he said, "Oh, but you don't want to hear about all that, now do you? Anyhow, as I said, he was in Victoria, where Helen was."

Helen again. I'd bet my last bottle of Kanonkop Pinotage it was the same Helen who used to be the head archivist at the U of S. I suspected it was she who created the treasure map. Had she given it to Walter? Or had he taken it?

"Was it Helen Crawford he was visiting?" I asked in a way that might have suggested I'd know Helen all my life.

I saw his near naked noggin move up and down just a nudge. "That's the Helen of course, but it wasn't any kind of visit he went for."

"Oh? Why do you say that?"

"She died. That's why."

I could hear a few pieces clicking into place. "So Walter went to Victoria to attend Helen's funeral?"

"Oh no. They weren't really close enough for that. They worked together for many years, but they weren't ever best friends. And after Helen retired a few years ago, they'd pretty much lost touch. Up until the call from the lawyer."

"An estate lawyer?"

"I suppose, I'm not sure what kind of lawyer he called himself. But he told Wally that Helen had left something important for him and did he want it mailed or couriered."

The treasure map. "But instead he flew all the way to Victoria to get it? Why would he do that?"

The old man made a noise that sounded like, "hehmphf", and I took it to mean my question stumped him. "I can't really remember why he said it was so important to go all that way. But Wally tells me my memory is failing...or he used to. I guess maybe it's true."

This was not a private investigator's favourite admission.

"Anyhow, I suppose he thought whatever it was she'd left him was too important to trust to Canada Post. Maybe it was something fragile? Like a vase or something? Maybe fruit. They have nice fruit out there, you know."

"M…Sven, did your husband ever talk to you about a treasure or a treasure map or anything like that?"

He shook his fragile head. "Can't say he did."

I hated mentioning this to the old fellow, but I had to give it a try. "What about blackmail?"

This seemed to get his attention. The eyes behind his thick glasses noticeably widened as he leaned forward to get a better look at me. "Blackmail? Did you say blackmail? Was someone blackmailing Wally?"

"Uh, no. I was thinking the other way around."

"What's that?" he turned up the volume on one of his hearing aids.

"Sven, I know what I'm asking may be difficult for you to consider, but, well, do you think Walter might have been capable of committing blackmail?"

The bald head swung back and forth. It was the swiftest movement I'd seen from the man since I'd arrived. "Oh no. Oh no. I may be old and hard of hearing and can't see much and maybe losing my memory, but I know my Wally," he insisted. "He was a good man. He would never blackmail anybody. He wouldn't be able to live with himself. I'm telling you the God's honest truth, Mr.…mister man. And I don't want to hear that you're passing around those kinds of horrible rumours about my poor Wally, either. That clear?"

"I'm sorry, Sven." I really was. "I don't mean to upset you with these questions. I don't know if what I suspect is true. But someone killed your husband. I'm just trying to find out who, and why."

He nodded a bit. "Well, okay then. But just forget about this blackmail nonsense. It's just not true."

I sighed. "Sven, is there anything you can think of that might help me find Walter's murderer?" I was going to suggest enemies, money problems, that sort of thing. But I didn't think it would do me, or Sven, any good.

"I'd have to say a big no to that, young man." He petted the nest of dog fur in his lap. "And so would Friedrich. Or is this

Kurt?" He stared at the animal. "Is that brown hair or red? So hard to tell in this light." He fiddled with one of his ear pieces, then said, "Mr. Quant, could I ask a favour of you?"

"Of course," I agreed, surprised he remembered my name when he'd clearly forgotten it earlier.

"Would you mind going into the kitchen cupboard and checking on how much dog food we have left? I can't see very well, you know, and I can only reach so high. I'm afraid to use the step ladder because I'm not too steady on my feet. I'm scared I might fall off. Wally did the shopping before he left for Victoria, but it's been a week. I don't know how much we've got left. Could you do that for me? I don't care about myself, but I don't want the kids running out of food."

While I scouted the kitchen cupboards for dog food, I took the liberty of assessing the people food supplies as well. By the looks of things, Sven was getting down to a diet of dry cereal and condiments.

About twenty minutes later, as I finished unpacking a few things I'd picked up from the corner store to restock Sven's and the Poms' basics, two Molly Maids from Ash House arrived. I made introductions, paid the cleaners including a hefty tip, and filed a mental note to have a talk with Ethan about Sven's future.

Churlish clouds filled the sky by the time I reached PWC. The temperature was dropping, the wind getting stronger, and I was almost out of time. Anthony and Jared's wedding was only hours away, and my meeting with Reginald Cenyk a couple hours after that. Maybe it was the weather, but a bad feeling was growing in my stomach. Was my archivist informant in danger? Was I? Instead of one murder, were we dealing with a string of murders? Was someone else about to get killed?

The news about Helen Crawford's death was interesting indeed. I now had a new twist to take into account. Had she truly died of natural causes, or was Walter Angel's death not the first murder tied to the Durhuaghe papers? Had someone killed Helen, then Walter? Were both archivists killed by the same hand? Was it

Durhuaghe? Maybe he'd lied to me. Maybe he'd been blackmailed by Helen all along. He'd have thought with her death the blackmail would stop. But to find it would continue—in perpetuity—because of the existence of the treasure map, might have been too much for him to swallow. He'd have realized that he would be forever under the thumb of whoever had the map. That couldn't be an easy way to live.

Tuxedo in hand, I quickly scaled the fire stairs to the second floor of PWC and made it inside just as the first of a series of roving showers dropped on the city. I hung the garment bag on the back of my office door and plunked myself down in front of my computer. As I typed away, I kept one eye on the time indicator on the bottom right hand corner of the screen.

It took longer than I'd hoped to find what I needed. I dialled the phone number as I stripped. An answering machine took my call. I left a brief message and my cell number and hung up.

All I had left to put on, other than my jacket, was the cummerbund. I remembered the handy rule of thumb—or should I say rule of crumb—taught to me by Anthony. If you consider the cummerbund as your crumb catcher, you'll always know to put the thing on with pleats open to the top, making it easier to catch crumbs in. I guess people at fancy events must be notoriously messy eaters.

I ran downstairs to check myself out in the full-length mirror.

Not too shabby. Anthony and Jared had selected cream-coloured tuxes with fawn accents for their attendants. It looked good with my not-yet faded Hawaiian tan and sun-bleached hair. I pulled up the jacket and turned around to assess the assets. Not exactly up to wonderpants standard, but the caboose was looking A-okay.

The Mazda was purring out of the parking lot a few minutes later when I slammed on the brakes. I raced back into PWC, opened the safe in my office, retrieved the wedding rings I'd been storing there for months, and galloped back to the car.

As an overcast sky continued to threaten rain, delivering every half hour or so, an anomalous mist swirled about the tents behind

Ash House in which one-hundred-and-fifty guests were gathered, awaiting the nuptials. The whole setting was beginning to look a little like a Sherlock Holmes movie starring Basil Rathbone. The only disparities in my foggy little dreamscape were Sereena's candy hearts, now set up on the lawn, bleating their sad-looking orange, yellow, and pinkness through the blur of grey. In its own way, it was a rather oddly beautiful scene. Not exactly the warm, dry, sunny day hoped for, but as Sereena always says, a sign of a person's intelligence is their ability to adapt.

I found Jared in a second floor bedroom, fussing with his bow tie.

"I told Anthony to go with the pre-tied bow ties," I said as I entered the room and took over the tying.

"You'd think as a former model I could handle this. But my fingers are all thumbs today." He laughed nervously. "Gawd, listen to me. I've been spouting clichés all day. Next thing you know I'll be hunting for something old, something new, something borrowed, and something blue. Do you think my hair looks okay I shouldn't have had it cut yesterday it always looks best several days after a cut it's too new I need some product and these shoes are killing me but you look great Russell I love your hair that way and can you believe the weather thank god for the tents I suppose we'll miss seeing the sunset now like we planned I mean what's the point of a sunset wedding if you're in a tent but we knew…"

"Jared. Jared. Jared!" I took hold of his shoulders and gave them a bit of a shake, setting his copper tinted curls to bouncing. I'd never seen the man so jumpy before. Ever. Jared was always the cool, collected one.

"I know, I know," he responded with a lopsided smile. "I've walked runway in front of thousands of people, and it never fazed me. But this…this getting married stuff is…well, it's just crazy. My heart feels like it's going to burst out of my chest. Imagine the mess!"

We laughed. Not because the visual was funny, but because we really needed to.

"Do you remember, Russell?" Jared asked, suddenly serious again. "A couple of years ago? After this." He indicated the scar tissue on his face.

I hardly noticed the disfigurement anymore. Jared's spirit, not to mention his killer smile and flashing green eyes, easily shone through anything any deranged attacker could have done to him or his appearance. When I looked at him now, I saw the same lovely face I saw, only inches from mine, on the day we woke up together in that country barn and realized we'd survived being abandoned and left for dead in a raging winter storm. I saw my friend. I saw a man I loved, who was beautiful inside and out.

"Remember," he urged again. "I came to you, and asked you to help me leave Anthony?"

I nodded. It had been a horrible, ugly time in my relationship with Jared. He'd decided that the mutilation had made him into a different person. That he was no longer the same man Anthony fell in love with. Anthony and Jared had long been admired for being one of the most strikingly beautiful pairs in all of coupledom. How they looked, how they dressed, how they lived larger than life, was hard to separate from their love affair.

Jared stared at his face in the mirror, unconsciously busying his hands by trying to straighten his curls. "After her original cancer diagnosis and mastectomy, I watched Kelly run away from Errall, from her life in Saskatoon. She escaped. She ran away and found another life. I envied her. It's what I wanted. I wanted it for Anthony too. I thought he deserved another chance with someone else."

"You were stupid," I said bluntly. And of course, the second after I said it, I realized it probably wasn't the nicest thing to say to a groom on his wedding day. But fortunately...

"I was stupid," he wholeheartedly agreed. "Kelly realized it too, didn't she? She eventually figured out that she ran away from the only thing she really needed. The only thing she couldn't live without. That's why she came back. To die with Errall back in her life."

More nodding from me. An impossibly huge lump was growing in my throat. I wondered when thoughts of Kelly would no longer do that to me. Probably never.

"She ran out of time. But I'm not going to wait that long. I love

Anthony. He loves me. My life could not be more perfect than it is right now."

I was in awe of this man, whose celebrated beauty had been taken from him, destroyed in mere seconds by a glassful of acid tossed into his face by another man with a damaged mind. He was getting through it. He was leaving it behind.

"It's time." Sereena was at the door.

I finished with Jared's tie, gave him a kiss on the cheek, then we were off.

It was a beautiful wedding.

Except for the plough wind.

The United Church minister was just getting to the good part when the sides of the tent began to quiver. Her voice rose to be heard over the bellowing wind. Guests on the outside aisles leaned away from the shuddering canvas walls. The only warning that bad was about to get much worse, was a menacing whipping sound that filled the air, like rope being pulled through giant eyelets.

And then the top of the tent disappeared.

Chapter 15

Cries of panic and alarm ripped through the air.

Thankfully, the driving force of the plough wind, like a runaway locomotive made of air, moved on as abruptly as it had arrived. Unfortunately, it took the top of the wedding tent with it.

By the time the crowd settled down, the canvas sheet was probably sitting in a field someplace far, far away like North Dakota. Surprisingly, pretty much everyone had remained where they were. So when the blustering wind suddenly died down to barely a whisper, everything looked just as it had before. Except, that is, for the great lengths of flower garlands, and anything else that was lighter than a human, strewn about the space in an unholy mess.

We all looked at each other, at first struck numb and dumb by the freakish thing that had just occurred. I caught sight of my mother across the room and expelled a sigh of relief to see that she was unharmed and seemingly unfazed. Slowly the tent—or what was left of it—filled with murmuring, reassurances that we were all okay. We stared up at the sky above us—now visible where the roof had been—almost accusingly, angry at the churning clouds, thick with rain, for what they had just done to us. Then murmur turned to mumble turned to all-out cacophony as people began to recount what happened, as if no one else had seen it but them. Eventually, that too died down. We fussed with our hair, straightened collars and hemlines, then fixed our gazes expectantly on the preacher.

Just as her mouth opened, so did the sky. The rain that fell on us was heavy but warm. We might as well have been in a shower, in a shower with our finest clothes on and eighty dollar updos. And two grooms waiting for the words they'd waited years to hear.

It was a disaster. The makeshift wedding chapel was in total disarray. The guests were soaking wet. The decorations were slowly making their way down stream to the South Saskatchewan River. The preacher was discombobulated, not knowing whether she should go on with the ceremony, try to turn some of the water to wine, or race for the hills. Everyone was looking at our grooms with pity in their eyes. Should we cry? Get angry? Scream in frustration?

I caught Anthony's eye. I was jolted by what I saw there. A gleam. A sparkle. The look of a man who knows, without doubt, what the important things in life are. Not only do you not sweat the small things, you don't sweat the big ones either. Just keep your eye on the prize. And today, his prize was Jared, and making that man his husband. No matter what. Everything else was just window dressing.

The sound that came next was the most unexpected of all. Anthony and Jared threw back their heads...and laughed.

They were laughing so hard, they had to hold on to each other to keep from falling down. Their upturned faces were being christened by sluicing rain, perfect hair flattened against their skulls, tuxedos soaked through. What a couple they made. Nothing on the outside meant a thing. Anthony, at fifty-eight, an aging James Bond, and Jared, the once breathtakingly handsome supermodel with a scarred face. They were perfect for one another.

No one knew what to do at first. But of course, there was only one thing left to do. We joined in. First me. Then the other attendants. The minister. Everyone else. I'm sure the gales of rollicking laughter could be heard all the way to that field in North Dakota.

And that was how Anthony and Jared became Mr. and Mr. Anthony and Jared Gatt-Lowe. Protected from a whirlwind of turmoil by a cocoon of love, our love for them, their love for each other.

As the wedding party, including me and Errall, made our way down the sodden aisle, out of that wrecked tent, a clear voice rang out. Someone was strumming a guitar and singing. I searched the space and found my sister, Joanne, perched on a stool in one corner, near a flapping gape in the tent wall. Her eyes were closed, head tilted slightly back, revealing tendons and muscles toiling at her slender throat. The song was unfamiliar to me. Something about her riding her pain like the wind. It was loud. It was inappropriate for the occasion. And it was perhaps, the most hauntingly beautiful sound I'd ever heard. It was her gift to Anthony and Jared. It was indeed the song of a wounded bird.

The major disaster that was the wedding weather, helped dwarf the minor one that occurred as I continued down the aisle. My cellphone began to jangle. Anthony and Jared were too busy smiling and waving and ducking confetti to notice a thing. The guests were entranced by the grooms and the music accompanying their first walk as husbands. Errall, walking next to me, was another matter however. I smiled weakly at her. She glared at me with something akin to murder in her eyes.

As soon as we breached the edge of the tent and were outdoors, I ran away. More to escape Errall's wrath, than to catch the call.

"Hello," I answered as I took cover from the insistent rain under the roof of a nearby gazebo.

"I'm calling for Russell Quant," a voice told me. "I hope I have the right number."

"This is Russell Quant. Who am I speaking with?"

"My name is Susan Crawford. Helen Crawford's sister."

Hallelujah. I thanked the woman for calling back and got right into it.

"Well, I don't know anything about a treasure map," Susan said after I'd finished giving her a quick rundown of the past week's events (just the parts she needed to know.) "But I am familiar with the Durhuaghe archive items you describe."

Double hallelujah.

"Helen swore me to secrecy when it all began. But she needed someone to talk to. Someone independent of the archives. Although we lived in different cities, and rarely saw one another in person until she retired and moved here, my sister and I have always remained close. We spoke on the phone several times a month." I marvelled at this.

"What exactly did she tell you about the Durhuaghe material? Helen found the journal and letters in the items he donated ten years ago, isn't that right?"

"I don't recall if it was Helen or one of the other archivists who first discovered the material," she said, "but I do remember that the discovery caused quite a commotion at the time. There was a great deal of disagreement amongst the archivists about what to do with the item in question. Should they destroy it, return it, or keep it in the archives in the spirit of full disclosure? You can see how opinions might vary.

"Helen took her stewardship role very seriously, Mr. Quant. She loved history. And books—she started out as a librarian, you know—and she loved the world of great literature and revered the people who created it. Simon Durhuaghe was among her favourites. To her, he truly was a god. She knew that by allowing the information in those journals and letters to become public knowledge, she would be responsible for a disastrous blow to Durhuaghe and his career. She simply couldn't bring herself to play a part in that.

"It took my sister weeks of intense deliberation and soul-searching to decide what to do. A minute in the shredder, and no one would be the wiser. Yet to return the material to Durhuaghe would make her an accomplice in a different kind of act she also could not stomach: subverting history.

"Helen was in a horrible bind, Mr. Quant. Although she didn't want the papers to see the light of day, she also did not feel she had a right to be part of making them disappear forever. We talked about this over the phone for hours and hours. Our phone bills were astronomical. Helen did accept that perhaps, one day, the information should be made known. Just not under her watch. She did not share her final decision with me. If she hid the journal and letters, where, or how, I cannot say, Mr. Quant. She considered that privileged information. But this map you talk about, the poem with the historic clues, although I couldn't swear to it, I wouldn't be the least bit surprised to be told my sister had created it. She was peculiar in that way. Using the past to hide the past, oh yes, there's a certain nice quality about that. Helen would have found great pleasure in it."

I was surprised by how much the sister knew, and disappointed by what she didn't. "If she didn't tell you about what she did with the material, why would she involve Walter Angel? I understand they weren't that close."

"My sister knew she was dying, Mr. Quant. She'd have known it was time to pass on her role as safekeeper to someone she trusted."

The time had come to ask Susan Crawford the same question that had upset Sven Henckell. But that's what PIs have to do sometimes: ask the tough questions others are afraid to.

"Ms. Crawford," I began, pulling the sodden bow tie from around my neck. "Did your sister use the material in the journal and letters to blackmail Simon Durhuaghe?"

"No," was her quick and unequivocal response. "She admired Simon Durhuaghe and his work. Certainly, she was gravely disappointed to find out what she did about his personal life, but she'd never have used it against him. To Helen, Simon Durhuaghe the great writer was very separate from Simon Durhuaghe the man. She did what she did to protect the one despite the actions of the other. What she did ten years ago, Mr. Quant, was to keep anyone from doing exactly what you're accusing her of."

"Can you be sure, Ms. Crawford? I know how close you were to your sister, but sometimes…"

"No, Mr. Quant, I have no doubt."

One more try. "It isn't inexpensive to retire early to Victoria."

"It is when you share a house with a sister and a friend who've also retired. The three of us lived simply, Mr. Quant. We just wanted to live out our years in a place we loved. We didn't travel. We didn't buy expensive things. We planned to live in this beautiful place, keeping each other company, reading good books, enjoying nature. She deserved more time to do all those things. People may tell you Helen was a bit odd, and she was. But she was a wonderful, thoughtful woman, Mr. Quant. I hope you believe me about that."

I sat in the gazebo for a while after I hung up. It was time to think outside the box I'd built around this case. I was so certain that whoever killed Walter Angel did so to keep him from using the Durhuaghe journal and letters to blackmail someone... Durhuaghe himself, or Sherry Fisher, or maybe someone else entirely? Yet, if I was to believe what I'd heard that day, the two likeliest blackmailers, Walter himself and Helen Crawford, weren't using the material that way at all. Instead, rather than using it to extort money, they were doing whatever they could to keep it hidden. If that were true, Durhuaghe, or Sherry, or whoever, had nothing to fear from Walter. Yet he'd been killed. And, Durhuaghe admitted that someone *was* blackmailing him.

My brain crept out of the box and came upon a realization: maybe the murderer wasn't someone who wanted to *prevent* blackmail. Maybe the murderer was someone who wanted to *perpetrate* it.

"Quant, how about getting off your ass and giving us a hand," came Darren Kirsch's delightful voice.

I looked up, startled. I was so deep in thought, I'd forgotten where I was for a moment.

"The chairs. We have to move chairs and tables into the house for dinner."

"They're going to feed a hundred and fifty people inside a house that isn't even finished?"

"No choice. Rain and no roof don't mix well. The caterers and servers are scrambling to adjust. It'll have to work somehow. And your sitting here having a little daydream isn't helping any."

An idea popped into my head. "Kirsch, did your detectives check the phone calls made in and out of Walter Angel's hotel room while he was in Victoria?"

The policeman's face and manner made a quick change. He was on alert. "What's going on, Quant? You on to something I should know about?"

"I don't know." I was so used to lying to the guy, I did it without thinking.

"Not much there," Kirsch said. "Just what you might expect, some calls home and to work. That's it."

That was enough.

Errall Strane has never been one to drink too much. I think it has something to do with the loss of control, or perception of it. And if there is one thing Errall loves, its control. But she is not without vices. Plenty of them. Her favourite is smoking. So when it was time for speeches and cutting the cake and she was missing in action, I had some good ideas of where to look for her.

I first tried the front porch, but she—and her curlicues of smoke—were nowhere to be found. Back deck. Gazebo. By the pool. Nothing. As a last resort I stepped through the doorway into the roofless tent. The place looked like a circus gone bad. Once lovely bouquets of flowers sat dejectedly in pools of rain water and mud. Chairs and tables that hadn't made it into the house were sitting at odd angles, some overturned, as if there'd been a race to get away from some kind of natural disaster (which wasn't too far from the truth). Kernels of popped corn, tossed over the heads of the newly married couple as they walked down the aisle, littered the ground like balls of hail that refused to melt. And amidst the chaos was Errall. She was leaning against an abandoned portable bar, lit cigarette and empty champagne glass in hand. She looked a little blue.

"You okay?" I asked, with the care of a crocodile hunter.

"This might have been our day, Kelly's and mine. This was our dream, you know."

I bobbed my head in understanding. "Yeah, I too have always

dreamt of having a freak storm rip the roof off my wedding chapel and soak my guests to the bone. I mean, who hasn't?"

Her eyes flashed. I was taking a chance. This croc was very capable of snapping my face off. Instead, I saw the corner of her lips turn up.

"They seem to be having fun all the same." This came from Anthony, who came up behind me with a fresh bottle of champagne in one arm and Sereena on the other.

"Aren't you supposed to be cutting the cake right about now?" I asked, accepting a glass of bubbly even though I knew I'd only have a sip. Or two. I still had work to do tonight.

"Anthony may be the one getting married," Sereena let us know, "but I'm the one organizing this affair. Nothing else has gone quite according to plan tonight. So I think we can afford to veer a little off timetable. Besides, your mother just brought out a roaster full of something called *nahlessnehkeh*?"

"I don't know what they are," Anthony said, "but people are wolfing them down like dogs on chow. Quite disturbing really." He poured Errall a top-up. "You okay?"

"Why do people keep asking me that?"

No one said a thing.

She regarded each of us in turn. "I'm fine. Really. I think finer then I've been in a long while.

"You know, Anthony, you and Jared taught me something tonight. You two had every right to throw a fit, stamp your feet, rage at God, whatever, because of what happened at your wedding. No one would have blamed you. Instead, you laughed. You laughed, kissed, and went on with things. And now you're married, with a houseful of wet, drunk, but basically happy family and friends, and a great life to look forward to. Nothing important changed, did it? No plough wind or rain storm or change of venue was going to stop you from getting what you always wanted. I know I can't have that with Kelly…"

"Oh, Errall…"

She held up a hand, traffic cop style. "No. Stop. No pity. That isn't what this is about. It's about the opposite of pity. I'm actually happy. Very happy. I finally figured out some stuff tonight. Bad crap can happen, but none of it has to stop you from getting what you want, from being happy. Maybe you don't get there quite the way you expected to, but you can still get there. *I* can get there."

"And this womenswear store is what will make you happy?" Anthony asked.

Errall scoffed. "Gawd no. I don't know what I was thinking. I love the law. I love fighting people in court. It's a good outlet for my aggression. It's hard work and long hours. I love that too." She turned to me. "And I love PWC just the way it is. I want you to stay, Russell. And Beverly and Alberta. I've had enough change in my life. I don't need any more right now."

"Are you sure?" I asked. "This is your big chance to get rid of me. If I stay, who knows when you'll get another opportunity?"

"Only if you promise me one thing."

Here it comes.

Errall's intense eyes fell upon me with the weight of blue steel. "Don't fuck this up, Russell," she said.

I stuttered something unintelligible.

"Russell," Anthony murmured, "you need to make a decision."

I backed away. How had this suddenly turned into being about me? I looked at the faces around me and they all said the same thing. I couldn't play stupid any longer. "I have to decide between Alex and Ethan."

"No," Sereena told me, using her low, coarse voice that scared me. "You don't have that luxury. You don't have Ethan. And, I'm afraid, you're about to lose Alex."

The harsh news was glaringly true, and awful to hear.

"You have to decide whether you're a man in love," she said, "or not."

"Maybe I'm not meant to be in love." There. I'd said it. It was a suspicion I'd been harbouring for years, even throughout all my time with Alex. And now, I feared I was going to be shown up for what I truly was: a man who could not love. "Maybe I'm just not wired that way anymore. There's got to be a reason why I'm running away from one terrific guy who wants me, to chase after another who doesn't. That's just sick, right?"

"Oh, puppy," Anthony said, making a tsking sound and laying a warm arm across my shoulders. "You're not sick. You're afraid."

I was. I was afraid.

Why couldn't my fairytale romance be as simple as it seemed to be for everyone else? Boy meets boy, boy falls in love with boy, boy marries boy, and they live happily ever after. Instead, my story was: boy meets boy 1, boy falls in love with boy 1 and meets boy 2, boy falls in love with boy 2 too. Boy 1 wants to get married and boy 2 doesn't know boy is alive, so boy buries head in sand.

I'd been living terrified of lifting my head out of that sand. But as I stood there that night, in that wedding tent disaster area, surrounded by my friends, I began to believe that maybe it wouldn't be so impossible to do. And moreover, I wanted to do it. I had a life story to get to. All I had to do was turn the page.

My fairytale story wasn't perfect. But that didn't make it any less a fairytale. Besides, what is perfect nowadays, anyway? It was time to figure out how to navigate my way to the happily ever after part. And to decide what, for me, that was.

What did I truly want my future to look like? Did I want someone to have adventures with? Someone to grow old with? Share experiences with? Did I want it to be stolen moments of idyllic romance on Hawaiian beaches with Alex Canyon? Or did I want it to be part of everyday life with someone like Ethan Ash?

This wasn't a simple question of quality over quantity, either. Both Alex and Ethan were quality men. And sure, the circumstances of any future relationship I might have with one of these men would be different, but that couldn't be the most important factor in deciding my romantic future, could it? Or should it be? Would Alex give up his international career to settle in Saskatoon? Would I give up my home and family and friends to be with him? Was Ethan emotionally available to fall in love with someone beyond his child? Was I willing to share that love? Did I even want a child in my life? Does love expect—require—sacrifice?

I needed to delve deeper.

What did *I* need? What did *I* want? What did Alex need? Had I ever asked him? What about Ethan?

Oh yeah, this was going to be real simple.

I was scrambling through the darkened parking lot adjacent to Ash House, trying to remember where I'd left the Mazda, when I heard the voices. It was odd, because as far as I could tell, the party was going so well, none of the wedding guests seemed even close to leaving. I was only going because I had a prior appointment to meet with my informant, Reginald Cenyk. I slid up against a handy Hummer and cocked my ear to get a better listen. There was only one person talking. And I knew the voice. Damien.

What was Ethan's boyfriend doing out here in the parking lot? In the dark? With someone who I knew wasn't Ethan. I knew that because I'd said a hasty so long to him before I left the house, with promises to make it back before the party was over.

An evil grin covered my face. The oh-so-perfect Damien was having an illicit rendezvous. And I was about to catch him with his pants down.

Pasting an I-just-happened-by look on my face, I swung around the end of the SUV and prepared to confront the lovers.

There was Damien. And next to him…Errall.

They were talking. Or, as I saw it, Damien was talking, Errall was consorting with the enemy.

"Russell, hi," Errall said the second she saw me. I don't think it was so much a greeting, as it was a warning message to Damien to shut up.

The boy turned and said hello.

I said hello back.

Silence for an uncomfortable beat.

"So what are you doing out here?" I asked. "The party's over there." Corny line, but I was doing the best I could.

"Damien's giving me a ride home," Errall explained.

I consulted my watch with great obviousness. "So early?"

Damien seemed to recover his sweet good nature. "I'm on shift early tomorrow morning. Those darn hospitals never close."

I'd overheard that he was a nurse or radiologist or some other such do-gooder.

I looked at Errall.

"And I'm just done." She never felt a need to give an explanation if she didn't feel like it.

"What about you?" Damien asked. "You're on your way pretty early too."

"I'm coming back," I told him. "I just have some work to do. A private investigator's case never closes either." Take that!

He nodded, then looked over at Errall. "Well, should we make tracks?"

We said our good nights and I watched as they got into Damien's Hyundai and motored off. I arched an eyebrow, pursed my lips, and squinted my eyes in a look that would send many a soap opera star back to acting class. My mind began to reel, wondering about what those two had been talking about. But there was no time for this now. I had work to do.

Another voice.

Jeepers, was the whole damn wedding party lurking in the parking lot?

"*Sonsyou*."

"Mom, what are you doing out here?" I asked when she appeared out of the shadows like a Russian barge through smog.

"I vant to see you before you go," she said.

"I just said goodbye to you in the house. And you and Joanne are coming into the city for brunch tomorrow, remember?"

"No, Joanne go home tomorrow."

"But that's not what sh..." And there I stopped myself, on the verge of bristling at the sudden, unexplained change in my sister's plans. Why was I pretending it was unexpected? It was exactly the type of thing Joanne excelled at. I needed to accept and embrace that about her. Or else let her go.

"Where exactly is she going?" I was concerned. Did she actually have a home to go to these days?

"Home. To Osoyoos."

"Osoyoos? She's living in Osoyoos? I don't even know what that is. Where is it?"

"BC somevhere, I tink, I don't know for sure, *Sonsyou*. Dat's okay dat she goes now. Eet's time for her."

I checked my watch, this time really needing to know the time. There was only barely enough time to get to my downtown appointment, but I couldn't leave my mother in the lurch. "Mom,

Joanne's been drinking and probably shouldn't drive. But I can't take you back to the farm tonight, so maybe the two of you could spend the night at my place. I can drop you off at the house right now or I can come back for you."

"No, no, don't vorry. Joanne stop dreenking now. She dreenks too much, I know, but she knows vhen to stop. Eeten says he only geeve her vater now."

"You're sure?"

"*Sonsyou*, I vant to tell you someting. I vant to tell you dat your daddy loved you and he vas a goot daddy. As deed best he could. He vas a goot daddy. A goot man. Mebbe not such a goot husband at first. But I vas so young vhen ve get married. He deedn't know about being a goot husband, and mebbe I deedn't know about being goot vife, either, I don't know. I deedn't ask."

I wanted to stick my fingers in my ear, sing "la-la-la" at the top of my lungs, and claim not to hear a thing. Maturity prevailed.

"And I'm to tell you, you are not like heem. Mebbe like your Uncle Lawrence, *tahk*, sure. But like Daddy, no. Joanne ees like Daddy, very much. She knows dees."

She'd heard.

Mom had heard Joanne and me talking—no—arguing, that night at her house. She'd heard Joanne telling me that our father was a cheater who couldn't commit, and that I was following right in his footsteps. And I almost believed her.

From the dark: "Mom? Is that you?"

It was now official. Party in the parking lot.

Joanne emerged from the shadows. I studied her and decided Ethan had been doing a good job; she looked almost sober.

"I lost you," she said. "Someone said they saw you coming out here. I didn't know Russ was with you." She looked at us back and forth. "So what am I interrupting?"

"I'm just saying gootbye," Mom claimed, reaching out to lay an arm around her daughter's narrow waist.

"I have to go back into the city for a while, for work. But in case you're not here when I get..."

"About brunch tomorrow, Russ..."

I waved it off. "Yeah, I know. Mom told me. You have to head home."

She lit a cigarillo. "I'd stay, but I just heard about this gig; have to get some stuff put together for that. And I think the cats are probably missing me by now."

I caught my breath and stared at my sister. She has pets, I thought to myself. This gave me pause. You don't have pets unless you have a home. You don't have pets unless you wanted to—and were capable of giving—love.

She chortled her trash can laugh. "All they do is ignore me when I'm there, but I set foot in that door after being away and it's like I'm the friggin' second coming."

"*Donya*, don't say such tings!" Mom scolded.

Joanne laughed and hugged Mom closer. They understood each other better than I ever would.

"I really have to run."

And then I did something I don't remember doing before. I pulled my sister into a hug. I whispered into her ear, "Love ya."

When I let her go, although I didn't feel her arms around me, I knew she'd wanted to hug me back. Fair enough, I'd taken her by surprise.

I tittered nervously. "But I have to find my car first."

"I saw it over there, next to the pink caddy," Joanne said, pointing, just as happy as I was to move on.

I gave Mom a quick hug, and dashed away.

"*Sonsyou!*" Mom called after me. "Be careful. No shooting!"

The four-storey parking lot where Reginald Cenyk wanted to meet had sat at the corner of 1st Avenue and 20th Street for a long time. It was one of those creepy places with ceilings so low that even in my itsy bitsy Mazda I couldn't help but feel the roof was going to scrape the top.

Reginald was right. Except for a few random cars on the first level, the place was deserted. At a snail's pace, I wound my way up to the top floor, unconsciously bowing my head in a futile effort to make the car smaller. I was pretty sure no one was following me, but I'd extinguished my headlights as soon as I entered the lot, just to be sure. It made the going excruciatingly slow, but if nothing else, I hoped it gave Reginald some comfort that we'd be alone.

It was dark outside when I pulled off the last ramp onto the rooftop level, grateful to be out from under the tomb-like ceilings. Conveniently, the southeast corner he'd chosen for our rendezvous, was just up ahead and slightly to the right of the ramp. I parked the car as directed, and waited. Over the edge, to my right, I could see the bright white and blue lights of the twelve-screen Galaxy cinema, and up ahead the cheery, neon, palm-tree-shaped sign of the downtrodden Capri Hotel. I looked down at my badly crinkled tux and muddied patent leather dress shoes. Ruining formal wear seemed to be a habit with me. At least this time there were no bloodstains. I lowered my window and drank in fresh, rain-scented air.

A few minutes later, my eyes glommed onto the rear-view mirror as a pair of headlights inched up the ramp behind me. Reginald wasn't being as careful as I'd been. Then again, I'm a trained professional at this kind of stuff.

I couldn't wait to hear what he had to tell me. I reached for the car door handle to get out. But I never made it. Instead, my body was violently thrust forward. I felt my chin crack against the Mazda's steering wheel.

White Truck.

Chapter 16

Dazed, I lifted my head just in time to see the headlights back away from where they'd just rammed the back end of my car. It was the white truck, with its silly front vanity licence plate: a row-boat and a beehive. I heard its engine roar. It was coming back for more. Uselessly my right foot slammed down on the brake—as if that would stop anything.

My fingers grasped for the seat belt doohickey. I had to get free before this idiot squished me into a pancake against the guardrail.

With the next impact, I realized in horror that wasn't his intention at all.

The metal bar made a ghastly groaning noise as the vehicle behind me pushed the Mazda against it with all its horsepower. My eyes widened in full horror as I watched the steel give way.

I was going over!

The convertible jerked forward in stuttering protest. The nose inched over the edge. A gurgling noise escaped my tight throat. Strangely enough, I found I could not scream out the terror I felt infuse my body like a deadly venom. I knew I would never survive the four-storey drop. Four words blared in my head: The End Is Near!

Further.

Further.

The car made a sickening thumping noise as the front tires rolled over the edge and the chassis hit cement. The nose began to teeter. It was only then, at that last, most desperate moment, that my fumbling fingers finally released the seat belt catch. I threw open my door.

Maneuvering my torso through the door, in preparation for...I didn't know what...I could see that the car had caught on a thick shard of twisted metal. I was saved!

No, I wasn't.

The killer truck had repositioned and was zeroing in for one last smack. With no time to consider options, my brain screamed, "ooooh noooooooo!" as I tossed my body from my car. The microseconds that followed seemed much longer, long enough for me to feel a keen sense of horror at what was happening to me, and a burning guilt for abandoning my car. I was a cowardly rat, jumping ship, not knowing if my own fate would be any less cruel than the one I'd left behind. But I had no choice.

I reached blindly into the air, hoping to find salvation. And I did. The fingers of my right hand fell upon an intact railing. Although it was hard and rough to the touch, the metal edge of it cutting into my skin, at that moment, the steel of that railing felt dearer to me than a lover's cheek.

As I took hold of the railing, my body crashed against the side of the parking garage, my legs flailing below me. My eyes jerked upwards in response to a horrible noise: the deafening sound of the final blow in a fight to the death. I watched as my sweet Mazda RX-7 convertible was viciously hit from behind. With a cry curdling in my throat, I witnessed the silver body nosedive into the back alley, far, far below. With a surprisingly muted wallop, the car crash-landed. One railing, one arm groaning with pain, were the only things keeping me from joining her.

I looked up to where the driver's side of the gleaming white truck had pulled up to the pavement's edge. With a benign whir, the window was lowered. An unsmiling face appeared. Reginald Cenyk, archivist turned murderer.

It wasn't exactly the best time for me to have a eureka moment, but there it was. It wasn't a rowboat on the white truck's licence plate: it was an ark. Like in Noah's ark. An ark and beehive. Ark. Hive. Archive. Sheesh. Reginald Cenyk, *cheesy* archivist turned murderer.

The truck door opened. Things didn't look so good for me.

I looked down. Deadly chasm. Nope, I still wouldn't survive the fall. I looked up. Killer who wanted to get rid of me because I'd found him out. Nope, things didn't look too good for me at all.

"What was that for?" I asked as if he'd just given me an unanticipated noogie. I sometimes react weirdly in perilous circumstances.

"I know you know," Reginald answered back, his pale face flushed with colour, thinning red hair fluttering in the wind. "As soon as you stepped into my office and started asking all those questions, I knew you knew."

He was giving me more credit than I was due. I actually didn't know anything for sure until his most recent phone call, when he specifically referred to a journal and letters. I hadn't told him what form the missing material was in. Then I learned Simon Durhuaghe *was* being blackmailed. But it hadn't started until after Walter's death.

Who else could have known about the content of the damning material without actually having seen it? If I accepted that Walter and Helen were innocent in all this, who else was a common denominator between them and the archival material? And, who knew that Walter had the treasure map and would be on that plane from Vancouver?

The answer to every question was the same: Reginald Cenyk. He'd been an employee at the archives when the controversial Durhuaghe material was first discovered. Walter had made calls to work from Victoria, no doubt to Reginald who he erroneously trusted.

What I hadn't known was that he'd try to push me off the top of a parking lot. I expected something less dramatic from him. Like maybe a gun or knife. I'd been ready for that.

Reginald stepped forward. "I hate this," he said, turning his baby face into a grimace. It seemed as if he was talking more to himself than me. "But it must be done. I have to get out of here."

From where he stood, and how I was positioned, hanging by a metal thread, he had a good shot at my forearm. And the bastard took it. Pulling back his leg, he let loose against my exposed, straining limb, kicking it as hard as he could.

I yowled in pain.

He readied for another kick. My arm couldn't take it. It would do me in. I was going to fall.

My eyes moved to a spot behind Cenyk's back. I screamed, "Darren! Help me!"

Startled, Reginald whisked around to protect himself from a rear assault. It gave me all the time I needed. I'd managed to secure a piece of loose rebar. Using my uninjured arm, I whipped it up and over the pavement ledge, and in the momentum of an arc, swung it with every muscle I had against the tender midpoint of Reginald's calves. I knew that's where it would hurt the most.

The slender man fell to the ground, his hands tied around his legs, mewing in pain. I bunched up my screaming muscles and used the leverage of the railing I was holding on to to swing myself up and back onto firm ground. I rolled up next to Reginald and jumped up, rebar still in hand. I raised it over my head, peered down at him and growled, "Don't move, you piece of shit, or I'll archive your ass!"

He didn't.

I fished my cellphone out of a pocket and dialled. *Now* I'd call for the help of my cop friend for real.

"I can't believe you," Kirsch told me in a tone of voice that left no doubt about how he was feeling about me at that particular moment. "You had me right there, you asked me for information, and then you went off to catch a killer on your own. Are you friggin' nuts?"

If you put it that way, perhaps, but I'm an independent kind of guy.

"I wasn't one hundred percent sure." I defended my reasons for leaving the wedding reception to meet Reginald Cenyk alone, rather than take the handy cop with me. "Only ninety percent, maybe even only eighty."

In reality, I was more sure than that, but I thought I could take him. He was an archivist, for Pete's sake. I'm a macho gay man detective. It should have worked out okay. I just hadn't considered the possibility that I'd be battling a six-thousand pound, three-quarter ton truck, rather than a ninety-eight pound weakling. Lesson learned.

We were in the police station outside an interrogation room. "So, what's he saying in there?" I asked, hoping to steer off the current topic. "You've had him in there forever."

Kirsch let out an exasperated sigh. He was too tired to resist me. But he wasn't too tired to be a thief. He snapped the fresh cup of coffee out of my hand, and took a long sip.

"I'm paraphrasing," Kirsch said when he was done, "but it seems he came up with the idea to use Durhuaghe's journal to subsidize an early retirement almost as soon as he and his pals at the archives found it. They debated what to do with it: return it to Durhuaghe, destroy it, or just include it with the rest of the material and let fate take control. Cenyk's vote was to put it into the archives along with the rest. Of course, he planned to steal it the first chance he got, and use it against Durhuaghe. Instead, Helen Crawford overruled him and hid the stuff."

"She wanted to protect Durhuaghe's reputation."

"Uh huh. Sounds like Cenyk harassed her about it over the years, hoping to trick her into revealing her hiding spot, but she never cracked."

"She knew what he wanted to do with it?"

"Not exactly, but she probably suspected. And if not Cenyk, somebody else might use it against her hero. She probably created the treasure map after she retired and before she left the city. It was her way of keeping the material safe, but still accessible after she died."

"Accessible only if whoever had the map had the smarts to figure it out."

Kirsch nodded. "I think she hoped it would be someone of her choosing, someone she trusted. But yeah, if the map ended up in the wrong hands, she didn't want to make it easy for them."

"That's why she picked Walter Angel to leave it to in her will. She trusted him to keep the secret."

"When she found out she was dying, she pretty much had to concede that it was he, as new head archivist, who should take on the responsibility of deciding the future of the material. Unfortunately, Walter in turn trusted the wrong person. He told Cenyk about the map, and that he was going to Victoria to retrieve it. Cenyk knew his only chance of getting his hands on it would be as soon as Angel stepped off that plane in Saskatoon. After that, Angel could hide the map and Cenyk would be no further ahead than he was when Helen was alive."

"How much money is this stuff really worth? In terms of blackmail cash, I mean."

Kirsch shrugged and handed back my nearly empty coffee cup. "Dunno. Cenyk suspected a lot. He suspected Helen was already blackmailing Durhuaghe—he didn't know about the baby—but he did know that Sherry Klingskill was Sherry Fisher. He thought that was how Helen could afford to retire early and live the good life on Vancouver Island. When she died, he decided it was his time for a slice of the pie."

"He was wrong about that, you know."

Kirsch nodded. "Still, he had to be furious when he found out that instead of him, Angel was now getting a chance at plucking the golden goose. He couldn't take it. That's when he decided to get the map no matter what, even if meant killing Angel in the process.

"But then along comes everyone's favourite snoop, always managing to get himself stuck in the middle of whatever mess is going down. Angel probably saw Cenyk at the airport. Maybe Helen Crawford left him a note, or her sister talked to him, I don't know, but he must have already begun to suspect Cenyk could be up to no good. He realized he needed to keep the map safe. So *you* end up with it. Maybe Cenyk spotted the two of you together at the airport. When he finds the map isn't in Angel's possession, he somehow decides he has to go after you."

I let out a nervous cough, and said, "There might have been a business card of mine in Angel's pocket."

"There ya go," Kirsch said, as if he expected nothing less. "In the meantime, even without the journal and letters in hand, Cenyk can't wait for a payday. He knows what's in the journal, so he decides to try an opening gambit with Durhuaghe to see what he can get."

"When he finds out I've solved the treasure map and found the journal…"

"At first he backs off, thinking the game is over, his chances gone…"

"…then I turn up at the archives to ask questions…"

"Yup, he knows it's only a matter of time before even someone with your limited abilities figures out a connection. Russell Quant has got to die."

"There's only one thing I can't understand."

"Whazzat?"

"Why did Molly have to die?"

Kirsch frowned and gave me a quizzical look. "Molly? Who the hell is Molly?"

I looked down at my feet. "I loved that car."

Tap.

Tap.

Tap.

It took some practice to get the pebbles to hit the third floor window.

Tap.

A silhouette appeared. I knew it wasn't Damien. I had seen him leave the wedding reception early. His working Sunday mornings was a bit of luck I intended to use to my benefit.

By the time things were wrapped up at the police station and I drove back out to Ash House, the party was long over. It was the middle of the night. The clouds that had caused such havoc earlier in the evening had evaporated, leaving behind a peaceful, star-speckled sky. For the next couple of hours I toiled. And now I was ready.

I was standing in the middle of the backyard, near the pool. I raised my right arm and gave the dark shape in the window a jaunty wave.

At first there was no movement from the lone figure. Then his right hand rose and began to move in a hesitant wave back. He had a right to be cautious, suspicious.

I stepped on a button on a control panel at my feet, never taking my eyes off Ethan in the window. At the extreme far end of the yard the smallest of Sereena's electric candy hearts lit up. "You're Sweet," it read.

Then another, bigger heart, lit up. "Hug Me."

And another. And another.

On and on hearts lit up behind me, until all twenty-four of them, spread throughout the yard, were blazing, with me in the middle of them.

Another toe tap on the controls.

I'd hoisted, with great effort and near misfortune, the electronic message board into a tree. Because of the parking lot incident, my arm was in considerable pain, but I was determined. Nothing was going to stop me. I'd attached it to the side of the tree house Ethan had built for his daughter. It had taken me forever to figure the thing out, then forevermore to choose just the right words I needed Ethan to read that night.

SORRY 2 WAKE U, it began.

I KNOW MY TIMING SUCKS.

IT'S THE MIDDLE OF THE NIGHT.

YOUR NEW HOUSE IS IN SHAMBLES.

YOUR BACKYARD IS A MESS.

YOU HAVE A BOYFRIEND.

I HAVE A FIANCÉ. Then came a lot of ellipses ....followed by: BUT I AM IN CRAZY LOVE WITH YOU ETHAN.

Another tap. The hearts began to flash on and off like some

wild valentine kaleidoscope. The light show was to give him a few seconds to digest what I'd just told him.

As I stood there, the absolute silence of the country night seemed impossibly inapt. With so much going on: the lights, the message board, the declaration of love, I would have expected the sound of blaring trumpets and crackling fireworks. But there was nothing. Just me in the dark, looking up at a man in a window, hoping.

I saw the figure move. My breath caught.

I watched as Ethan shifted from one side of the window to the next, almost as if he was pacing, uncertain of what to do. Can't imagine why.

Another foot tap.

I EXPECT NOTHING FROM U.

I JUST WANTED U TO KNOW.

Another tap. The lights stopped flashing.

I APOLOGIZE TO U AND DAMIEN.

FOR BEING SUCH A JERK.

DOING THIS BEHIND HIS BACK.

IF U LOVE HIM.

I PROMISE TO LET THIS GO.

IF YOU DON'T...

Ellipses indicate the omission of words needed to make sense. Perfect. Life, I'd come to realize, doesn't always make sense. Happy ever after isn't always what you thought it would be.

Tap. The lights began a riotous dance, wildly flashing on and off to some rowdy, unheard rhythm, filling the yard with candy heart colours. And then I did what only the bravest of men have done before. In that shrivellingly cold night, I slooooowly stripped naked.

When I was done, I stood there, straight and proud, hands at my side. I gave the control board one last tap.

ETHAN...

WILL YOU TAKE A LEAP OF FAITH...

AND GO OUT WITH ME?

And with that, I performed a near perfect backflip into the icy pool behind me.

Honolulu in late August is hot. Thirty degrees Celsius hot. That sounds even hotter when converted to eighty-seven degrees Fahrenheit. But I love the heat, so it didn't bother me much.

Not surprisingly, Alex had sounded a bit taken aback by my request to meet on the island again so soon. I had to see him. I knew it wasn't easy for him to get away. He could only commit to one night, then he'd have to catch a plane back to Australia.

I chose a spot we knew well. It was a picnic table just off the beach, in the Fort DeRussy park area between the Waikiki Shore Condo building and the Hale Koa military hotel. I told him I'd be there at seven p.m. sharp, long after the sunset watchers would have headed back inland for dinner. That way I knew we'd have some privacy.

At five-thirty p.m, as Alex's plane landed, I was headed for the Daiei grocery store on Kaheka Street. I wanted to pick up a few supplies for our picnic, including some of his favourite marinated, fresh, raw fish poke.

With my nose pressed against the fish man's glass display case, focused on deciding between the shoyu, kimchee or just plain ahi, I heard a loud crash behind me. I straightened myself and turned around to find that another shopper's cart had collided into mine.

"Sorry," the man said, a big grin on his face.

"No problem," I said distractedly. I was about to turn back to my selection process when I recognized the guy. "Hey, you did that on purpose."

Kimo's smile widened. His teeth were big and strong and dazzlingly white. "Maybe. Who's gonna prove it?"

"I'm a private detective," I told him. "Sounds like a job right up my alley."

"I'm a cop," he shot back. "I could take you in for illegal parking of a shopping cart in the middle of a grocery store aisle."

"Are you kidding me?" I complained in mock outrage. "I'm parked well to the side. There's plenty of room for others to pass by. I think it's you who should be charged for pushing a cart like it's his first day behind the wheel."

We stared at one another, each kind of dumbfounded at seeing one another again, and how happy we were that it happened.

"I'm surprised to see you back on the island so soon," Kimo said. "Don't tell me it's your honeymoon already."

"Nah, nothing like that." I made a show of peeking into his cart. All beer. No food. "You know they sell beer at the ABC store. No need to pretend you're shopping for bread and milk when all you're doing is picking up party supplies."

He laughed. "Visiting a buddy who lives near here. I don't shop here usually."

"Boyfriend kind of buddy?"

Kimo made a noise that sounded kind of animalistic. And sexy. Then he asked, "Do you wanna get a drink or something?"

"I thought you were going visiting."

"Oh, yeah, that's right. How long you in Honolulu for?"

"I leave tomorrow, Mr. Kapachakalakawei."

"Back to Saskachakalakawei?"

"You got it. Everything turn out okay with Huei?" That was the guy I'd helped Kimo and his partner take down at the airport.

"He's taken up residence in a nice cell with a view."

"You know what they say, no use staying in Hawaii without a view."

"You're different this time," he said out of the blue, studying my face like he was seeing something there he hadn't seen before.

"How do you mean?"

"You know, last time, when we met at the airport, and you told me you were getting married and all that? I doubted you, *brah*. But now, I got ya, I can see it."

"See what?"

"You're bad in love, *brah*. Baaaaad."

"Yeah," I told him. "I really am."

Kimo gave me a wink and began to move away. "Too bad for me then. I'll see you around, Russell. *Aloha*, my friend."

"*Aloha*."

I poured the last of the POG and vodka from the Thermos into my plastic cup at about ten o'clock. At first the passion-orange-guava concoction tasted fresh and tangy, now it was warm and sickly sweet. The outside temperature had settled into a comfortable mid-seventies.

I sipped my drink and gazed at the water, even though with the sky so dark I could barely make out where sand met ocean. The beach and sidewalk had grown busy again with diners returning to their beachside hotels and lovers taking romantic strolls along the crashing surf. Everybody had somebody.

Except me.

I was alone. My sad little picnic sat uneaten. I'd been stood up.

Alex Canyon never showed up. Somehow he'd figured it out. Somehow he'd known this impromptu get-together I'd arranged was for me to give him back his engagement ring. To end our relationship. Maybe he'd called Sereena, or Anthony, and they'd said something by mistake. Or on purpose? It didn't matter now.

I fought back tears and wondered if I'd made the right decision, asking him to come all this way, only to tell him it was over? Now here I was, sitting on my own, looking like a loser, feeling like stink. Feeling…heartbroken. Did I even have the right to feel heartbroken? I'd come to Hawaii to break up with him, yet I was feeling like *he* broke *my* heart? Alberta might say this was karma taking a nice big bite out of my ass.

Despite it all, I knew I'd done the right thing. I'd done the best I could in a bad situation. This wasn't something to be done over the telephone or with a pithy email. I owed Alex that much. I owed telling him face to face that I loved him. Just not enough.

In planning this, I never thought beyond saying those words to him. I thought about it now. Would we sit and have a good cry together? Probably not. Would he yell and scream at me for being such an asshole? Not his style. Would he take the ring and toss it into the ocean, a dramatic gesture symbolizing how I was throwing away our relationship? Nah. He would have simply gotten up, kissed me once on the cheek, wished me well, and walked off into the sunset. I'd never see him again. And I would cry.

But none of that had happened. Instead, there I sat. All alone on my picnic bench. A bit unsteady from too much vodka and POG. A tropical breeze played with my hair and filled my nose with smells of the sea. I watched people passing by, hand in hand, arm in arm, in love. People who weren't me.

And suddenly I realized something surprising.

I was happy.

I was unafraid.

Sure, I was alone. And maybe I'd stay that way. But it felt good to have my head out of the sand. It felt good to feel my heart hurt. It felt good to ask myself the tough questions about love and have an answer that I wholeheartedly believed in, no matter the consequences.

Weaving only slightly, I took my drink and crossed the sidewalk to the beach, and headed for the ocean. The closer I got, the lights of the public walkway faded away, and dark enveloped me like a soothing hug. The sand felt gritty and wonderfully abrasive against the skin of my bare feet. When the first tendril of tingly cold water rushed across my toes, I stopped. I threw back my head and pulled in a deep breath of sea air.

Nothing had ever felt better than that moment.

Until the next one.

My phone vibrated against my thigh. I pulled it from my shorts pocket and saw that a text message had just arrived. It was from Ethan Ash. After many ellipses, it read: "..I WILL."